# The Legend of See Bird: Kiamichi

## Karl L. Stewart

Publisher Page
*an imprint of Headline Books, Inc.*
Terra Alta, WV

*The Legend of See Bird: Kiamichi*

by Karl L. Stewart



To order additional copies of this book or for book publishing information, or to contact the author:

Headline Books, Inc.
P.O. Box 52
Terra Alta, WV 26764
www.headlinebooks.com

Tel: 304-789-3001
Email: mybook@headlinebooks.com

*Publisher Page is an imprint of Headline Books*

ISBN 13: 9781951556198

Library of Congress Control Number: 2020938258

PRINTED IN THE UNITED STATES OF AMERICA

*This book is dedicated to all those "Old Timers," men and women who inhabited a predigital world. Though times could be harsh, they endured, never expecting life to give them a free ride.*

# 1

**December 24, 1924.**
**Along the White River in Indiana.**

The wind didn't so much howl as hammer at the canvas sides of the two mule-led wagons creeping along what passed for a road, jolting over each frozen rut. The rider of the snow-spattered chestnut leading the small caravan peered to each side, leaning far over the saddle, squinting his eyes, teared up from the icy blasts. There were farms out there, for sure, somewhere, hidden behind the thick curtain of blowing snow. But, the man on horseback thought, they might as well be a hundred miles away.

See Bird swallowed hard, a bitter taste filling his mouth. Had everything gone as planned, his entire family would be safe in Oklahoma by now. But then, he smiled wryly, a lifetime of experience had taught him that things seldom go according to plan.

Huddled in his saddle, his broad-brimmed black-slouch hat tied down over his ears, he waited for Charlie to draw the wagons up and pictured his old family homestead nestled neatly along the banks of the Kiamichi River in southeast Oklahoma. It was a land of laughing water where he played for endless hours growing up with his twin brother See Right. It was the river where he learned to swim and first experienced the strange God-given gift that blessed him. It would come upon him suddenly, sweeping over and through him – taking possession of him, endowing him with a sureness and a power to save, that certainly was not of his own device.

It was also a land of long grass, hardwood forests, and people from his own stock, the Choctaw, a good people who greeted him as one of their own, with an open raised hand and a heart-felt "Halito." And in this season, even though they had little, he knew they would be quick to share. Amongst them, he would no longer need to stay cloaked, to be wary of each spoken word, to wonder what thoughts lay hidden as though in deep grass, behind hooded eyes. True it was that he made his way in the white man's world. He earned the respect of many, treasured the friendship of a few, and found love with one.

His horse bobbed its head and snorted, impatient with this man sitting so impervious to the storm sweeping down on them. See Bird leaned and patted the big horse's neck. "You don't like it either, do you, boy?" he muttered and reined around to face the approaching wagons.

Another blast drove shards of ice like glass against his craggy face. If he felt it at all, he did not let it show. He shifted in his saddle and looked hard at the wagon's driver. He could not see Charlie's face, shielded as it was behind his lowered hat. But then he did not need to see his son-in-law's face to know how he would look right now. Shoulders hunched, teeth clenched, his worried eyes mere grey-blue slits; his face pure concentration. Because, behind him in the wagon, huddled beneath a pile of blankets would be See Bird's adopted daughter

Gertrude, Charlie's wife, now entering her last month of a troubled first pregnancy.

See Bird raised a hand to bring Charlie's wagon to a halt and caught a glimpse of the trailing second wagon. His eyes glowed with pride as he considered the petite woman who drove it. Sally stood only barely over five feet tall and with a slight frame to match. But she was no woman to be trifled with nor underestimated. Men had learned this – to their dismay – more than once. Her luminous brown eyes would alter in a moment to granite if she felt her family threatened. Then those same soft pool-deep eyes would flash a fearsome flame, sparks from stone. Right now, her face would be set, warm lips drawn tight in determination. He imagined the firm set of her jaw, her unruly flaxen hair, torn loose from beneath her shawl, covering, then uncovering most of her face, and her small hands, bundled in mittens, expertly working the reins.

This was his family, he thought with a wild pride. These few wagons struggling across a wind-whipped, frozen landscape as a brutal winter descended upon them, carried everyone he held dear to his heart in this life.

The crow's feet deepened at the corners of his eyes as he wondered again, for probably the hundredth time, if he was doing the right thing by yanking them from their roots, sunk so deeply in West Virginia hills. Would they ever be as content when they traveled across the Mississippi to settle in a strange land? Could his people ever become theirs?

True, the four of them had discussed this very issue over many a cup of Arbuckle's back in Warm Holler, and all agreed this was something they were willing to do. Surprisingly, Charlie was the first to leap at the idea. A veteran of the Great War, he had witnessed carnage in Europe that, when he tried to talk about, choked him into silence until, with a frustrated shake of his head, he would give it up and walk away. He had gone off to war an eager young soldier and returned sixteen months later, a man ridden by demons that only the bottle seemed to keep at bay.

Charlie's love for Gertrude was as strong as ever, perhaps even more intense than before, as though he needed desperately to stay connected with this loving woman. He may have been driven by demons, but See Bird had never seen Charlie even raise his voice to Gertrude, much less a hand in anger. In her turn, Gertrude loved Charlie unreservedly without descending into pity. She spoke with Sally frequently. See Bird could only assume it was to gain perspective and understanding of her troubled husband. And, See Bird admitted to himself, Charlie certainly could do a day's work, always sober, at least until the job was done. Perhaps, See Bird considered, Charlie saw this move to Oklahoma as an opportunity to make a clean break with the past, to start life anew.

The wagons halted, and before See Bird and Sally could climb in, Charlie dove through the canvas folds into the interior. Gertrude was moaning in pain. Despite the bitter cold, sweat matted her black curly hair.

The family conference within was short by necessity. The wind buffeted the canvas sides of the wagon. The ropes needed tightening and the horses and mules needed tending. See Bird sensed the decision that needed to be made and sighed resignedly. He spoke without enthusiasm but with conviction. "The fact is the weather's too foul for us to continue. We have to try to return home." He glanced from face to face. "And even so, there's no guarantee we'll make it before the baby comes." See Bird avoided stating the obvious, that as weak as she was now, losing strength every day, his daughter maybe was in more danger than anyone would care to admit. He gathered himself up and straightened his shoulders. "But there is no time to waste, especially with Gertrude in such a delicate condition. If we turn south, there is a good road down to Cincinnati. We can take stock and regroup there."

"You got my vote, Bird," Sally spoke up and added, in an attempt to temper his disappointment, "We could try again next year and get an earlier start. Gertrude needs a doctor. We can't risk her life and the baby's to boot." There. She had brought it out into the open. She studied the small circle huddled beneath blankets. Gertrude tried to speak, but only managed to sob, "I don't want to make us give up and go back. I'm so sorry, and I'm so tired." She groaned, and nearly too weak to continue, leaned against Charlie. "But I don't think I can make it to Oklahoma." She completely broke down, sobbing and shaking, hunched over in silent tears.

Charlie cradled her head in his lap as he gently rocked. He eyed See Bird and Sally, straightened himself up and announced, "You folks will think me nuts for sure. You know I want to go on more than anything." Nodding to his wife, he added, "She knows it, and that's why she's hanging on so hard to going." He snuggled her closer in his embrace. "But she's right. She won't make it. And if I lose her, nothing else will matter. See Bird," he looked deeply at his father-in-law, resolve replacing fear, "take us home. The sooner, the better." His tight lips stretched into a grim smile, "Let's turn and run with the wind." See Bird nodded. His shoulders sagged just a bit.

Two weeks later, the brittle north wind at their backs, the family slowly made their way across the new bridge at Cincinnati, linking Ohio with Kentucky. The icy, black Ohio sluggishly flowed beneath them. The snow had stopped, and the day was clear and cold. They would make camp on the Kentucky side of the river until Gertrude gathered strength enough to resume the journey home. The frozen rutted road had sapped her of all her reserves. Clearly, she had made it this far on willpower alone.

Having led the bedraggled band across the bridge, See Bird directed the wagons off the road and down between two wooded hills not far from the river. To Charlie, he pointed out a cluster of homes in the distance, smoke curling from the chimneys. "That's Covington. It ain't much, but I'm betting it's got a doctor. Get down there, find him, and bring him right back. I'll set up camp. Do it now. Your gal needs him more than I need your help setting up. Go." See Bird watched Charlie hurry his horse through the barren trees. "Sally, give me a hand with this tent, would you?" he called.

Just before a dull steel sunset on a short winter day, See Bird, Sally, and Gertrude heard the sound of an engine approaching the snug, thick-walled tent See Bird had built for their traveling accommodations. The engine coughed to silence and See Bird hurried to the tent door, yanking it open to see a smallish man wearing a heavy black coat and carrying a handbag step out of and slam the door of a Model-T Ford. He did not pause at the tent door, but strode directly past See Bird into the tent. Charlie tied his horse to the rear bumper and followed. The doctor took but a moment to survey the interior, and apparently finding it acceptable, perfunctorily turned to shake See Bird's hand but focused his gaze on Gertrude lying on a heavy quilted mat while Sally mopped her head with a towel. Sally stood and wiped her hands on her dress. "I know all about birthing, doctor. I'll be helping with the baby."

"Of course you will," he replied briskly and shoved his spectacles farther up the bridge of his nose. Turning to See Bird and Charlie, he added, "You men can make yourselves scarce. Excuse us, but we've work to do." As Charlie and See Bird made their way out through the door flap, they heard the doctor speak to Sally. "Clean hot water? Fine. And towels. Excellent. Okay then, madam, let's get busy."

See Bird and Charlie tended the horses and made a small fire on the lee side of the tent, close enough to hear whatever transpired within. Their fitful attempts at conversation wilted and died before they could firmly take root. Mostly they sat in silence. See Bird worried that in his desire to go to Oklahoma, he had endangered the ones he loved the most. Charlie stewed over every decision made that put the woman he loved in danger. Both wondered what could possibly be taking so long inside the yurt-like tent. Occasionally Gertrude would cry out and Charlie would surge to his feet, only to be restrained by See Bird's grip on his arm, drawing him back to the log. "That doc seems to know his way around womenfolk. Let's not get hasty and get in his way." Charlie sank back down and resumed his fretting.

The night was pitch black. Charlie hunched over, his eyes fixed on the small fire, staring at nothing. See Bird, relying on habit long-established, glanced all about the area and beyond, never staring at the flames. He always felt vulnerable when a campfire stripped him of his night vision. He was wondering if perhaps the two of them would have to remain outside until dawn, shrouded in their blankets. He had long since lost feeling in his toes. But he scarcely noticed. Suddenly, both men leapt to their feet, shucking their blankets. A howl like that of a baby coyote rent the air. Before they could get to the tent corner, there stood Sally, totally exhausted, hair askew, a weary smile on her face. "Charlie," she said softly, "why don't you go in and meet your beautiful new son?" Seeing his concerned look, she added, "And Gertrude too. They're both fine. Go on in now." He stood as if transfixed. "Go on. Git." Sally smiled at See Bird and stepped aside as Charlie broke the spell and rushed past her.

"That's okay, Sal," See Bird said with a slight wave of his hand. "She needs you too. I'll be right in." She raised her chin, smiled wearily in acknowledgment, and turned back into the tent, leaving See Bird alone with his thoughts. "So, this is how it's gonna be," he said to himself. And as he turned to go check on the horses once again, he murmured a prayer. "Well, Father," he said to himself, "I tried. I do so love those prairies and hills. And I'm gonna miss them something fierce." The old horse seemed to catch See Bird's disappointment and draped his head over the Indian's shoulder as the man brushed his mittened hand along the horse's still powerful neck. And there in the dark of a cold Kentucky night, by a crackling fire, See Bird stood and, staring through the flames, remembered another fire from long ago and far away.

# 2

## North Dakota Badlands 1903

Though it was late-summer, it was a cool evening in the North Country. The small camp-fire See Bird made suited his needs, which were few. A pot of perked coffee, a spit to roast a hare he shot from the saddle, a touch of warmth. It was enough. And it was more than enough. Kiamichi blew contentedly from the shadows just beyond the flames. Life was good.

After finishing his sparse meal and tossing out the rest of the coffee, See Bird shook out a large loop from his lariat onto the ground and carrying his gear, carefully stepped inside it. Inside the loop, he unrolled his bedroll and lay back, resting against his saddle with arms folded beneath his head, taking in the show above him. Across the black velvet sky splashed the Milky Way, like a broad trail leading him to the northwest. A dim green fluorescent, stellar curtain took shape and slowly waved near the end of that trail, the heavenly lights beaconing him to some vast city, just beyond the horizon. Unblinking stars and constellations greeted him like old friends. Back in West Virginia, hemmed in amid the hills and forested mountains, one would never see a grand display such as this, could scarcely even imagine what splendor the night sky could offer.

Back there Sally, his wife of less than a year, would be asleep, having tucked her little daughter Gertrude into her bed in the loft, finished whatever household chore she had been working on, and blown out the light as she slipped beneath the thick hand-made quilts into the bed he shared with her. His heart welled with love for this small woman with hair yellow as flax and brown eyes so deep that when her eyes met his, he sometimes feared he would lose his balance and tumble in. Her very soul seemed to open to him.

Following their wedding, he tried mightily to harness his wanderlust and live the life of a West Virginia farmer. He plowed several acres and planted some tobacco. But Sally sensed his unhappiness and frustration. In her deep love, his young wife released him, as she put it, "to go rodeoing." She reasoned that, with her extended family living in the neighborhood, they would stop by frequently, helping out as need be. The Hatfields were good people who took care of their own. Her uncle, Devil Anse, respected See Bird for his loyalty and good counsel, and in his absence, would allow nothing amiss to happen to Sally and his grand-niece Gertrude.

So early one summer's morning, See Bird rose and slipped into his moccasins, collected his gear, packed it in his 'wargrip,' and strode to the corral. Kiamichi, reading his man's body language, knew something exciting was about to happen and called to him, stamping and racing around the corral until See Bird swung open the wooden gate and stepped inside. Whereupon Kiamichi stopped his prancing about and stood stock still, his ears locked on his man, belying his attempt to appear disinterested. See Bird chuckled to himself as he walked over to the horse, set his saddle down for a moment, and went through his routine of stroking his sorrel from front to rear, all 14.5 hands of him, checking each hoof, all the while speaking gently, getting Kiamichi's permission to saddle up. The horse was so eager to go that See Bird could feel the animal's skin quiver in anticipation. When the saddle was placed on his back, he nickered and hop-stepped a few times before settling. See Bird chuckled again.

The chestnut, or sorrel as the Westerners called him, was a handsome animal. The power of the quarter-horse was evident in his rounded rear haunches, which gave him the ability to accelerate instantly. The thoroughbred gave him the beautiful symmetry, size, and grace. God had given him his intelligence, which See Bird had come to recognize as more than mere 'horse sense.' More than once, Kiamichi had surprised his man with his keen awareness and understanding of a difficult situation. See Bird thought his horse must be at least the equivalent of the smartest dog he had ever known, but coupled with a personality that belonged to Kiamichi alone.

As he cinched it up, See Bird noted Kiamichi was not even holding his breath and made no attempt to inflate his chest. Perhaps he realized it would be futile. But maybe he just wanted to leave this corral as much as did his rider. In any case, once See Bird cinched up, he didn't have to drive out his steed's breath and recinch the saddle a notch tighter. Soon he slid into the saddle, his 'wargrip' tied down snugly behind. His Winchester, a gift from Sally's uncle Devil Anse, rode in its soft, tasseled leather sheath by his left knee. His looped lariat hung from the saddle on the right side. See Bird responded to his horse, and excitement, like electricity, surged throughout his own body. Kiamichi danced a circle once full around. See Bird squeezed his knees gently, directing the animal toward the gate. Kiamichi needed no further urging and cantered forward. With a whoop and a wave at his wife and child standing on the front porch, man and horse exited the Warm Holler farm, headed west.

At Huntington See Bird hustled his horse up a ramp and onto a Chessie freight car of a train chugging as it built up steam, preparing for the journey down the Ohio to St. Louis. He dropped his gear in a corner of the same car, made sure Kiamichi had fodder, oats, and fresh bedding, wiped him down, refreshed his bucket of water, and only then did he see to his own needs.

Two days later, as dawn broke, See Bird woke and felt, as well as heard the train slow, stop as though testing its footing, and then resume its creeping forward motion. Sliding open the freight car's door, See Bird stood and watched the glorious scene unfold before him. Far beneath his feet swept the mighty Mississippi, carrying the last of the late spring snow-melt from up north. The long train inched its way across the iron-trestled span, making its cautious way toward the sprawling city on the Missouri side of the river. St. Louis, gateway to the west, it was called. But it's just as much a gateway for those going the other direction, See Bird thought, remembering his lonely passage east several years ago. At that time, he thought he would probably never return to a land where he had lost his first love, and with the closing of the Chisholm Trail, his very life's work.

But displaced cowboys such as himself found a new way to make more money in a day than droving cattle herds on ranches would earn them in a month. After the train pulled into the bustling St. Louis station just on the south side of downtown, not far from the river, and jerked to a brake-squealing halt, See Bird led a nervous Kiamichi carefully down the ramp and off the platform. He wondered aloud to his horse as he was prone to do, "Who would have thought it, big fellow?" Kiamichi, in reply, snorted. See Bird laughed. "Who would have thought that cowboy shows would catch on like a prairie fire? And that city-slickers would pay to watch such shenanigans? You and me now, if we do well, we can make enough this summer to see us all through 'til next year. You game? Are you, boy?" His excitement was contagious. Kiamichi blew and vigorously nodded his head as if in agreement. "I thought so." As See Bird swung into the saddle, he leaned over to speak softly into his steed's ear. "Well then, let's go find us a rodeo."

Now, three months later, with a summer's worth of winnings carefully tucked away inside his 'grip, Kiamichi quietly grazing nearby, See Bird lay on his saddle blanket inside a circle made by his rope's loop to ward off snakes, enjoying the North Dakota night sky. A falling star, and then a second one streaked southeast across the inky firmament, the direction home, to Sally. The ghostly green curtain still waved slowly across the sky to the northwest. Slowly, he stood, stretched, and brushed himself off. In the far distance, up in the hills, his sharp eyes caught the flicker of a small campfire before it winked out. "Another soul like me," he thought, "appreciating what money can't buy." By now, his fire had died to deep crimson embers. His soul moved first and then, completely unselfconsciously, he straightened up, hooked his thumbs in the waist of his trousers, stepped over the rope, and began to dance around the dying fire to a song so ancient it was old before the white man set foot on this continent.

# 3

**Earlier that summer**

From St. Louis, he rode southwesterly, heading in the direction of the family homestead near Dexter, Oklahoma. Approaching Springdale, Arkansas, he came upon his first "Cowboy Stampede," arriving near the end of the second day of a three-day event. The town reminded See Bird of some big, colorful bird, all aflutter, seeking a place to alight. He registered under the name of Red Carpenter for the third day's competition, paid his fee, and then ambled over to find a spot along the rail to watch a nightshirt race, in which riders in various stages of sobriety, wearing nothing but what any respectable man wore to bed, engaged in a chaotic two-mile race. With no boots to hold feet in the stirrups, nor spurs to goad the horses, riders relied on whooping and whistling to generate speed and their knees to control the direction of their confused steeds.

The horses, unused to such a lack of control, took full advantage of the situation, and periodically one or another would break from the pack, taking off at a diagonal to the rest of the racers, bringing its rider to the point of screaming frustration and the crowd to a state of breathless hilarity. With all the bumping and jostling going on, it was only a matter of time before the laughing crowd saw a rider's legs fly up over his horse as his feet slipped from the stirrups, only to watch as the unfortunate man was then unceremoniously tossed into the dirt. In the stands and along the fences, tears of laughter ran in rivulets. While the "Cowboy Stampede," as it was called, was mostly a display of man conquering beast, events such as the nightshirt race gave the beasts a chance to gain some measure of revenge. The audience roared its approval. See Bird, considering it from a cowboy's angle, was glad to see the embarrassed racer pick himself up, dust himself off, and gingerly limp barefooted back to the arena, apparently none the worse off, considering that serious injury from such a spill was more than a remote possibility.

By signing in under his nickname 'Red,' See Bird passed as a white man and thus had the run of the grounds and did not need to bed down in the area 'reserved' for native riders. That area lay just beyond the 'stampede' grounds, but the segregation was more than just racial. See Bird felt that it was part of a systematic attempt to make any native rider, no matter how skillful a horseman he was, feel intimidated and inferior. But, he noted, the ruse seldom worked. Indeed, as often as not, it backfired. Then, a rider inflamed by the slight might ride as never before, just to demonstrate his skill and worth. In fact, there were many successful Native Americans in these rodeos. In a society where they had been stripped of many of the trappings of manhood, native rodeo competitors won more than their limited numbers would have suggested. Still, See Bird had learned to tread lightly in the white man's world. He would generally avoid trouble, go where they went, see what they saw, and learn what he needed to know in order to improve his chances for success.

If the cowboys were local, they slept at home. The faded two-story wood-framed hotel was most likely filled, and if it wasn't, the thought of sleeping in a sagging, squeaking, bedbug-infested mattress for two bits convinced See Bird to unroll his blanket and nest in a soft pile of clean straw, in the livery. That way, he would also be near Kiamichi, contentedly munching oats on the other side of the stall divider. Tomorrow they would compete in the 'fancy roping' and bull-dogging. Both were events that See Bird felt confident he and Kiamichi would do well in. He was a perfectionist with the rope, and Kiamichi was unmatched working cattle.

Dawn broke pleasantly warm. After tending to his and his horse's needs, See Bird strolled down the main street to take the pulse of the place. The aroma of coffee and bacon drew him into a corner café, and soon he found himself seated at a small, oilcloth covered table. The waitress, a young freckle-faced woman with red hair tied back, flashed him a welcoming smile. "What'll it be, cowboy?" and slapped a pot of coffee down in front of him.

"I'll have whatever it is what dragged me in here that smells so danged good."

Her smile stretched even wider. "Be right back." She pivoted and walked away. Something about her reminded him of another red-haired girl from a different time and state. Mattie had that same saucy way about her, confident and charming, and with a smile that blew him away. But that was before one terrible night on a moonlit trail nearly cost her life. Something changed in her after that. She became more wary of people, less prone to take risks. But See Bird didn't really blame her. How long, he wondered, would it take a woman to recover completely from something like that? Maybe she never would. Still, Mattie was strong and married his best friend, Luke, with See Bird's approval, if not his blessing. He sighed and downed the coffee. You simply cannot predict real life. You just ride the trail, never knowing what's around the next bend.

"You here for the 'Cowboy Stampede'?" The perky waitress was back, filling up his table with piles of bacon, fried eggs, hashed brown potatoes, and toasted bread. Lastly, she set down a bowl of whipped butter, blackberry jam, and a fresh pot of coffee with cream. Taking a step back, the young woman blew a strawberry lock off her forehead and surveyed the display with satisfaction.

See Bird ostentatiously looked around. "Pardon me miss,"

"Molly," she interrupted. "Just call me Molly."

"Well, Molly, you must be expecting a crowd to sit here with me 'cause it would take a crew of hungry cowboys to eat all this. But I don't see anybody rushing over here. And yes, I am here for the 'stampede.' But if I was to eat all this, the only way I'd break a bronc would be because I'd weigh so much I'd bust that poor critter's back."

Molly put her hands on her hips and cocked her chin. "Well, mister…"

"Red. Call me, Red."

"Well, Red," she continued with a wink, "I figured you for a real cowboy, not some local hayseed. But you got to admit there ain't a whole lot to you. I thought maybe you could use some beefing up."

At that, they both laughed. See Bird picked up a fork and pointed at her. "Just you remember, gal, what they say. It ain't the size of the dog in the fight that matters. It's the fight in the dog." With that, he stabbed at an egg.

"Hah." Molly turned and strutted away. Barely slowing, she turned her head and flashed See Bird another smile. "And good luck, Red."

He watched admiringly as she passed through the kitchen door, then bent to his meal. Maybe she was right. Maybe he needed some luck. But See Bird was never one to rely on it. Preparation and hard work beat luck anytime. And considering the hundreds of hours' worth of work he and Kiamichi had put in back in West Virginia, and knowing his horse as well as he did, See Bird smiled to himself. "Let those other fellows depend on their luck. They're going to need it." He then set to his breakfast in earnest.

Bulldogging was the first event See Bird had signed up for. A slight early summer's breeze played in the dust of the arena, chasing it one way, then another, like small children playing tag in a schoolyard. He recalled with a wry smile the early days of the rodeos, down in Texas, when the ranch-hands would get together just to raise Cain and show off their skills. There were no fancy arenas built especially for these early 'cowboy contests,' or rodeos as they were more frequently called as of late. There had been no chutes, no gates, and no time limits. The animal, bronc, steer, or bull, was blindfolded and snubbed in the center of the arena. The cowboy climbed aboard, and the beast was set free. At least that's how it was supposed to go, but often didn't. Just mounting the animal could be problematic. How is a cowboy supposed to grab ahold when the bronc or bull starts dancing? And when does the timer start?

As See Bird walked Kiamichi in the direction of the chute, he caught some nearby chatter from a couple well-dressed 'cowboys' leaning on the rail. "You joshing me, old son? He actually did that?" the taller one asked the other.

"Sure enough did. Up in Cheyenne. They say he bit that bull right on his lip. The critter was so stunned, he fell down on the spot and Bill Pickett won the prize money." The shorter one carefully removed his spotless, flour-colored Stetson and flicked dust off it before tenderly resetting it squarely on his greased and slicked-down hair.

"Well, I'll be danged. No white man would have thought of a fool trick like that. But leave it to a 'coon.' Still, you won't catch me locking lips with such as that." Silence as both men tried to visualize what must have happened up in Cheyenne. See Bird and Kiamichi continued past. "He bit that bull?" the taller one asked again and paused to try and picture it, "Well, Lordy, I ain't never heard the likes of that."

In the chute, See Bird settled himself on Kiamichi's back. Catching the wild eye of the young bull in the neighboring chute, he remarked, "Now don't you be getting no ideas. I ain't Bill Pickett, and I got me a young gal in West Virginia that I do all my kissing on. So don't look at me thata way." He nodded at the 'hazer' mounted in the chute on the other side of the bull's chute. When the bull bolted, it would be the hazer's job to keep it running straight. Everything set, the bull's gate flew open. The burly creature saw a chance for freedom and took it. An instant later, Kiamichi was after him. His powerful quarterhorse hindquarters did not so much dig in to provide thrust as they simply rocketed both horse and rider forward at an astonishing speed.

See Bird, completely at ease with his powerful steed, within seconds pulled alongside the thundering bull. Squeezing Kiamichi with his knees, he reached over and down, grabbing the horns of this creature that outweighed him by 400 pounds, slid out of the saddle while Kiamichi ground to a halt a few feet away, beyond reach of those horns. As his feet hit the ground, See Bird immediately dug in his heels and twisted the bull's head toward him to stop its momentum and wrestle it to the ground. For the merest instant, it seemed steer would win the match. But See Bird's leverage won out over the steer's size, as it thudded to the ground, all four legs facing away from him. See Bird released his grip and stepped back to hear his time called. This was it, he thought. A lifetime compressed into six heart-thumping seconds. No other life could be worth living. Kiamichi stood, proud as a statue, just as he had been left until, on an unspoken hand signal, he stepped forward, allowing his rider to retrieve the reins and glide back into the saddle. He seemed to understand that this triumph was as much his doing as it was his rider's.

Horse and rider took a quick turn about, See Bird doffing his uncreased black slouch hat, acknowledging the applause, whistles, and hoots from the crowd as the announcer called his time again. Along the fence stood the two men whose conversation See Bird had overheard earlier. "Now, that's how it's supposed to be done. He didn't need no fool tricks, Lemuel. That's a real white man," said the taller one, emphasizing his comment with a playful punch to the other's shoulder.

See Bird dismounted as he passed through the gate, smiling to himself. "Howdy, boys." He touched the brim of his hat and paused a second. The two clearly admired his ride, but their words scratched him like a briar. "Having a good time?" he asked, eyeballing their shiny boots and new dungarees.

"That's for sure, mister. Where we hail from, there ain't much rodeoing."

"Oh, Where's that?"

The first would-be cowboy tilted his hat back for its effect and said, "Oxly, over by the Mississippi. Nothin' but small-timers there. Posey here is a teller in the bank. Me, my pa owns the only hotel in town. We heard about this show, dropped everything, and well, here we are." He concluded with a wide grin and assumed a stance that he must have thought resembled a real cowboy. "How about you, mister Carpenter? Where do you call home? And where'd you learn to ride hell-bent-for leather like that?"

See Bird studied his own well-worn boots a second before raising his eyes and replying. "Lot of questions, boys. But I'll tell you. I'm not from these parts. I started out down by Dexter – a crossroads town between Fort Smith and the Red River."

The second man interrupted, "But ain't that down in the Indian nations?"

"Shore 'nuff is, boys." See Bird swept off his hat as if to dust his britches with it, allowing his straight black hair to sweep down along either side of his face. "Choctaw country, to be exact. C'mon, Kiamichi. We gotta get set for the fancy roping." He took a step forward and his horse fell in behind him like a called dog. See Bird glanced over his shoulder at the two stunned faces. "I guess my people are just naturals on horseback. 'Chi pisa la chike.' See you around, boys."

As he walked Kiamichi down the dirt track that passed for the main street back to the livery, See Bird was aware that few people took notice of him. Everyone seemed to be preoccupied with their own business, bustling about, a wagon being loaded with farm supplies in front of the general store, and a few other couples entering and leaving the café he had eaten at a few hours ago. His rumbling stomach reminded him that he would soon revisit it and wondered if that same red-haired waitress would be there. It was only as he passed by the saloon that he caught the eye of a slack-jawed loafer leaning against the wall.

Perhaps the conversation he had just had with the fellows at the rodeo still rode him hard, or maybe he was just hot from the noonday sun. Whatever the reason, as he drew abreast of the loafer and their eyes met, See Bird swept the hat off his head, wiped his forehead with his cuff, and looked away, presenting a pure profile of an Indian man in his prime, riding a handsome horse. Caught unawares, the loafer threw the splinter he was using for a toothpick onto the boardwalk in disgust and turned abruptly, passing through the door into the saloon. 'You didn't like what you saw, did you?' See Bird thought to himself. 'Well, that's just too bad. And, if the Good Lord's willing and the creek don't rise, I'll take some more of your money this afternoon."

Back at the livery, See Bird flipped the stocky attendant a silver dollar and instructed him on caring for Kiamichi as he gathered up his lariat. He dallied a loop as he walked out behind the station. A few hip-shot horses lounged lazily in the corral. Beyond the livery low, wooded hills broken by a few open farm fields lay before him.

If See Bird loved riding, 'fancy roping' was something he did in his spare time just to relax. It required all his focus, and he could get so lost in the rhythms of twirling, that Sally more than once, to his chagrin, and her irritation, had to repeat her call to dinner. Inclement evenings might find him in the house, braiding a rope or shaking out a loop and twirling for hours, working patterns just to please himself. Sometimes the air hummed with music as the rope spun, songs only he heard, and which stopped instantly when the rope did.

Back at the rodeo, locating the announcer of the events proved to be no difficulty. A big red-faced balding man, wearing a calico shirt and wielding a megaphone, took the script See Bird used and briefly scanned it. "You really gonna do all this, pardner?"

"If I don't mess it up, I will," See Bird replied semi-seriously. "We'll see."

"We'll work you in, right after the bronc bustin', cowboy. Good luck." And See Bird made his way down to the arena.

A lady bronc rider was just picking herself up from the dirt to a nice round of applause and limped her way out through the gate past See Bird as he stepped in. The announcer was in full throat. "And now, ladies and gents, prepare yourselves," he called. "Red Carpenter, the West Virginia Whiz, is about to delight you with some fancy ropin' never before seen west of the Mississippi. Let's hear it for Red Carpenter."

A polite smattering of applause greeted him as See Bird walked out to the center of the arena, a small man, scarcely five and a half feet tall and tipping the scales at a hard 140 pounds. He was the third and final twirling contestant of the day. He had not caught the shows of the other two. His concern was only with himself and his own performance. It was important to give these people a show they would not soon forget, something they would talk about at their supper tables tonight and in the saloons and churches where they gathered.

While he waited for the announcer to call his first 'stunt,' he shook out the noose in his lasso and warmed up a bit. The rope felt stiff at first. He realized, with all these people watching, he was a bit self-conscious and needed to relax. And he needed them to relax, as well. He started with a flat spin, twirling the rope in front of his feet, then passing it under one leg to the other hand behind his back, where the right hand picked it up again. Grace and timing, that's it, he thought and smiled. He had done this a thousand times back in Warm Holler. Finally, he was starting to feel energy flowing up through the dirt beneath his feet, up his legs, powering his arms, extending through the fibers of the lasso, giving it a life of its own. The loop followed the motions his arm was making in the air. It shifted directions from flat to vertical. See Bird hopped through the loop several times before it played itself into a new shape – the Texas Tornado. He worked the rope the way a master musician would his instrument, finishing up his figures by creating a double loop that settled over his body and dropped to the dirt. The folks in the stands and around the fence were now paying attention. The enthusiastic applause proved it. A few whistled. See Bird raised his hat to the crowd and nodded in the direction of the announcer who called out, "For his first stunt, the West Virginia Whiz will lasso a horse running full speed."

The gate banged open as a horse and rider charged toward the small man. See Bird, now having reformed the loop perpendicular to the ground, skipped through it, seemingly oblivious to the onrushing horse and rider. Then, with a flick of his wrist and extension of his arm, the loop enlarged even more, drifted out and settled around the steed's neck. Dancing a step to the side, See Bird tightened the noose as the rider drew his horse to a stop. The crowd responded with appreciative applause.

As the rider turned his horse back to the gate, the voice in the megaphone called, "Next, Red Carpenter will demonstrate his command of the lasso by throwing a figure eight, capturing both the head and the legs of the oncoming horse." At this, the rider pivoted his horse and charged once again toward the man with the spinning rope. And, once again, with amazing grace, that man fed out a large loop, made a figure eight in the air with his rope arm, double-looping the lasso, and exactly as the horse and rider reached him the horse stepped through the lower loop while the upper loop dropped over its head. He had the crowd's complete and rapt attention now.

It quieted in anticipation as the rider reset his horse before the gate. See Bird picked up a second rope. "Watch as Red will now use two lassoes, roping the cowboy with one and his cayuse with the other." This was one of the more difficult stunts, requiring the rope artist to be equally dexterous with both hands, sending out two ropes at the same time. See Bird occasionally missed this in practice. Now a bead of sweat formed on his upper lip as he concentrated. Rolling out two loops, See Bird found a moment where they seemed to be slightly out of sync, a warning of danger. But as the rider guided his horse at a gallop once more towards him, See Bird breathed deeply and smiled. "It's not me. It's the rope," he thought, launching both at once, capturing rider and horse with moves as graceful as a professional dancer.

As See Bird retrieved the lasso from the horse to a rolling thunder of applause, the rider reached down, handing the second rope to 'The Whiz.' As he released it, he said with a smile, "Mister, I never seen the likes of that before, and I used to work with Buffalo Bill. My hat's off to you." Tipping his John B. to See Bird, he then turned and trotted his horse from the arena.

At the same time, the gate opened and a young

man entered bearing a long, coiled rope and leading Kiamichi. That was the next signal to the announcer. "Ladies and gentlemen, did you see that? Well, hold on to your parasols and hitch up your britches." The fellow was really into it now. "'Cause The Whiz is going to finish up with one of the most difficult rope tricks imaginable. He is going to twirl, from horseback, a 90-foot loop. Attendant, please present the rope." The fellow presented it to See Bird, who took one end and said, "Please take the rope up the aisle," and pointed. At this, the young man climbed from the arena up the aisle, through the crowd, to the back of the stands, unwinding it completely. The announcer sang out, "Ladies and gentlemen, as you see, this rope is indeed 90 feet in length." See Bird recoiled it and mounted Kiamichi.

Man and horse moved to the center of the arena, where he began by shaking out a small vertical loop. Then he enlarged it a bit and slowly lifted it over his head. Continually feeding out rope, the circle grew larger and larger. The new hemp glistened beautifully in the sun. See Bird nudged the horse forward toward the crowd. The loop expanded, drifting over the heads of those in the front row. From the crowd, someone who couldn't stand the tension released a raucous whistle. Unfazed, See Bird edged forward until Kiamichi's muzzle was nearly touching the fence. The rope was now fully extended in a near 90-foot loop, humming just over the heads of the entranced audience. Magic was in the air. Then slowly, steadily, Kiamichi began backing away until See Bird was once again in the center of the arena in the center of the lasso's circle. At that point, he released his end of the rope and dropped it in the dirt. Kiamichi dropped and knelt on one knee while his rider waved his hat to the standing, stomping, and whistling crowd.

"Let's hear it one more time for Red Carpenter, the West Virginia Whiz," the announcer called as See Bird, with a cowboy whoop, exited through the arena gate on a prancing Kiamichi.

# 4

**Fort Smith, Arkansas**

"'Hell On The Border,' folks used to call it." See Bird did not think it at all strange to talk with Kiamichi as he rode down out of the Ozarks toward the confluence of the Arkansas and Poteau rivers. In fact, he would have considered it unfriendly not to talk things over with his horse — the animal reciprocated by twitching his ears and occasionally giving out a friendly blow. Life is good; he seemed to be saying. See Bird picked up the conversation as he followed the trail into Fort Smith. "Judge Parker used to hang people by the dozens down there. It was a mighty rough patch of ground. Look at it now, all citified."

He pulled up as he entered the town, bustling with activity. The old fort still sat on the bluff, but around and below it spilled a growing city. From the train station down by the river, a tram carried passengers to the upper part of the city. A noisy engine nearby, sounding a bit like a toy train, caused Kiamichi to hop a few nervous steps before See Bird could reassure him. "Whoa. That's okay, boy. That's a horseless carriage. Folks say they're the future, and the likes of you will soon be put out to pasture." He patted the steed's neck and grinned as some machine that did indeed resemble a wagon minus a horse stuttered and popped its way along the brick street. It was not traveling at much more than a slow walk. That was because in front of it walked a man waving a small flag, warning people out of the way. See Bird shook his head. "But don't you believe it, boy. You're safe with me. That thing looks like a boondoggle." He watched it putter down the street, causing minor disruptions as, on occasion, the shaking machine would backfire. Horses at hitching posts would side-step nervously, to get out of the way and to strain to glimpse the contraption. "Yup, boy. It's a new century. Who knows what they'll think of next!"

They stayed only long enough for See Bird to purchase some needed supplies. Then they hit the trail again, clearing town before the evening set in. He was so used to sleeping under the stars, with his horse nearby, that the prospect of sleeping on some noisy, vermin-infested spring bed, in some creaky-floored hotel, waking up every time somebody came or went, was markedly unattractive. There just seemed to be no privacy in them.

Several days later they made camp in the Ouachitas, a beautiful range of low, forested mountains in south-east Oklahoma. From Choctaw words 'ouac', meaning buffalo and 'chito,' their word for large, in other words 'large buffalo,' the range stretched out, oddly enough, running from east to west, rather than north to south, like the Rockies or Appalachian Mountains. "But all the buffs and elk are gone now. Too bad."

See Bird and his twin brother See Right, in days long past, used to hunt along these hickory, oak, and juniper-forested ridges, and fish in streams so clear that man and beast both would drink their fill from a boulder-strewn river. As evening settled in, See Bird drew to a halt along such a stream and after both drank as much as they wanted, See Bird filled his canteen and stooped to pick a handful of watercress to add to his supper. “Do you know where we are, big fella?” Kiamichi shook his head as if in the negative. “No, of course you don’t. Well, take a good look, boy. This here ribbon of water is your namesake, the Kiamichi River. Every time I say your name, it reminds me of this place.” Nearly overcome for the moment, he squatted on his heels and just listened to the sounds of the forest and the water — his horse, less impressed, set to munching some rich, new green grass along its bank.

“Tomorrow, we’ll reach the homestead.” Kiamichi lifted his head and appeared to pay attention. See Bird rose, flicked a blade of grass away, and tended his mount. “Don’t rightly know what we’ll find. Last thing I heard, Pa was still trying to run some cattle. But that was a long time ago.” He brushed him down, fed him a handful of oats, and ground-hobbled him for the night. “We’ll see what tomorrow brings us.”

See Bird was antsy with eagerness and was up before dawn to break camp. Pushing hard, it was nearly evening of the following day when they crested a low ridge along the river and took in the scene below them. A curl of chimney smoke from a small house with a shingled roof, the very one he remembered growing up in, carried the pleasant aroma of wood-smoke their way. In a corral out behind the barn, a piebald horse stood alert, its ears pointed their way. A dog barked.

“Look there, boy.” See Bird pointed toward the river. “Over thataway is the swimming hole where my brother and me played around on days like this. Should we drop by and see who’s home?” Kiamichi nodded his great neck. “Well, alright then. Let’s go down and knock on the door." And with a nudge to the horse's ribs, they started down the hill. The dog must have seen them. It now began barking in earnest.

As the approaching rider showed no sign of stopping or turning back, the dog, a handsome mid-sized black and white collie, nipped at the horse's hooves until a near-miss of a quick kick sent it sulking off towards the barn. See Bird paid it no mind. A low fence set off a patch of space that could scarcely be called a house-yard surrounding a grey clapboard affair that appeared not to have seen a splash of paint in a long while. The gate hung permanently open, dangling by one hinge. See Bird reined up outside the fence but remained in the saddle, vaguely disturbed and anxious. "Hello, the house," he called. He thought he detected a rustle by a window curtain, but other than that, there was no response. "Halito, Pa. You there?" The door squeaked open on rusty hinges, but the words he was forming froze in his throat. He found himself staring down the business end of a double-barreled shotgun.

The woman stood there, balancing the shotgun on her hip like she had fired it before. No need to aim. See Bird knew that from this distance, she could scarcely miss. She knew it too. "Don't get down. Just sit and say what you want."

She clipped her words like the girls he remembered from the mission school, but she spoke good English. "Ma'am, I used to live here as a boy, and I would greatly appreciate it if you would just lower those barrels a mite. Here are my hands." He rested them on the saddle horn. "Empty. I promise I'm not here to hurt anybody."

The woman sized the rider up and sensing no threat, slowly let the gun sag, relaxing her grip. Holding it in one hand, with the other she tucked a strand of jet-black hair behind one ear. What might have been a slight smile formed and disappeared. "I'm listening," she said.

"Name's See Bird, ma'am, and I'm of 'the people' too. Fact is, I was birthed in that house behind you. Last time I was here, my pa was trying to farm cattle. I left nigh onto twenty years ago and didn't look back. I was just in the neighborhood and thought I'd see how things were."

The woman turned and stepped back through the door. For a moment, See Bird thought she was going to shut the door on him, but a few seconds later, she returned – without the gun. "Well, step on down, See Bird, and halito. Why don't you tend your horse out to the stable while I perk some coffee, and then I would like to hear your story. Pardon the shotgun, but I don't get much company, and a girl, living alone, can't be too careful. My name is Leaping Water, 'Talulah.'

Having settled Kiamichi into a stall, brushed and fed for the night, See Bird stepped out of the stable to see the Piebald standing near a pile of tossed hay. He had to admit the animal had good lines and was a bit larger than Kiamichi, but it appeared a bit too high strung for his liking, ears flicking every which way, tail continuously swishing, even at this late hour. "You've got something to settle, don't you, big fellow?" See Bird grunted and made his way to the house through the dusky air of evening.

The wonderful aroma of fresh perk greeted him before he stepped up onto the porch. As he passed through the door, he automatically looked to its right to see two wooden pegs attached to the wall, pegs his father had whittled for him and his brother See Right to hang their moccasins on when they entered the small house. The sound of bubbling coffee drew his eyes to a cast-iron stove in one corner, on which the coffee pot sat and sang, in the very place where one just like it had sat many long years ago in this, his childhood home. See Bird was surprised and nearly overwhelmed by the memories and emotions that surged through him. The years between then and this moment dissolved, leaving him choked up and momentarily speechless.

Leaping Water noticed his discomfort and smiled as if to say, "I understand." She finished pouring two cups and set them on a small wooden table. She sat, and with a wave of her hand indicated he should do the same. "It's getting late," she said, almost apologetically. "I don't cook much on hot days like this, so you will have to make do with the food you carried in with you. Bed down in the stable, if you like."

"That'll be just fine, ma'am."

"Please, don't call me that, mister. You look to be ten years older than me. Should I call you 'Sir?' Folks hereabouts call me Ta-lu-lah, 'Leaping Water.'" When she smiled at his discomfort, See Bird was surprised at her transformation and could see that she was indeed an attractive young woman. The lines about her mouth and eyes disappeared. Deep brown eyes set in a round face, which at first glance had seemed suspicious and hostile now seemed alight with good humor and curiosity. Fingering her cup, she said, "You started in on a yarn about growing up here. Tell me the rest of it."

She leaned forward as he shared the stories of his youth, of growing up in a land that was to be reserved forever for the red man. Her sincere interest sparked in him a desire to communicate, and he found that in the telling, he was defining his life. He spoke of his twin brother 'See Right,' how he had rescued him from the river one hot summer's day. He told Talulah of the Christian mission school he had attended through the sixth grade and about how the sudden death of his mother marked the end of his formal education.

He explained how his father seemed to never recover from the loss of See Bird's mother and how, several years later he left his father and brother behind on the family homestead to make his way in life as a cowboy, wrangling cattle and training horses down in Texas before drifting east. He knew his people, the Choctaw, were originally from the land east of the Mississippi before they were forced out, and he desired to see it for himself. It was down in Texas where he discovered his gift for working with horses, even those ranchers had given up on. He told her that it was on a ranch near Waco that he had met his present horse, Kiamichi, trained him, and then was made a gift of the steed before the young man left.

Finally, he shared with this young woman about his recent return to the west from West Virginia in order to compete in the newly forming rodeo circuit. "That's about it. Maybe someday I'll bring my family out here. Now you know as much about me as I know myself, girl. What's your story?" And he settled back in his chair, a coffee mug cradled in his hands, waiting.

"What's there to tell?" She pushed herself away from the table and walked over to the stove. She held her hands out and counted off on her fingers. "I got me a farm I can't work, cattle I can't use, and a horse I can't ride." She laughed at See Bird's confusion, and See Bird joined in. She carried the pot back to the table and poured him another cup of coffee, then sat again. "Seriously, about a year ago, a fella rolled in on the Frisco train from back east. Said he wanted to 'make a go of it, old chap.' That's really the way he talked. Said he was from some island across the ocean where everyone talked English the way he did. I can't see how they understood each other. Anyhow, he read a book by some Buntline fella and decided 'The Wild West" was the life for him." See Bird knew of this Ned Buntline. He once picked up a pulp novel Western written by the man, but after a few pages, tossed it aside laughing at such foolishness and though he liked to read, never picked it up again nor any other book by Ned Buntline.

"He got to New York and bought a ticket west. He told me he kept going until he found a place that reminded him of home said these hills reminded him of the 'Cotswalds,' whatever they are. He met me down by Dexter when he got lost tramping about the woods and stopped for directions at my family's place." See Bird nodded. It was a fact he was well aware that a person unfamiliar with the heavily forested mountains, could easily get turned around and wander aimlessly for days. "He stayed overnight and fell in love with his 'Indian Princess,' as he called me. He bought this place, cattle included, for a good price from a young man and his wife. Sorry. They don't sound like kin of yours." She shook her head. "He never seemed short of money. We married and moved in, all within a month of his stepping off the train."

"You should have seen him wearing what he thought were cowboy duds. He wasn't a whole lot taller than you, but when he put on his fancy boots and hat, he acted like he was six feet tall. And those chaps. When he walked in them, it looked like two sheep taking turns stepping forward. He was having a great time playing cowboy. And I played along. It was the first time in my life I ever had anything." She dropped her eyes then raised them quickly, looking out the window toward the corral and barn. "What brought him back to the real world was that horse out there." She nodded her head in the direction of the piebald. "Lucien Hobbes. That was the man's name. Behind his back, folks called him 'Lucy.' He even wanted me to call him Lucien." She shrugged.

"From the books he read, taming a wild horse sounded easy. He claimed any 'real Western man' could do it. So, Lucien bought one and had it delivered. 'It certainly is a big brute,' he said to me. 'Wish me luck, my charming Indian maid.' He pushed his glasses way up on his nose, grabbed a saddle he found in the barn and carried it out into the corral. Then he tried to throw it onto the horse's back. The animal screamed and ran away. But Lucien was determined. You should have seen him in his fancy get-up chasing that crazy animal around the corral, tossing the saddle at it, picking it up again, shouting at the horse, then chasing it some more. Once, he nearly got it cornered and moved in with his saddle. Only the horse had other ideas. It reared up, knocked him down, broke his glasses, and bruised his ribs. When I doctored him up, all he could talk about was how this was not the way he had pictured it back home in England. 'It's all so exhausting,' he said. 'Perchance, I was not meant to be a lowly wrangler of cattle by horseback.'

"To Lucien's credit, he tried the next day and the day after that again. I could count on it every day that when I looked out that window, I'd see him chasing and cursing that horse around and around. And him wearing those heavy sheepskin chaps. I swear that horse was laughing at him and must have thought it was all a game." She shook her head. "Then one day he came in, slammed his saddle down by the door, and announced, 'My dearest Princess Leaping Water, I have come to a conviction that this is, indeed, not the life for me. I have taken legal pains to commit all of my property to you. It is all yours, this domicile, the livestock, lands and crops, even that wicked animal out there.' He stood right there and waved his arms around like this was some huge English castle or something. He went into the bedroom and when he came back out, he was dressed in the same clothes he was wearing the day I met him, including his derby hat, wool suit and vest, and his black walking stick with a silver tip. He was wearing a red scarf he called a cravat and walked to the door. I did not know what to say, but I'll never forget what he said. He bowed and clicked the heels on those black and white shoes. 'Do not weep for me, my darling. For I must go where my dreams do beckon.' He spun on out, and the last I saw of Lucien Hobbes, he was striding down the trail to town, singing to the skylarks. And that was over a month ago."

See Bird leaned back in his chair and thought about all he had just heard. Clearly, the girl opposite him expected him to say something. The glimmer of a plan was taking shape in his mind, but it all meant nothing without her approval. He cleared his voice. "Well, Talulah, that is about the gol-dangedest tale I ever heard. And I don't rightly know what to make of it. I cain't stay and work your farm, but if you don't mind, I'll stick around a little while to fix things up a bit for you and tame that handsome devil out yonder. Then we can take him and the cattle in your pasture into town and probably sell them for a decent horse and buggy so's you can get around. Right now, though, I'm about done in. So, if you do not mind, I'm gonna go turn in. I'll see you in the morning. That'll give you some time to think over my offer. Just let me know. I'll be satisfied with whatever you decide." With that, he stood, picked up his hat, and stepped out the door into a warm summer night. "Good night now, Talulah, and don't worry too much. I'm sure you'll work it out just fine."

"Wait a minute. Here, See Bird," she said softly from the door. "Take this lantern so you can find your way." She handed it to him. Then the door closed and he was alone with the night.

# 5

"I think your man Lucien, maybe by fool's luck, maybe because he knew something about horseflesh, went and bought himself a pretty good animal." See Bird stood with one foot on the bottom fence rail and leaned against the top, cradling a mug of steaming black coffee handed to him by Leaping Water. "See that? He's studying us right now."

"I do not think so," she responded. "He is looking the other way."

"Don't look at his eyes, Talulah. Watch his ears. They're pricked and turned to the side, facing us. And don't you be fooled by which way his head is pointing. Except for right behind his rump and right in front of his face, he sees everything with those big beautiful eyes. He sure 'nuff sees us."

"You musta broke in a lotta horses, hey?"

"I've ridden thousands, I guess. But I never broke a single one. They're by nature friendly critters, but they gotta watch out for wolves, bears, cougars, and the like. So, they're pretty quiet and mighty careful about their surroundings. They usually talk to each other with their bodies. If you study on it just a bit, you can learn their language." Leaping Water glanced up sideways at this statement. "I dumped my saddle and gear out in the corral last night so's he could see it and get used to it. Horses will spook over some of the silliest things. I once had a horse who gave up one day on coming over to one side of the corral. For days he avoided it like the plague. Then I noticed and removed an old plow someone had recently leaned against the fence, and he came back right away. He didn't know it and didn't want to give it a chance to attack. Your horse figures that pile is no threat to him now, but he's still suspicious, so he's pretending to ignore it." See Bird chuckled. "That'll change." He handed the mug back to Talulah and bent to climb through the fence. "I might as well start earning my keep," he said as he slowly walked towards the center of the pen. "Let's get introduced to each other," he called out to the horse, who immediately stopped grazing and gave him its full attention.

She didn't know what to expect, but what did happen was definitely not anything Leaping Water would have contemplated. See Bird walked to where his gear was stacked. After a few minutes of seemingly meaningless hand actions on the horse, he picked up a line of rope and pitched it towards its rear, driving it away. "Well, I'll be," she muttered. "That's just silly." Still, the man stood in the center and pitched the rope toward the horse as it circled the pen, looking to get away. After five or six revolutions one way, he changed the pitch and sent the horse moving the other direction. After only a few minutes of this, See Bird stopped and coiled the line with his eyes on the ground, looking away from the horse, who had stopped as well.

At this point, See Bird made his move toward the horse, but not directly, moving in almost a half-circle to it. Anxious, the animal moved a few steps away. See

Bird uncoiled some rope and they played pitch for a few more laps. "Watch this now, Talulah. You're in for a treat." See Bird turned and kept his back to the horse. In a few moments, it walked up to the man and reached out, bumping his shoulders with its nose. See Bird reached up and rubbed the area between the beast's eyes while walking away in circles. The piebald followed like a puppy. "That's enough for now," See Bird said, walking toward the fence. "We'll play again later," he said as he climbed back through the fence. The horse, seeing the man leaving, watched him with those same huge, limpid eyes, then turned and wandered over to the other side of the corral, as calmly as if he played pitch rope every day.

"Horses are naturally sociable critters," he said to break the silence. Leaping Water was speechless. "They don't yammer on like we do. But if you know how they operate, you can talk to them as easily as you do to your kid," he looked at the attractive young woman in embarrassment and muttered, "if you had one. And they'll talk back, but, like I said, with their bodies. Now that one's a good boy. He doesn't want to hurt anybody. He was just scared – and maybe a mite lonely. He will appreciate getting to a place where he'll have some company. In the wild, horses band up. Back home, Kiamichi here has two mules and a mare for company. It keeps him healthy upstairs, if you get my drift. By the way, what do you plan on calling him? He'll learn his name if he hears it enough."

"I don't know. I was thinking of 'Cobb.' It sorta reminds me of my crazy husband, Hobbes. And then some fellas in the general store were talking about somebody they heard of back East by that name." She looked up at See Bird with a twinkle in her eye and a smile. "It sorta stuck with me."

See Bird noticed how she always clipped off the words ending in 'ing.' 'Something' became 'somethin'. 'Thinking' became 'thinkin'. It was strange, he thought, how he had not been aware of it before. It just sounded so natural. "I don't see that there'll be much of a problem getting a saddle on Cobb then," See Bird noted. "He'll just need a little patience and respect."

She glanced up and met See Bird's warm eyes. This was a man worth the title, a man worth waiting for. He broke the look with a smile. "Now, gal, how about some breakfast. If I'm to get a saddle on Cobb there, I'll need some vittles and another cup of Arbuckle's." Together they turned and headed back to the familiar house. Leaping Water noticed that the gate now swung easily open on two stout hinges. The border collie bounced along with them.

See Bird spent the day working with Cobb at a leisurely pace. By the afternoon, he had him saddle-broken. By evening, with See Bird firmly aboard, the two were jogging around the corral. Once Cobb had figured out that the strange creature with unreadable ears wanted to ride on his back, he was more than willing to cooperate, at least for a couple of rubbery carrots.

After supper, See Bird brought out Kiamichi and called Leaping Water to climb aboard while he sat on Cobb. "I thought I would show you some of the neighborhood hereabouts where I grew up," he said as she climbed competently into the saddle, western style, showing considerable leg. My horse, Kiamichi, is named after that river over yonder. Just thought I'd visit the old swimming hole and give him some exercise so's he don't get all lazy on me."

As the two turned to ride away, the frisky watch-dog, who had been hiding out under the porch during the heat of the day, decided that this outing looked like too much fun to miss, squirmed out of its hole, and dashed up alongside Kiamichi as if they were bosom buddies. Then, with a friendly 'yap,' it raced ahead, frequently glancing over its shoulder to ensure it was leading them in the correct direction.

After a few minutes, it became obvious to See Bird that Cobb would have provided a fine ride for Leaping Water. True, it might have been larger than a woman like her would have chosen for herself, but Cobb was eager to please and responded well to his rider's desires. They reached the river bank and turned upstream. See Bird became lost in memories of the place, and in the playful voice of the young Kiamichi River. He could hear the voices of young boys squealing with delight and calling out to each other. He was surprised at the flood of childhood detail that washed over and through him. Then they rounded a bend where the river curved under a cut-bank. A deep pool eddied and the clear water circled slowly. The river's voice dropped to a whisper. The two riders pulled up, and See Bird spoke softly. "This is my favorite place on Earth, I think. As boys, See Right and me would come up here every chance we got from work to goof off and cool down. We taught each other to swim right over there." He nodded towards a boulder protruding from the long grass by a cut-bank. "We would dive off that big rock over there." He slid out of the saddle. Leaping Water followed quickly. Together they walked over to it and sat. Leaping Water shifted her weight, brushing lightly against him. Suddenly, See Bird became aware of her nearness and of how strongly he desired to share with this lovely woman just how much this place meant to him.

He found himself wanting to lean over in her direction, could see in his mind's eye how she would close her eyes and lean into him, how their lips would meet, and then what would follow there in the soft grass. Then, her image faded and there beside him was Sally, and it was her brown eyes searching deeply into his, her blond hair drifting in the evening breeze like spider silk, and her lips waiting for his. How could he think of betraying the love and trust she gave him? How could he even daydream about inflicting so much pain on one he loved so much?

Ashamed, he continued his lean forward, past Leaping Water, down, picking up a twig and tossing it into the river. "Go get it, boy," he called hoarsely to the dog. The eager animal leaped to his feet and raced past the seated couple, into the water with a splash. Both people were keenly aware that the intimate moment had passed, one with disappointment, the other relief.

# 6

Several days later at breakfast, See Bird announced, "Leaping Water, I think it's time we headed your beeves into town. I've pretty much got Dog trained to herd 'em. He took to it like he was born to chase cattle. I've tidied up the place as best I could, and it's past time I fetched out to go rodeoing. What do you think, gal?"

She took her customary seat opposite him at the table, and for a moment just savored the morning, the early slanted sunrays cutting narrow beams through her flowered window curtains, the aroma of fresh coffee and bacon, the voice of this good and loyal man. "Yes, of course, See Bird. It's time. For sure, it is past time. I've held you here as long as I can," she smiled, "but I know you have other responsibilities and a lucky woman waiting for you back to your home." She paused. "So soon's I clean up here, let's go to market."

Herding Leaping Water's cattle to Dexter was just as easy as See Bird had expected it would be. To call the time spent with Dog over the last couple days 'training work' would have been embarrassing. The animal was so eager to learn and responded so quickly; it was as if he had been waiting all of his life to learn commands. If Leaping Water were to hold onto the property, she would need help. Dog would prove valuable to her.

Mostly, he loped along beside the riders trailing the small herd. Occasionally, when a cow would show a spark of independence or absent-mindedly wander off the trail to crop some grass, See Bird would whistle and point. Dog would then leap into action, joyfully dashing over to yap in the cow's face, heading her back to the herd. If she were a laggard, Dog would nip at her heels. He worked tirelessly, even as the morning grew longer and the heat of the day increased. Upon completing one task, he would then resume his place alongside See Bird and Leaping Water, just waiting for any opportunity to display his worth.

Having spent his youth in the area, See Bird shared memories with and gave ranching advice to Leaping Water. One concern he did not share with the Choctaw woman had been gnawing at him for several days, but since he could think of no solution, there seemed no point in bringing it up. She was alone. Her family was a long distance off. Neighbors were scarce. Sure this was a new century and all, but still, she was a woman alone, with only a dog for help. They had talked it over one evening. She was adamant about staying and keeping the place, and See Bird felt he had no right to insist otherwise. Still, he was concerned.

Dexter came into view first as a huddled collection of wooden shacks bordering the river, between it and the Frisco railroad tracks. As they drew nearer, it became more defined. The village was much the way See Bird remembered it as a young man. On the east end of town, as they approached, was the livery-stable, with its corral and holding pens out back, providing easy access to the railroad. The village proper didn't amount to much. It slouched alongside one dirt road, with the buildings pretty much all on the same side.

Two sawmills, one on each end of town, with their accompanying storage and work sheds sprawled along the riverside. As one would expect in a lumbering area, the buildings along the main street were mostly all of wood, single stories with false-front second stories except for the hotel, a new-looking, two-story red brick structure. Other than that, the three blocks of the main street were filled with two general stores, the sawmills, a café next to the hotel, and a saloon. A white church's stubby steeple topped by a white wooden cross poked above the roofs a block off. The rest of the village of probably fewer than 250 seemed huddled around the church's skirts. On the far end of town, where the street turned away from the river, stood the blacksmith shop.

As they neared town, See Bird moved ahead and seeing a middle-aged man in bib overalls and a big-brimmed hat forking hay into the corral behind the livery, he signaled with a whistle and a wave to open the gate. The worker, seeing the approaching herd, returned the wave and moved to swing the gate opcn. See Bird then rode back and helped drive the cattle in. The attendant closed and latched the gate and walked back into the livery. See Bird and Leaping Water followed, walking their horses behind him.

The shadowed livery-stable felt ten degrees cooler than the outside, and the two riders were grateful for the shade as they stalled their mounts and turned to the man who greeted them with a raised hand and a friendly, "Halito." See Bird was about to comment on the heat, but the words froze in his mouth. What he said instead was simply, "Pa." The liveryman stood as if glued to the spot while he composed himself. See Bird stepped forward and the two embraced. "It's been a while," was all he could say.

A few minutes later, as the three sat on several overturned pails, See Bird and his father filled each other in over the events of the years past. See Bird spoke of his cowboy days down in Texas, his travels east, and his meeting and marrying Sally. As the years sailed by, he had wondered increasingly about whatever happened to his father and brother, See Right. "You don't have to wonder about that anymore," his father interjected. "After your mom died and you left, my heart kinda went out of ranching. See Right wanted to travel too. When he came back from wherever he went, he brought a wife with him. He always was right handy fixing things but not so much into working with cattle, so it didn't take long before we sold the spread and moved into town. Got a good price for it. I bought out the livery-stables at this end of town, and if you just mosey down to the other end of town, you'll find the blacksmith shop. Like as not that's where you'll find your brother, in his leather apron, pounding out a horseshoe or something. Now that we got both ends of town covered, I figure we'll get everybody coming and going." He laughed. "And we're doing okay." He stopped and glanced at Leaping Water. "You mentioned a wife back east. Then who is this young woman?" he asked, not unkindly.

"Pa, this is Leaping Water Hobbes. She married an English gent a while back, but it appears he lit a shuck for parts unknown, leaving the missus here with the land and cattle off'n our old place. I swung by to check it out, found her, and have been helping out for a bit, sorta working to get it up and running proper. She wants to stick it out but doesn't even have a buckboard. That's why we're droving her cattle in, all but one milk cow and a young bull. She needs to sell these beeves. Do you know, is there a market hereabouts?"

"I surely do, son. I'm it. The Frisco line runs right through town. It seems that back east, folks are developing a real taste for western beef. I believe I can get you a good price for that herd of yours, Mrs. Hobbes," he said as he turned to Leaping Water.

After some quick calculations and a handshake to seal the deal, See Bird and Leaping Water rode down the main street in her newly purchased buckboard drawn by a pair of sturdy if undistinguished horses. She exchanged her cattle and the piebald for the buckboard, two lesser horses, and enough cash to stake her for a while as well. They pulled up in front of the first general store they came to and stepped down to the fresh smell of sawdust and sounds of saws working the rough lumber across the street at Clayton's Lumber Mill. "You go on in and get what you need," See Bird instructed. "I'm going to take a little walk down to the blacksmith shop." He smiled. "Seems like this is my lucky day. I didn't know what to expect, coming into town, but this sure wasn't it. I'll meet you over at the café by the hotel in half-an-hour." He touched the brim of his hat and walked away. Leaping Water watched him wistfully for a moment and then looked nervously at the storefront with its pickle-barrel in front and the dry-goods in the window. Then she steeled her nerve. "If I'm gonna be an independent woman, I gotta start now. So here I go." She gathered her skirts and, with determination, stepped up and through the open door into the general store.

The clang of hammer on steel greeted See Bird as he approached the blacksmith shop. It stood at the west end of the thoroughfare, nestled beneath a giant cottonwood on the bank of the river. The road out of town turned to the right directly before it. "Halito, See Right," he called as he stepped inside. There was no mistaking his identical twin shaping a horseshoe on the anvil. Bare-chested but for a well-worn leather apron, he eyed the man stepping out of the bright sunlight into the shop for a few careful moments. Slowly, he set the hammer down, wiped his hands on his denims, and walked over to him. "Brother," was all he said, and the two men locked forearms in greeting.

Time flew. The two men were so natural together that it seemed to See Bird that it might as well have been only yesterday since they had parted. "Do you remember that time when we were just kids and Pa brought us into town for supplies? And while he was in the general store, the two of us were just playing around, crawling under the boardwalk and such like, looking for toads?"

See Right grinned and picked up the thought, "And all the sudden there was more shouting and yelling and shooting than I ever heard. We crawled out and hid behind the water trough to see what all the commotion was about."

"And it's a good thing we did," See Bird interjected, "'cause Curly Bill Brocius was robbing the bank and the lead was a flying."

See Right nodded. "I could hear bullets smack into the water in the trough, thought it sounded like hailstones."

"After him and his crew rode out, Pa found us huddled there, packed us in the buckboard, and we all headed on home just as if a holdup happened every day. He didn't even seem particularly worried about our safety. He said he figured we were smart enough to stay out of the line of fire. Too bad for Curly Bill that he picked a fight with Wyatt Earp later on. I don't think Pa ever told Ma about the shootout."

"If he had, she probably wouldn't of let us come back into town ever again."

They laughed and settled down to quietly filling each other in on their lives since they had parted. "After Ma died and you rode off," See Right said, "Pa sold the place and moved to town. I got antsy and moved on, over toward Durant. I found me a good woman but didn't want to ranch, and there just didn't seem to be anything else open for me. Pale skins were already starting to fill up the place. When we came back here, old Jasper Collins, who used to own this shop, up and died. Pa bought it with some savings. We found us all a house over by the church and that's where we call home now." He shook his head slowly. "I didn't know if I'd ever see you again."

They were distracted by another person entering the shop. "Excuse me, See Bird," Leaping Water interrupted with a hint of irritation, "But it was getting hot out there. I got everything I needed from the store all loaded up, and it's been nearly an hour." Her glance traveled to his mirror image, forcing her to do a double-take. "Oh, my goodness. It's true then. There are two of you." Catching herself, she apologized, "I'm sorry. I didn't mean to interrupt. You must think…" She tried to drop her eyes, but could not stop staring.

See Bird laughed. "It's okay. I'm the one who's sorry. I lost track of time. See Right, this is Leaping Water Hobbes, the lady who bought our old spread. I been helping her out a bit 'til she gets on her feet."

The two men stood. "Glad to meet you, Mrs. Hobbes. Listen, why don't you and See Bird come over to the house. Pa and I sometimes shut down for an hour or so when it gets hot like this. How about let's take a break and make something to eat. We can't afford to eat out every day."

See Bird turned to Leaping Water. "How's that sound to you, Mrs. Hobbes?"

"It sounds just fine, See Bird. But it'd sound a whole lot better if you stop calling me Mrs. Hobbes. I do not imagine I'll ever see Lucien again." She turned her attention to See Right. "My name is Talulah. It means "Leaping Water" in Choctaw, and I would love to meet your wife, See Right."

The directness of this attractive, round-faced woman took him aback briefly. His face darkened momentarily. "I'm afraid you will not be able to meet my wife, Talulah." He looked at See Right. "She died two years ago giving birth to my son. He died too. They're in the graveyard behind the church." There was a very awkward moment of foot-shuffling. Then See Right brightened. "It was not easy for a while, but it is better now. Please, let us go meet Pa." He smiled again and ushered them out. See Right closed the door and bolted it behind them. Then all three climbed onto the seat of her newly bought and fully loaded buckboard with Talulah happily positioned between the two reunited twins. With a flick of his wrist and a click of his tongue, See Right turned the wagon and walked it down the street and around the corner.

# 7

"Well, it won't be long before this whole country is crisscrossed with railroad tracks," See Bird thought as he drew Kiamichi up short of the slightly raised gravel roadbed that wound its way in a generally western direction from Dexter. "This sure wasn't here the last time I passed this way. Of course, it's been a while," he spoke to his attentive horse, who bobbed his head in response. Reining Kiamichi to his right and heading north alongside the tracks, he thought out loud, "That would've been when we were following old Jesse Chisholm's trail north, pushing a few thousand cattle for Big Jim McCarty. Remember him, boy?" Kiamichi blew as if in response, and See Bird drew up short. "Are you understanding me, boy? Seems to me like that you are." He chuckled to himself. "Seems to me you're as smart as most people I know and don't interrupt nearly as much. That's probably why you are such good company." He patted the side of his steed's neck and squeezed its ribs gently with his knees, encouraging Kiamichi to pick up the pace a bit.

Sensing See Bird's eagerness, the horse broke into a gallop, See Bird letting him have his head for a bit before slowing to a walk once again and resuming his conversation. "I was a mite worried about leaving

Talulah in such a bind back there, but if I'm not mistaken, See Right was more than willing to check in on her once in a while like I asked him to, and she seemed more than willing that he be the man to do so. Yes sir, I do think that might work out just fine for the both of them." Rounding a small hill, he spotted a water tower in the distance and some out-buildings that hinted at a town nearby. Peach orchards lined the trail. A short time later, his suspicions about a town being nearby were confirmed.

Winnewood was the town, and as See Bird walked Kiamichi down the central thoroughfare, it looked as though a party was about to break out. Merchants stood in their doorways, and customers strode back and forth to their hitched wagons, loading goods and chatting with passersby. See Bird turned his head at the whistle of the Atchinson-Topeka and Santa Fe engine chugging into the newly built station. Some young men were hoisting a temporary sign above the entrance to a solidly constructed building – 'The Hotel Eskridge.' Energy charged the atmosphere like electricity as See Bird dismounted, threw a quick slip knot over the hitching post, and strode inside to the front desk. A smiling clerk with a poor complexion, slicked-back hair parted in the middle, and a red garter on the left sleeve of his red and white striped shirt greeted him. Only one other person, a portly middle-aged man wearing a tweed suit and a huge handlebar mustache, clearly a boarder, sat reading a newspaper in a dark blue velvet chair.

"I'd like a room, a bath, the name of a good place to eat more than trail dust, and someplace to tend my horse." See Bird used his black hat to brush the accumulated dust off his clothes. Upon recognizing See Bird's native heritage, the smile on the clerk's face disappeared, replaced with a frown of unhappy disapproval. "I'm sorry, sir," he huffed, "but we're all booked. We have nothing available."

See Bird bristled. "Pardon me, mister. This must be a thirty-room hotel. I've been riding for a couple days now, and I believe my money is just as good as the next man's." He plunked down a silver eagle. "I'm tired and hungry. Now, please, check again."

"There is no need for that. I am certain that we do not let out rooms to your kind. There is a livery stable that will let you sleep with your horse if that is your preference, but you must understand…"

"Now hold on there, Marlin." The deep voice interrupted the clerk. It was the newspaper reader. He stood and carefully folded the paper, tucking it under his arm before walking over to the counter and addressing the frowning clerk. "How long have I been rooming here, and how do you like the articles I've been writing about your town?"

"They're fine, Mr. Buntline. We all appreciate them."

"Yes. Well, it seems to me that you would not want to read back in print what I just heard emanating from your lips. Neither would the owner of this fine hotel, a man I know quite well, take kindly to learning about how you take it upon yourself to turn away paying customers. This man is seeking only what is reasonable and what you profess to provide. He seems willing to pay for it, so I suggest you accommodate him – pronto. And do so with a smile." He turned his head for the first time and addressed See Bird.

"Mister, I do not know your name, but I do know ignorance and ill-will when I see it. I am just an itinerant writer collecting material for future books, I hope. In this American West I have learned to be tolerant of a good many things. But some things are intolerable anywhere. I believe you and I shall both be glad to shake the dust of this town off our boots." With that, Mr. Ned Buntline slapped the counter with an open palm, glared at the ashen-faced clerk, pronounced a "Good day to you," and with an unhappy grunt strode out the door.

See Bird turned his attention to the chagrined clerk. "I believe we must have had a misunderstanding. About that bath. I like it real hot…"

See Bird awoke refreshed. He had slept well. The bed was surprisingly comfortable and devoid of any vermin. The clean floral window curtains were a feminine touch, nicely added. After a hearty breakfast in a nearby café, he retrieved Kiamichi and led him to the depot in order to catch the 9:50 AM to Oklahoma City, figuring that from there, he would follow his nose to points west. The train was nearly on time, and except for a brief instance when Kiamichi balked boarding at the train whistle blast, all went smoothly. See Bird had considered riding coach, but his cash had been draining at an alarming rate, and since Kiamichi had nearly spooked while boarding, he was glad he decided to ride 'horse-coach.'

The day was warm and sunny, and See Bird was content to sit in the open cargo door, his moccasin-clad feet folded beneath him while he whittled away at an interesting chunk of wood he had picked up outside the blacksmith's shop. The natural curve of it was becoming, ever so slowly in his patient hands, the neck of a gallant chestnut stallion. He held it in outstretched hands and looked at it, almost surprised. "Big fella," he said to the horse munching oats in the corner of the car, "you must have given me this idea, so I think I'll give it to that gal of mine back home. She really likes this kind of stuff." He smiled as he thought of Sally, then stood and gently secured his project in a pocket of his saddlebags. Retrieving a whetstone from his 'wargrip,' he resumed his seat by the door, gently stroking the blade of his Arkansas toothpick to a razor's edge. Finally satisfied, he carefully tucked it in its sheath behind his left hip and lay back, hands folded behind his head. Quickly he fell into a restful nap, lulled to sleep by the gentle rocking of the train.

He awoke as a hazy evening descended. The train rocked its way steadily north as currents of cooling air braided streams through the still warm and heavily layered air. The atmosphere surrounding the train became nearly luminescent. After a supper consisting of a can of beans and some jerky, he stood at the partially open door, entranced by the silvery scenery, the shallow valleys filled with the long grasses and prairie flowers. Suddenly, the scene before him changed, and the thought crossed See Bird's mind that his eyes must be playing tricks on him. The air now filled with sparkling, dancing lights, as though the travelers were riding through a million campfire sparks, but he smelled no smoke. He rubbed his eyes to clear them, but when he looked again, the lights, like a galaxy of soft stars, still lay just beyond the door.

He came to a silent awareness of what he was seeing, fire-flies. There must have been millions of them, miles thick and filling the shallow valley. He stood in awe for minutes, silently watching, wondering if the paying customers in coach were even cognizant of the incredible beauty lying just beyond their windows. "Probably not, Kiamichi, probably not." He spoke as much to himself as to his horse as he gently slid the door partially shut, leaving it open just enough so that he could stand there and enjoy the enchantment. “We pen ourselves in and turn up the light so we can see better. We blind our own eyes, don’t see what really makes the trip worthwhile, and then wonder what it’s all about.”

# 8

From Winnewood, See Bird and Kiamichi rode north and then west toward Denver, the new metropolis of the West, sprawled high up on the east side of the Rockies and boasting of a population over 130,000. They arrived in time for what was starting to be referred to as 'Cowboy Christmas,' a time of almost constant rodeos in the Denver area. The two did well and See Bird's winnings grew apace. Following each rodeo, he would convert much of the coin into high-denomination bills, carefully tuck the greenbacks into his third pair of socks, and then snuggle that deep in his 'wargrip.' For while most of the rodeo contestants were honest men just trying to earn some money doing what they knew best, See Bird was well aware of those hangers-on who lurked at the fringes of any such large and raucous gatherings of people. Men in tight suits with their practiced smiles and fast fingers.

Nor did the young man seek out those establishments where such men and the easy women were always more than happy to separate the cowboy from his money. Those hard-won dollars hidden deep in his gear were meant to provide for all the needs and a few extras that he and Sally would live on until the next summer.

He marveled at the changes he was seeing - paved

streets, electric street-lamps, handsome buildings seven and eight stories tall, streets clogged with both foot and vehicle traffic, and the air punctuated by the clanging of trolley-cars. It appeared as though the nature of the American city itself was changing. And although horses still seemed to be the preferred mode of transportation, See Bird had to be alert for the sudden occasional appearance of some foul-smelling horseless carriage, rattling as though it would shake itself apart at any moment. And, as See Bird found out personally, should any pedestrian be so inattentive as to step in front of one, the driver would lay on the horn angrily, honking in such a manner as would wake the dead.

"If they're not careful, somebody's liable to get hurt by one of them contraptions, boy. I imagine a person could get injured real bad. Still, that thing is kind of ingenious, isn't it?" he asked, following one such encounter. "I'd love to take one apart to see what makes it tick." Kiamichi calmed back down and shook his massive head disgustedly in reply.

They did not remain long in Denver. The 'Mile-High-City,' as it was starting to call itself, was getting as pricy as cities back east, and See Bird's stash of winnings did not seem to go quite as far as he hoped it would. Also, his wanderlust was kicking in again. One evening, after what started as a particularly good ride on a particularly bad bronc named Nightshade, and ended with See Bird being tossed smartly into a fence rail, bruising two ribs, but luckily fracturing none, he spoke as he checked a loose horseshoe on Kiamichi's front right hoof. "Fella," he said with a grimace, "I'm thinking it's about time we pulled stakes and lit a shuck for parts north." As he released the hoof with a groan and massaged his chest, he added, "I heard me some talk today about some towns that are really getting serious about these 'cowboy stampedes.' So, tomorrow morning, assuming I can still walk and ride, we'll leave and head towards Greeley and then maybe Cheyenne. Who knows where we'll go from there? One thing's for darn sure. This is one mighty big country to ride a horse across. I don't think this rodeoing business woulda worked without that train. What do ya say? Up for another ride?" Kiamichi just munched his oats thoughtfully.

They disembarked from the northbound one evening later in Greeley, at the confluence of the South Platte and Cache de Poudre rivers. If See Bird had been expecting to meet the Old West there, he was disappointed. Electric street lights lit the downtown, not yet settled in for the night. And rodeo excitement was in the air. Banners welcoming cowboy contestants and touting the events spanned the main street and hung draped from buildings.

After seeing to Kiamichi's immediate needs, See Bird wandered down the street. His nose led him to peer through the door of a small hotel to see a nicely appointed lobby. Off to the right was a door to the hotel café, where the clinking of dishes and the mouth-watering aroma of steak enticed him. "There is something to be said for the comforts of civilization," he thought to himself. To the businesslike clerk at the counter he said as he plunked an 'Eagle' down, "I'd like a room and a bath. And then I think I would like something better than jerky and beans for dinner. How late is your dining room open?"

The clerk slid the dollar into his hand and replied, "The room is only two bits, mister. You've got fifty cents coming back at you. Your room is 210, right up those stairs. There's a bath at the end of the hall. Dining room's open for another hour and a half. Welcome to Greeley. Enjoy the 'cowboy stampede.'" With that and a smile, he handed the cowboy his half-dollar change and a key to his room. Before See Bird could say another word, the busy clerk turned to deal with another customer.

"Well, Greeley may not be much to look at, but it sure beats some of the other places I've lit," he thought as he climbed the carpeted stairs. His room was spare, but clean, furnished with only a bed, one chair, a bureau, and a small closet. He dropped his grip on the floor and, hearing a pair of loud popping noises from down in the street, moved cautiously to the side of the window. Peering through the curtains, he relaxed and smiled to himself. It was only a cowboy letting off steam. Already, a pair of the man's friends were laughing and supporting him between them as they led the staggering young cowboy back into the saloon. See Bird noticed approvingly that one of the man's friends had taken the drunken cowboy's firearm and stuck it down the back of his britches. 'Good move,' he thought to himself.

The next day See Bird made a rare slip-up while attempting to rope a steer and finished out of the money. Upon release of the rope, he felt his ribs tighten up as a sharp pain laced across his chest. He apologized to his horse. "I knew I shoulda rested a few days more to let them bones heal up, but resting don't pay the mortgage. Still, I do not relish losing my entry fee." Kiamichi seemed to nod in agreement. "Just when I'm thinking we'll always win…we don't. One of the first lessons I ever learned back in Texas was, 'There ain't a horse that can't be rode, and there ain't a man what can't be throwed.' 'Pears to me I had to relearn it. I'm so embarrassed. I think tomorrow we'll just light out again. I heard that up in Cheyenne, they got them a shindig starting up that's fit to beat all. We'll rest a few days up there and then hit it fresh. Sound good, big fella?" See Bird asked as he brushed down his traveling companion and patted him into his stall for the night. "Right now, all I need is a bite, a bath, and a bed," he muttered to no one as he left the livery.

Later, sleep descended upon him as he lay in his darkened hotel room. He thought of his home in the West Virginia hills and of the woman whom he knew was leading their daughter in a prayer for him as she tucked the child in before climbing into the bed she shared with See Bird beneath the loft. "Well, Sally, a bite, a bath, and a bed. That's all I need." It was his final thought before sinking into a deep sleep.

The Northern Pacific Railroad crossed Crow Creek, and there it was that the huffing black locomotive slowed to enter Cheyenne, Wyoming, jerking to a halt at the large, new station. From Cheyenne, the Northern-Pacific rails ran east-west as well as south to Denver. Passengers hustled about on their various journeys, rushing to make their trains on time. It seemed to See Bird that many more were coming to the city than were leaving. Most were folks from the surrounding area, come into town to share in the excitement. Liquor flowed and fueled behavior that would not be tolerated in more peaceful times.

The first evening in town, See Bird killed some time sitting on a backless bench in front of the hotel, whittling away with his Arkansas toothpick on his 'Western scene.' His blade was a nearly Bowie knife-sized blade that he kept stowed in a sheath behind his left hip when not in use. Now it rested in his hand as he picked uncertainly at the wood.

He looked up from it, his attention drawn to a scene unfolding on the boardwalk. A young woman, almost certainly one of the cow-girls in town to compete in the riding competition, was striding in his direction. But her eyes were fixed straight ahead and scarcely noticed him. Clad in denim blue jeans, a flowered long-sleeved shirt buttoned at the wrists, boots, and a cream-colored John B. Stetson pulled down over her straight black single-braided hair, she was moving with purpose, her boots thudding on the boards.

Closely following her was a pair of nondescript men, one young pimply-faced fellow, and his companion, an older fellow with a nose that looked as though it had been poorly reset a couple times. Rushing to catch up with the girl, the older man grabbed her by her elbow. She reacted by cursing him and yanking away. The men laughed and fell in behind her as she strode on. See Bird thought he detected a flicker of fear in her eyes as she approached, reminding him of a fawn being harassed by hounds.

"Hey, girlie, why'd you go and do that for?" the young one prodded. "We don't mean you no harm, at least not much." They laughed lewdly. "We're just curious about what makes you such a good rider," he added with a poke to his friend's ribs. "You must have strong thighs. If you're real nice to us, why, we might even let you have a swig from our bottle." The two could scarcely contain their mirth. "Yeah," the older one added with a backhanded swipe at his nose, "we might even let you wrap those sweet lips around it."

See Bird felt an embarrassment for the girl and an anger rising at the aggressively crude language and actions of the two men. He had met their like many times in his life. Men, who when sober were mealy-mouthed cowards, but when fortified with alcohol, found at least a make-shift and temporary courage. And they were closing in, once again, on their prey. She rushed by. See Bird stood suddenly, nearly colliding with the drunken louts. They barely pulled up in time to avoid a collision, staggering to a halt before him.

So intent were they on their pursuit of the young woman, they stared past him until she disappeared around a corner, then turned to See Bird. The elder one clenched his fists. "Just what do you think you're doing, blocking the way? We got business with her," he slurred.

"Boys," See Bird said quietly, "you got no business with that woman except to apologize."

"Apologize? To her? For what?" They took one angry step towards See Bird.

He planted his feet and continued in the same calm voice. "You men are drunk." His knife-hand hung loosely at his left side. He gestured with it as if he was not aware of its presence. But four other eyes fixed immediately on it. "What you should do now is turn around and go back the way you came. Sober up a bit and then go crawl back under the rock you crawled out from." He touched the tip of the knife to the front brim of his hat, smiled, and dropped into a 'ready' position, taking a half step backward. "Don't that sound like good advice to you boys?" he asked with a quiet intensity.

The two who so shortly before had seemed staggeringly drunk, sobered instantly and backpedaled quickly. "Mister," the one with the broken nose pointed a finger and said, "we don't know what your stake in this is, and we don't care. We'll go, but we don't forget."

"That's right," the younger one chimed in. "You

don't look like you'd be much without that big knife, and we got friends. We'll see you 'round." They backed away.

"That's okay," See Bird said, relaxing now that he saw the way things were going. "You may see me around. Just make sure it's from a distance." He watched the young woman's would-be assailants as they turned and stumbled hurriedly away, then resumed his seat on the bench. Picking up his wood carving and studying it for a few moments, he turned it in his hands and mused, "Now doggone it. I very nearly clipped the ear right off'n this horse. Those old boys upset me so."

Several minutes later, he was concentrating so hard on cutting a groove in the mane that he failed to notice the girl standing there until her shadow blocked the sinking sun. Carefully replacing the knife in its sheath, he rose, doffed his black slouch hat and smiled. She returned the smile as she extended her hand to shake his. "Mister, I don't know why you did what you did back there, and I probably didn't need your help." She paused a moment and then went on. "But I surely do appreciate it. My name's Clara Lazetti. Mind if I buy you a cup of Joe?"

"Glad to meet you, Clara. I'm See Bird. Folks sometimes just call me Red. And no, I don't mind. I'm just about ready to call it a day. I'd love you to buy me a cup, if you let me buy you the second."

"It's a deal, See Bird," she replied as he ushered her past the hotel and through the open door of 'Angela's Home Style Restaurant' next door.

The harried waitress took their order and closed the door on her way to the coffee pot. "Seems to get a bit cool when the sun goes down up here," he said, making small talk.

Clara flashed a wide smile. "Sometime, some

nights. And then again, there are summer nights up here in Wyoming that could almost, I said almost, make you wish for winter. But you're not from these parts are you, See Bird?"

"Not hardly," he said. "I'm from Oklahoma by way of West Virginia." Uncomfortable talking about himself, he asked, "Lazetti does not sound like a name from these parts either."

The waitress put two cups down and splashed them full of coffee. Clara pushed her cup around the saucer before responding. "I guess not. My folks came to this country from Tuscany, over in Italy." She swung her head as if Tuscany were just across the street or around the block. "We had nothing. But my pa always dreamed of owning some land, somewhere. The steamship tickets alone used up all his money, I was a baby, and we had nowhere to go. Some folks in the Italian neighborhood of New York City pitched in, found Pop a job helping some ward alderman or suchlike, and before you know it, he had saved us up a stake so's we could buy some land out here in the West. That's what Pop always said he dreamed about, owning some land of his own."

She paused as if to stop, but See Bird pursued. "But how did you come to be way out here in the Wild West?"

"Well, See Bird, it's funny you should put it like that. Buffalo Bill's show came to New York on its way to England, and we got to see it. It's one of the first things I remember. I still get goosebumps from it, all the cowboys and Indians shooting it up and chasing around and the cavalry busting right in to save the day. Just a bit after that, Pop put us on a train for the Dakotas. He'd heard that with the Indian wars all over, there was land for the taking. But when we got there and saw what kind of land it was, Pop just kept right on moving until we came to Cheyenne."

"On the day we got here, he saw a flier posted that advertised some range land for sale. He threw in on it, and here we are. There've been some real skinny times, I tell you, but Pop pitched right in like he was meant to do it, and Ma worked right alongside him. I grew up riding and roping 'til I do believe I'm as good at it as any man." She stopped fiddling with her coffee cup, picked it up, and looked See Bird straight in the eye, before taking a drink. "I'm riding in the bucking horse competition tomorrow, and I intend to win."

"I sure hope you do, Clara, but you know there's a number of others who most likely feel the same way."

"Oh, I'm aware of that, for sure, See Bird, and I've been thrown more than a few times. But I've grown up with and know almost all the girls who'll be riding out in that arena." Fact is, most of the bucking horses they learned on were the ones their big brothers figured were too easy to bother with. So they saved them for the little girls. But nobody ever saved the easy rides for me." She leaned back and laughed out loud. See Bird laughed with her, delighted in her openness and confidence, intrigued by her competitive nature. He was about to ask her if she would like him to walk her to wherever she was going when her eyes lit up in delight. "Ah, here comes the cavalry. There's someone I want you to meet, See Bird. My little brother."

Following her gaze, See Bird saw a young cowboy enter the restaurant and approach the table. He had the same fiery black eyes and hair like his sister, and his tanned face broke out in the same jaw-stretching smile Clara wore. But there the similarities ended. Where she was fairly short and strongly built, he was tall, rangy, and looked rawhide tough. His appearance reminded See Bird of those years he had spent working cattle, and the men he got to know then. Real cowboys always had that certain look and that certain walk gained from long hours spent on horseback. It set them apart from city-slickers everywhere. "See Bird, this is Louis. But you can call him Louie." The two shook calloused hands.

"Sis, how come you didn't show? We were going to work tightening up your fist grip, remember?" Louis asked.

"Louie, you wouldn't believe what happened to me this evening. See Bird, here rescued me from a fate worse than death." She then described what had happened, how she had peeked around the corner and seen See Bird back the two would-be rapists down as if he did such things on a daily basis. Louie's face darkened as she related the men's words and actions. "Did they hurt you in any way, Sis?" From Louie's tone, See Bird got the distinct impression that the question was more than academic and that the well-being and possibly the lives of two men may have hung in the balance.

"Not at all, though I was starting to get mad. That's true. I almost kicked the one that grabbed me like you taught me, but he let go." See Bird noted to himself that perhaps Clara had been telling him the truth when she said that she could have handled it. She certainly seemed self-confident enough. But then again, there's many a woman lived to rue the day they tried to take on men with bad intentions and some that didn't.

"Just the same," Louis added, "I'll be there to keep an eye on things. If you see either one of those hombres, point him out to me. I'll take it from there."

"You got it, little brother, but See Bird chased them off with their tails between their legs. I doubt we'll be troubled by that riff-raff again."

Brother and sister left together. See Bird sat and

thought for a minute, then left for his hotel room, wishing he shared Clara's confidence.

# 9

The waning moon hung low and dull in the sky as See Bird stepped out on the boardwalk. He always checked in on Kiamichi before he turned in. It just seemed the friendly thing to do, and besides, he found that talking things over with his horse helped him sort out issues and make better decisions. Looking down and paying particular attention to where he was stepping in the dim light, he turned a corner and headed down a short alley toward the livery stables. Four shadows loomed before him and to either side. "Hold it right there, you little pip-squeak," a mocking voice ordered from directly ahead.

An ambush. This was exactly what See Bird had been wondering about in the restaurant. After their earlier encounter, he thought there were three possible courses of action Clara's assailants could take. The first was that the two would go sober up and forget about their earlier humiliation. The second was that they would try again for Clara. That thought had troubled him the most. The third option was that they would come after him. Clearly, that was what they intended. And the two had found a couple others like themselves who were not squeamish about taking such a cowardly course of action.

Bent Nose, as See Bird thought of him, could not resist taunting his victim. Perhaps he wanted to hear him beg or see him shake. In any case, See Bird did neither, nor did he stop walking. Instead, he unexpectedly sped up and before Bent Nose could adjust, the Indian lashed out with the heel of his hand to the base of the man's nose. He heard a crunching sound and felt the splash of fluid moments before the man's voice erupted in a string of pained obscenities. Seamlessly, not wasting a moment, See Bird spun, slamming a sidekick into the upper chest of a man closing in on the left, narrowly missing the man's windpipe, but knocking him back and breathless. But before he could turn to face his other attackers, he felt a crushing blow to his back, driving him to his knees.

"Now, you piss-ant Indian, you're really gonna get it." The pimply-faced young man from earlier raised a hefty piece of wood over his head, preparing to crush See Bird's skull.

"Drop it," a hard voice interrupted. Then there was the sound of a fist meeting flesh.

"What the…?" Another thud.

See Bird staggered to his feet, clearing his head. Someone else had joined the fray, and while he would have loved to sort it all out, he needed to get back into the fight immediately.

The stranger wrenched the board from Pimple Face's grip, swung it twice, missing the first time but then connecting with a 'thunk' to the man's head. But once was all that was needed. The man dropped like a puppet with his strings cut. "Okay, See Bird." It was Louie. "It's only three against two, now. Let's finish these bushwhackers off. Ya-hoo," he shouted with joy, landing a stiff right cross.

The two of them waded into the other three with fists and feet flying. See Bird may have stood at only five-and-a-half feet, but in that small frame was packed 140 pounds of rodeo-riding gristle and hard muscle. He and Louie, standing nearly a half-foot taller than him, granted their opponents no quarter. Once, See Bird was not quite quick enough to avoid a stinging blow to the side of his head. Reacting instinctively, he ducked to avoid a roundhouse right coming from the other direction, then suddenly grabbed the man's head with both hands and drove the top of his own head into the underside of the chin. The would-be ambusher's head snapped back as he tumbled into the dirt, not to rise again anytime soon.

Louie and See Bird drove against the two remaining men, pummeling them relentlessly. At one point, with a hard-case's back against a wall, Louie took up a boxer's stance, left leg forward, and delivered a series of punishing jabs to the man's face, until, trying futilely to protect his ravaged visage, the man raised his arms to shield it. Anticipating just such a reaction, Louie moved in close and landed a series of devastating blows to the midsection. With an audible 'oof' of releasing air, the fellow dropped his arms to hold his stomach, crumbled to the ground, and curled up in pain, also out of the fight.

It was becoming crystal clear to Pimple-Face, the last remaining fighter, that somehow these two men had beaten them all, and his spirit collapsed, the fight seeming to go out of him. He began whimpering as See Bird pressed the attack, "Please stop. Stop. I quit," he sobbed. See Bird relented and stepped back, catching his breath, seemingly off-guard. As he did so, his opponent seized the opportunity and bull-rushed him, clutching for See Bird's shirt in a final attempt to disable the smaller man. However, See Bird smoothly stepped back and to one side, spun, and delivered a chop with the blade of his hand to the onrushing man's throat.

Gagging and choking for air, the man fell to his knees. See Bird knelt in front of him and drew his knife from its sheath. The deadly weapon glinted dully in the dim light. "Do you see this, you scum? I should scalp you now and end your miserable life." His voice quivered in anger. Louie walked slowly over to where the two men knelt facing each other. See Bird slowly reached out and grabbed the last assailant by his hair, and yanked the man's head up. The tip of the knife pressed against his forehead hard enough to cause a bead of blood to form. "But I'm not gonna, this time. I'm a Christian Indian. I believe in forgiveness." He stared into the man's terror-stricken eyes. "Do you believe in forgiveness? Do you, you waste of a man?" The bushwhacker's Adam's-apple bobbed soundlessly. "Because if I ever see you around here or around that girl again, I'm liable to lose my conversion. Do you understand me? Do you?" He shook the man's head by the hair, withdrawing the blade only slightly. See Bird smelt the sudden aroma of urine and smiled. "That's what I thought. You do understand."

The miserable bad man sagged into a faint, See Bird releasing him to fall into his own muddy puddle. Then he rose, sliding the knife carefully into its sheath. Louie looked at him a moment before asking with puzzled amusement, "You mean to tell me you had that pig-sticker the whole time and never used it. Why in heaven's name not?"

As the two men emerged from the alley, See Bird shrugged and answered lightly, "I only use it to open tin cans and carve Western scenes."

Louie chuckled. "Well, it sure put the fear of the Lord in that fella. I think Sis won't be troubled by their likes again," Louie added. "And where'd you learn to fight like that, See Bird?"

"My Uncle Isaac taught me. He went off to fight in the War Between the States, and when he came home, he showed me some tricks he learned somewhere – from some Chinaman, I think. He told me I'd never be a man-mountain, but I surely could be a man, and if I'd learn how to move right, I'd be able to stand with anyone. He told me that if I found myself up against a bigger man to make him pay for every pound." He shrugged and changed the subject. "I'm a mite curious, myself, about where you picked up those nifty boxing moves."

"Oh, that's nothing. Pop used to fight sometimes back in New York. You know. Bare knuckles. Anything to put food on the table. There's some mighty good Eye-talian fighters back east. Maybe someday one'll be the world champ. Who knows? He learned a lot the hard way, and he taught me what he learned." He rubbed his jaw in remembrance. "Durn near knocked my head off a couple times."

By now, the pair had nearly reached the livery. They stopped. See Bird extended his hand. "Thanks, Louie, for pitching in. You sure saved my bacon."

Louie laughed that friendly laugh of his. "You're welcome, See Bird. But I gotta tell you; it was a whole lot of fun. I haven't been in a good knuckle-buster in quite a while. And it was worth it just to watch you handle that punk." Both chuckled.

"I'll see you tomorrow," Louie said with a wave of his hand. "Sis will be in the 'lady broncs' right before the 'male saddle-broncs.' Good luck."

"Yeah, and good luck to Clara. Your sister has some grit," he called as he wiped a drop of blood off his lip.

# 10

See Bird woke the next morning with a groan. His shoulders still ached from when he was slammed in the back down in the alley. It was a slight consolation for him to consider that had the blow been merely two inches higher, he most likely would have suffered a broken neck. As it was, the day was still young enough that he had plenty of time to work the stiffness out of his back. His knuckles also needed some time to heal, but he was grateful to his Uncle Isaac for teaching him how to fight more effectively, how to use his whole body as a weapon, not just his fists. As he slipped his arms into the red rodeo shirt he pressed overnight under the mattress, he smiled wryly, considering what Louie's hands must look like this morning, his fists bloody, scraped and swollen. After he was fully dressed, he topped off his rodeo outfit with fancy leather gauntlets he made the previous winter and his beautiful, hand-tooled leather chaps. "That's what bare-knuckles fighting will do to a man," he thought as he carefully topped off the ensemble with his uncreased black slouch hat, crowned with a turkey feather. Carefully closing and locking the door behind him, he descended the stairs to the lobby and then walked out to the street, directly into chaos.

There was no question as to which way he should

proceed. The entire city of Cheyenne appeared to be moving en masse in the same direction. Somewhere in the distance, a brass band played. Buckboards and buggies full of country folk wound slowly through the crowds that spilled from the boardwalks. Chatting couples strolled along, bowlegged cowboys strode afoot or rode horses, giggling children dodged between their elders, while merchants in bowlers spoke in excited tones. All moved as if summoned by the pied piper himself, playing in some distant band.

After retrieving Kiamichi from the livery, See Bird climbed astride and fell in with the crowd flowing along toward the sound of music until the shadow of a massive construction loomed directly ahead. There the sea of people split and flowed either to the right or left. See Bird finally worked himself to the front of the crowd, reined in, and took stock. He found himself gazing over a fence into the grandest arena he had ever seen. The covered judges' stand was a small tower to his front left. Draped in red, white, and blue bunting, it stood some ten feet high, providing a clear visual line of sight for the entire arena floor, all seven acres of it. A double-decked spectator stand of bleachers, capable of holding several thousand, stood sheltered beneath a sloped roof running the arena's entire length. See Bird had never seen anything like it.

"Would you look at this, old boy?" he asked his nervous steed, stroking its mane. "Sure seems a long way from where we started back in Texas."

In spite of killing blizzards, mine failures, and land so flat it made See Bird itch to see a hill, clearly this rodeo, called by the locals, 'Frontier Days', was an enormous hit. Despite brutal recent winters which left whole herds of cattle frozen where they stood and the played-out mines, folks from these parts were more than willing to part with some hard-earned greenbacks or silver dollars for the promise of exciting entertainment. And by their fashionable clothes, quite a few certainly did not look like they were locals at all. See Bird recalled that the Northern Pacific train he rode north from Denver had been packed with well-heeled passengers, all excited about going somewhere. Now he understood where they had been headed. He felt a churning like butterflies in his stomach and wondered for a moment if something he ate the day before was causing him problems, but finally reconciled himself to the idea that it was just anxious worry.

Kiamichi seemed affected by it too. He stepped nervously from hoof to hoof. "Easy boy. Let's just settle ourselves down a bit." See Bird slid out of the saddle, looped the reins over a fence rail and climbed up, making himself comfortable along the top. He watched the crowds filling the stands while listening to the noise swell, creating a sound like a waterfall. He wondered, for a moment only, whatever had become of the men who had set upon him the night before. He shrugged the thought aside. It did not seem likely that they would present themselves here today. Their humiliation had been complete, their beatings thorough. Most likely, they were having their wounds tended to, or perhaps they had simply slunk off, looking for easier pickings.

Amid the din, a burly middle-aged man, wearing a slightly too small Stetson and carrying a megaphone, strode purposefully across the arena floor towards the judges' stand. He disappeared through the only door and a few moments later appeared on the upper level. He waved at the crowd, trying to get its attention, and amazingly, some responded. It seemed to See

Bird the noise level declined, at least marginally. He raised the megaphone to his mouth, took a deep breath, and called, "Ladies and gentlemen, welcome to the Cheyenne, Wyoming, Frontier Days Celebration." A stagecoach entered from the far end and made its way toward the tower. "You are in for the time of your life, the greatest show on dirt. The judges are now approaching to take their positions up here with me." A smattering of applause. The stagecoach pulled up alongside the judges' stand. The doors popped open and two suited men emerged wearing bowlers. Both looked to stand well over six feet. One was smooth-faced and the other wore a handle-bar mustache that hid most of the lower half of his face. Neither looked as though he was enjoying the experience. They wore the suits uncomfortably tight about the chest and shoulders and took positions, standing ramrod-straight by either door, scanning the crowd. See Bird thought they were the most unlikely pair of rodeo judges he had ever seen.

It gradually dawned upon him that these two were guards, but why would rodeo judges need bodyguards? As the men stepped down onto the arena floor, the announcer bellowed, "Let me introduce today's judges. First, is Tom Corman, manager of the 'Flying T' ranch out of Cody, Wyoming." A bandy-legged man with a weathered, flushed face waved to the crowd from the stage door and stepped down. "Next out is Brandon Willoughby, our own dear City Marshall. He used to ride in events such as this 'til a bull named Switchback abruptly altered his career." A few good-natured catcalls and whistles greeted the man as he entered the tower. "And finally, ladies and gentlemen, let me present to you our honorary judge of the day's contests, the former North Dakota rancher and Rough Rider himself," he paused to fill his lungs once more and let the suspense build a little before he bellowed, "the President of the United States, Theodore "Teddy" Roooooosevelt."

If See Bird had thought the crowd was loud before, the sound now hit him like a crushing wave, causing him momentarily to grip the top rail so as not to become dislodged. The deafening roar reached avalanche strength as the President stood momentarily in the door of the stagecoach, clutching his hat in one hand and acknowledging the adulation of the crowd by pumping the other fist in the air, all the while beaming in pure delight. See Bird found himself rising to his feet with the crowd and doffing his hat in respect. For the briefest moment, it appeared that T.R. saw him standing there and nodded. See Bird beheld a man with a powerful jaw full of frightful teeth. Then the beaming gaze moved on. See Bird looked over his shoulder as if to explain to his horse, "He's a good man," was all he said. Then he sat.

Meanwhile, President Roosevelt bounced out of the stagecoach, strode a few steps and then also disappeared through the door to the judges' stand. He climbed the interior stairs and shook hands with the announcer, who handed him the megaphone. Roosevelt turned to face the crowd and lifted the megaphone to speak. Miraculously, it seemed to See Bird, the roar subsided and the crowd quieted. The stagecoach rounded the judges' tower and pulled away in the direction from which it had entered. The two bodyguards took up their positions, one just outside the door while, See Bird surmised, the other would also be standing directly inside the same door.

Teddy Roosevelt spoke. "Fellow citizens of this

American republic, I am dee-lighted to be here today. It is my privilege and honor to welcome you to Cheyenne and to this bully spectacle. I will do my level best to deliver fair and honest judgments upon the proceedings with the able assistance of these fine men, and if any man here would challenge our decisions, well then," he paused for effect, "that man must needs be a Democrat." Laughter rippled through the multitude.

Roosevelt, See Bird thought, must be the most dynamic speaker he had ever heard. It wasn't that his voice was resonant, or the words elegant. It wasn't and they weren't. But the man seemed completely convinced that what he had to say was vital. It was obvious to everyone that he loved what he was doing, punctuating his words with vigorous nods and thrusts of his head. Leaning his whole body forward, he spoke with conviction and power. Quickly, he drew to a conclusion. "So I say, in this magnificent state, where strong women stand on equal footing with strong men, let the contests begin, and may the best men – and women – win." With that, T.R. reluctantly handed the megaphone to the announcer and took a step aside, waving to the adoring multitudes.

"And now, ladies and gentlemen, you'll need to cinch it up tighter, because we have a surprise for our illustrious guest. Please direct your attention to the far end of the arena as the gate swings open. It is my great pleasure to present to President Roosevelt a few men who just happened to be in the neighborhood and thought it would only be polite to drop in and say 'Hello.' Without further ado, I present to you the heroes of San Juan Hill, some of the men Mr. Roosevelt personally recruited for that late war with Spain, 'The Rough Riders.'

The great arena resounded to the thunder of hooves,

a cloud of dust, the yelling of boisterous cowboys waving their hats in the air, the stamping of thousands of feet in the viewing stands, and the renewed roar of thousands more voices, all screaming, whistling and hooting their approval. Perhaps a hundred or more ‘Rough Riders,’ led by a cowboy carrying a large American flag, galloped once around the circumference of the arena and then brought their horses to a walk. Slowly, with respect, they filed past the judges’ stand, where T.R., reaching far over the rail, leaned down and shook hands with each man, sharing a few words with some. When the last rider rode past, the President stood back up, withdrew a handkerchief from a pocket and dabbed at his eyes. The crowd loved every second of it.

“Well, Kiamichi, that takes the cake. I never saw anything like it in all my born days. Now, what say we go and earn us some money.” Kiamichi shook his mane and blew. “And remember, be on your best behavior. The President will be watching.”

# 11

However cool and bright blue the day had begun; it all had completely disappeared by the time the calf roping began. Gritty dust clung to every surface and hung in the arena air under a white-hot bowl of a sky as See Bird walked Kiamichi into the chute. The Choctaw cowboy was tempted to cover his mouth with a neck-kerchief, as he had so many times while riding herd in Texas, or bringing cattle up the old Chisholm Trail. But everyone else seemed to be 'grinning and bearing it,' except for the rodeo clown whose face was nearly hidden behind the huge tablecloth of a scarlet and white striped kerchief he had draped around his neck, so See Bird left his unused as well.

Three riders had already completed their events, two of them turning in respectable times of around eight seconds. The other rider had gotten off to a quick start, but that was the problem. His start was too quick. In calf-roping, every second counts. So the cowboy must bring his horse to a gallop before the chute ever opens, in order that his horse will be running at full speed when the twenty-eight-foot rope attached to the calf triggers his gate release. Timing is everything. Unfortunately, that cowboy was the victim of bad timing. His ten-second penalty for a too quick-release certainly put him out of the money. See Bird knew he would need for things to go perfectly for him to win this event. He glanced over at Kiamichi and saw the sorrel was twitching with excitement. But his eyes and ears were rock steady. "We got 'em, boy. Don't we?" He stroked the muscled shoulders of his steed, but he might as well have been stroking a carved statue. Kiamichi stopped twitching and stared straight ahead between the boards of the gate; his huge brown eyes focused intently on the arena floor. He was ready. See Bird felt humbled and grateful to Kiamichi for bolstering his confidence.

'Beans' Toohey, a young Texan who had once worked cattle alongside See Bird, was a man with a severe overbite and a voracious appetite for books. On a long-ago evening, as the men sat around a campfire yarning, he suddenly popped to his feet, waving a worn-out book at them, so excited he stuttered. "W –would you believe this? It says r-r-right here that the horse has the b-b-b- biggest eyes of any animal in the world, even the e-e-l-l ephant. How about that?"

Harley Souk, a scruffy veteran of many trail drives, was the only man to even raise his head to meet the eyes of the excited young man. He stared at Beans with his beady eyes, swallowed a mouthful of biscuit, and said, with the barest hint of a smile, "I ain't never seen me an elephink, much less every animal on this here earth." Pointing with a spoon, he asked, "You ever seen one, boy? No? I didn't figure you had either. That's what you get fer sticking your nose in a book and picking up some useless piece of gobbledegook that's most likely a lie. I don't know or care if a horse got the biggest eye in the world, but there ain't no doubt about it that a horse can crap more than any other critter on the planet." The rest of the men stirred and chuckled. "Yessir, I'd bet my bottom dollar on that. It's a regular crap machine."

See Bird had laughed along with the other cowboys, but somehow that tidbit of information had tucked itself away in the back of his brain, and like an itch between the shoulder blades, no matter how he twisted for it, he never could scratch it, and always wondered about it. So he took to studying on it the way he usually did, in his own patient manner. He knew that horses were prey and so had to be wary. Their big eyes stood out so that they could see things as well behind them as they could to the front. He had learned long ago that it was nearly impossible to sneak up on one because of that. But as to why those eyes wore lashes so beautiful, and how those eyes could express emotion so clearly, "Well, I guess that's just the way the Creator done it," he muttered to himself as he mounted and prepared for his run. "It must have pleased Him."

See Bird settled into the saddle and bit down on the 'piggin string.' He wasn't nervous. He and Kiamichi had done this too many times for that. But he did feel a tug of anxiety. So many little things could go just wrong enough to put them out of the money. And the money he was piling up in his wargrip would have to be enough to see him and Sally through the winter back home in West Virginia. He nodded his head when ready, and a cowboy yanked open the calf's chute gate. He nudged Kiamichi into a gallop, and when the calf reached the end of the twenty-eight-foot rope, it triggered the release on his gate. Just in time. The timer's watch began counting. Within a heartbeat, Kiamichi was at full speed, hooves thudding rhythmically in pursuit of the fleeing calf.

Quickly, See Bird fed out a loop on his lasso and as

quickly launched it. The rope settled perfectly around the calf's neck. Kiamichi came to an immediate stop, but not so quickly as to toss the calf. He took one small step backward, maintaining tension on the rope. See Bird flew to the ground and raced down the rope to the calf. He picked it up, all two hundred pounds of squirming bovine, and dumped it to the ground, dropping it onto its side. With the 'pigging string' he tied three legs together using 'two wraps and a hooey,' as a half-hitch knot was commonly called. Instantly, he threw his hands in the air, the signal to stop the clock, as Kiamichi slowly backed away, keeping up a steady tension on the rope. But the event was not done yet. He returned to his horse, mounted and stepped it forward, relaxing tension on the rope. The timer waited six more seconds. If the calf should kick loose, all the beautiful teamwork between man and horse would have been for naught.

"7.2 seconds for Red Carpenter, the West Virginia Whiz," the announcer bellowed. "That's got to be the time to beat today. Let's hear some appreciation for our new leader, Red Carpenter." The crowd cheered and clapped enthusiastically for See Bird. But the cowboy competitors and those who knew horses whistled and cheered just as loudly for Kiamichi. They knew that without an outstandingly focused, trained, and intelligent animal, the rider would have accomplished little. Kiamichi seemed to be aware of his contribution, as well. See Bird chuckled as he felt the swagger in his steed's step as they exited the arena floor. He reached down and patted Kiamichi's withers. "Good job, big boy," he said. The muscular chestnut bobbed his head and blew, as if to say, "It was nothing. I could have done it in my sleep."

After seeing to Kiamichi's needs, See Bird returned

and relaxed at the rail alongside the other cowboys, watching the remaining contestants. A couple good times were turned in, both around eight seconds. The best-timed rider received a ten-second penalty when his calf wriggled his legs free before six seconds had passed. But even he would not have beaten See Bird on this day.

"Nice ride there, Mister," said a tall young cowboy with blond curly hair poking out underneath his John B. "That's quite a horse you got there. Been riding him long?"

See Bird considered his response a moment. "I made his acquaintance down by Waco mor'n a few years back. We hit it off right away. Been together since. You ridin'?"

"Not in this. Don't have me the horse yet. I'll be ridin' saddle broncs later. Right now, I'm just waiting to see the ladies try their hands at the bucking horses. Should be fun. Have you seen that Clara Lazetti? That gal's so good she could ride with the men and beat most of them. She drew first lot." His voice softened, he almost whispered, "I shore do wish I could make her acquaintance."

See Bird glanced about them. Scanning the crowd was difficult, if not impossible. The arena was so huge and the crowd so thick, it was difficult to make out individual faces. Couple that with the ever-present dust and the heat rising in waves from the pounded surface, and the task of finding a couple bad apples became nigh impossible. He reassured himself with the thought that Louie, and probably a few of his other friends, would be watching Clara as well. Bullies and bushwhackers were cut from the same cloth – all cowards, all moving toward weakness, always away from strength.

Just then the chute slammed open and Clara flew into the arena, wearing a cream-colored shirt that matched her Stetson, and mounted on a non-descript mixed-breed with serious attitude problems. Raking its sides vigorously, she quickly found the beast's rhythm and rode smoothly in the saddle. See Bird chuckled as the blond cowboy standing to his left, lent his motion to hers, leaning first one way and then the other, oblivious to anyone else except the girl fighting to stay in the saddle.

Having successfully completed her eight seconds, another mounted cowboy swiftly moved alongside Clara. She released her grip on the bronc and wrapped her arms around the rider's chest. As he put distance between them and the still bucking horse, she stepped lightly to the ground, flashed a smile that See Bird caught, even from halfway across the arena, doffed her hat, and executed the sweetest combination of a curtsy and bow to the crowd that he had ever seen. By their reaction, it was clear that the spectators approved her effort. The Indian did not know if her ride's score would hold up throughout the competition, but there was no doubt that she had won over the crowd.

"Hot dang!" her curly-haired admirer shouted, banging his hat against his legs. "Ain't she just like I told ya?" Without waiting for an answer, he exclaimed, "I just got to meet me that gal," and stomped off, muttering to himself.

The older cowboy to See Bird's right watched the scene unfold and added with a touch of disgust, "May be that I seen me better rides, but I never seen a man so in love. It's downright sickening." He spat a dark wet spot of tobacco juice in the hot dust and turned back to peer over the rails into the arena. See Bird smiled and began making his way to the chute area.

Teton Mama was the bronc See Bird drew, somewhat to his disappointment. He didn't know the horse from Adam's off-ox, and he was aware that mares could be excellent bucking horses. Still, there was just a bit of stigma attached to riding a mare instead of a stallion. And a name like Teton Mama was scarcely one that evoked fear and trembling. To top it off, as he climbed aboard, he took note of her size and appearance. She was a dun-colored nobody, slightly smaller than average. Bucking horses were often taken from draft stock because of their strength and durability. See Bird had no prejudices against any horse, but he was well aware of the fact that no matter how well he would ride, if the mount wasn't up to it, he would never get a good enough score to win. Half the points he would earn in the bucking competition came from the horse's performance. He was mulling that over when the little mare turned her head to eyeball him. He detected not a hint of fear, just a touch of curiosity, a considerable amount of humor, and a wealth of animosity. Then she tried to bite his leg. "Whoa, Mama," he thought, "there may be more to this here animal than meets the eye." He settled in, nodded, and the gate sprang open.

A bronc rider's initial score is tallied on the first jump out of the chute. He must 'mark the horse out' by raising his feet over the horse's shoulders giving the bronc the initial advantage. Then he must rake the animal with his spurs in a sweeping motion from shoulder to flank. The longer the stroke, the higher the score. Lest someone should fear that the 'raking' hurts the animal, the fact is the rowels on the dulled spurs must roll against the tough hide. A rider could be disqualified if his spurs are sharp or the rowels are stiff. Owners of good bucking horses make plenty of money off of them and will not tolerate anyone abusing them.

Teton Mama entered the arena on the fly. The mare's elevation put her above the top rail and stunned See Bird as well as the audience. Her compact power drove him back into the cantle for a moment before he could adjust. His boots were definitely above Teton Mama's shoulders, his toes pointed out, so his rake was a long and good one. That this man was still on her back after her explosive entry infuriated the mare. When she came down into her 'front end drop' her hindquarters nearly slammed into the back of See Bird's head, rattling his teeth.

It appeared that the bucking horse was determined to turn and bite the man who rode her. She leaped into the air, twisting first one way and then the other. Sunfishing makes it extremely difficult for the rider to find a rhythm that enables him to work with the horse. But Teton Mama didn't care about pleasing her rider. Sometimes a rider will have to shift his weight around in order to encourage bucking. Teton Mama needed no encouragement. Finding See Bird still in his perch after another tooth jarring leap and landing, she fairly screamed in rage, leaped in one direction, landing stiff-legged, then leaped in the opposite direction.

See Bird was learning quickly this horse had no pattern of behavior and began to anticipate the unexpected. As he became more familiar with her tendencies, his original grimace was threatening to become a smile of admiration. Then, mercifully, the ride was over. Time was up. Even after he was eased out of the saddle, Teton Mama continued to buck. It took several riders to rope and guide her out of the arena.

See Bird watched her exit and lifted his hat to her in tribute. He wasn't sure how many points he himself had earned, but no horse here today, he thought with confidence, could give more than this mountain mare.

# 12

A clean ninety points earned him the victory, though for the life of him, he couldn't figure out how he could have lost all of ten points. It was obvious to him that Teton Mama put her heart and soul into it and deserved to have maxed out her fifty points. That would mean he had ten points deducted from his fifty. Man and horse points were added together for the total score. He admitted that he may have lost a point or two on the entry. Her explosion into the arena had taken him completely by surprise, but after that, he believed he gave that mare all he had to give, making perhaps the best ride of his entire life. "Maybe it did all come down to her size, sex, and appearance," he thought with disappointment. "It ain't fair, but then the world often ain't fair if you're not big and beautiful or manly-looking, if that's what they want. But one thing is for sure. There ain't no better bucking horse in all Wyoming. There can't be."

So preoccupied was he with his ride that he nearly banged right into Clara Lazetti as he was leaving. She, too, had won her event. "Whoa there, cowboy. Where you goin' in such an all-fired hurry?"

He looked up to meet sparkling eyes and that wide-open smile of hers again. "Well, pardon me, Clara." He touched the brim of his hat awkwardly. "My mind must still be all cobwebby from that pounding I took back there."

She put her head back and laughed that clear laugh of hers that reminded him of a mountain brook in springtime. "From my spot on the rail, it looked to me that you gave that witch all she could handle. That horse is probably still trying to figure out how you did it." She spun around and locked her arm in his. "I'll tell you what. We both earned us some shiny eagles today. Now, I insist that you share dinner with Louie and me. I was going to meet him down at 'The Atlanta Restaurant' after I collected my winnings, and now I get to thank you properly for what you done for me the other night." Seeing he was about to protest, she cut him off. "You can't say 'No.' Louie and I do not get into town all that often, and we are mighty proud to count you as one of our few friends."

"Now, Clara," See Bird interjected, "I have a hard time believing you don't have a hundred friends in this town, especially after the show you put on out there today. I know for a fact, there was a tall drink of water standing next to me, watching your ride who thought mighty highly of you, a blond, curly-haired friendly young man…"

Clara interrupted with a soft chuckle. "That's Noah Moore. The Moores are small-time ranchers with a big-time family. He was the eighth son in a row. Word is that when he was born, his ma took one look at him and said, 'No more.' His dad thought it was kind of funny and so the name stuck. It must have worked because there've been no more kids from that family. I went to school with him, even beat him in a spelling bee, but in spite of all my attempts to get him to notice me, he was so shy he wouldn't give me the time of day."

The two strode along the boardwalk, arm in arm, like old friends, Clara chatting away, See Bird seeming to listen to every word. In fact, he liked the sound of her voice, but often had no idea what she was palavering about. It reminded him of the song of the Meadowlark on a summer morning back home in Warm Holler. His thoughts drifted back home and to his Sally.

"Well, speak of the devil," Clara called out to the young man she saw looking to cross the street ahead of them. "Hey you." The cowboy looked around to see who she was calling. "Yeah, you, Noah Moore. Hold on a cotton-pickin' minute." The young man in the street, realizing he had no chance to escape by pretending he had not heard her, swept his hat off his head, revealing a mop of blond curls, and raised a shy hand in silent greeting.

Clara stopped before him, See Bird in tow, tilted her head so that her raven hair fell behind her neck, draped across her shoulder and said, "Noah, don't you think after all these years it's about time we had us a friendly chat?"

See Bird watched the man struggle with himself for a moment and watched as he gathered himself together as if fighting to overcome some huge internal obstacle. Apparently winning that battle, he exhaled and composing himself, carefully placed his hat back on his head. "That would suit me just fine, Clara. Maybe I'll see you this Sunday at church."

"Sunday?" She questioned. "My papa says to make hay while the sun shines. So I'm thinking maybe we should have dinner together, right now, just me and you and Red and Louie. As a matter of fact," she added before he could object, "we're on our way right now to meet Louie and celebrate our wins. So join us, okay?"

Without waiting for a reply, she linked her other arm in his and set off with both men in tow. "Did you see me?" she asked with a smile, bumping Noah's hip with hers. The three of them together made for a curious trio of walkers, the diminutive Clara between the compact Choctaw Indian on her left wearing his tall black slouch hat and the towering blond Viking on her right.

"Why I guess I did. But I didn't win nothing, Clara. I was one second short when my dang boot slipped out of the stirrup on a spin."

"Noah, you can't help it that you're too tall. Everybody knows you long boys tend to get spun around too easy."

As they made their way along, See Bird thought to himself with a smile, "That tall young man has just got spun dizzy, and I don't think his head is going to clear up any time soon, not if Clara has in mind what I think she does."

# 13

$678.87. Even after all the expenses he incurred, and the shortened season due to the time he spent down in Oklahoma helping Talulah and visiting with his family, $678.87 was still a fine pile of money. With it, he and Sally would be able to make it through until next summer just fine, and perhaps they would even be able to buy that twenty acres of woods along Blackberry Creek. His wife's uncle, Devil Anse Hatfield, owned it and had hinted it might be available. Sally loved to walk those woods with her daughter, Gertrude. The little girl was born, the daughter of Frank Osborn, the High Sheriff of Logan County and Sally's first husband. He was shot dead while trying to arrest some moonshiners, leaving Sally a very young widow. When See Bird married Sally, he adopted Gertrude. In truth, he loved the child as though she were of his own blood. And she loved him in return.

Mother and daughter would talk and walk and never return home without having found some treasure, be it a colorful bouquet of daisies and columbine for the entry table, a basket of herbs and mushrooms, or berries and nuts. Once a pink-cheeked Gertrude carefully lifted from the basket an Indian arrowhead and gave it to her pa for his inspection. He was truly moved. He was also certain both of his 'gals' would be thrilled with the land purchase. It may be that, if he bargained hard, he would even have enough to buy another mule to help put in a few more acres of tobacco.

These were his thoughts as he sat cross-legged in the cattle car on a pile of clean straw, his wargrip beside him. Kiamichi munched oats contentedly in a corner nearby. Hiding his earnings in a sock had by now become a joke. It would be the first place someone with fast fingers would look. So he had converted most of the money into a few big bills back in Cheyenne and then carefully removed several stitches along the inside of his 'grip,' inserting the bills into a false side pocket. They didn't rattle or clink, nor did they take up much space or weigh very much. He used old thread so the pocket wouldn't draw unwanted attention should he meet up with bad hombres. Unlike many cowboys, See Bird had never taken to haunting those places where fast talk and slippery fingers worked, but still sometimes, he was well aware, they can seek you out.

See Bird was a trusting man, but he was also a realist. He knew that rodeos, cowboy festivals, wild-west shows and the like, attracted some mighty unsavory characters, each one with a slick smile and a scheme for separating a man from his hard-earned money. Whether it was whores, flim-flam men, bunco artists, or card-sharps, at heart they were all best avoided. He had learned that from riding herds years ago up the Chisholm Trail for Big Jim McCarty. He had watched as men lost every penny they had risked their lives for in a single night of debauchery at trail's end. As he tied off the thread knot, he considered, "This may be a new century, but human nature still hasn't changed much, if at all, if I been reading the Good

Book right, since Jesus walked the earth." He carefully repacked his grip, securing most of the remaining $78. in the third sock. With a sigh, he lay his head against his bundle and listened to the wail of the Northern Pacific engine pulling east against the oncoming night.

From Cheyenne, he worked small-town rodeos and rode the rails north towards the "Big Sky Country." On arriving in Custer, Montana, he heard that a couple cowboy contests were supposedly cranking up if he only traveled east through North Dakota.

The first river he crossed upon entering the state was the Little Missouri, a shallow but lovely winding little river, dotted with sandbars. The land on either side was strikingly purple in the evening light. Cottonwoods and thin strips of meadows lined its banks. Behind these were stark cliffs and grassy plateaus, an altogether unique landscape. As the engine slowed down to stop in the sleepy village of Medora, See Bird decided this area was worthy of more of his attention, and so, for no better reason than whimsy, as the train pulled out of the village, two passengers, See Bird and Kiamichi, stood by the tracks and listened to the lonesome whistle bid farewell.

# 14

The small campfire was starting its final decline into crimson embers. Three men sat around its perimeter, two of them gazing off into the darkness, alert to any sound that may have been out of place, their senses keyed to any hint of danger. Not that they were expecting any trouble. It was more the habit of alertness that came with their job, protecting the person of the third man in their group, a shorter man, older than either of them by several years, at least. He looked to be in his mid-'40s, tanned and robust, with a barrel-chest. Sporting a two-day-old beard, at first glance, he could have been mistaken for some rancher out looking for strays. But that impression would last only until he inserted his pince-nez monocle over one eye and flashed a frightening grimace, exposing a jaw-full of powerful teeth.

"What do you think, Rowelly? Are we closing in on them?" he asked without taking his eyes from the dying fire. Absent-mindedly he poked at the fire with a stick, then impatiently tossed it into the flames, causing a cluster of sparks to rise and flicker away into the blackness.

The man he addressed hesitated a moment before responding. Down in the valley, perhaps a mile away, another campfire flickered in the darkness. Perhaps it belonged to those they hunted. 'But no,' he thought to himself, 'horse thieves would know better than to build a fire out in the open like that. Most likely, it's just some ranch hand working a fence line.' "Maybe," he replied. "They had about a ten-hour head start on us. But stringing along a half-dozen horses, they can't travel as fast as us. With luck, we'll catch up maybe tomorrow evening or the next day. That is if they don't up and do something smart, like unload them on some unsuspecting buyer, or pack them on a train headed elsewhere." With a hint of exasperation, he added, "I still think we should just have telephoned ahead. We know the direction these rustlers took and authorities could catch them. This is not like the old days. There's telephones now, at least in some places." He returned his gaze to the shallow valley below them. There was no trace now of the fire he had noticed earlier. He imagined the ranch-hand down there peacefully asleep, without a care in the world to trouble his dreams.

"Perhaps you are correct. But suppose the authorities up ahead have concerns of their own. Unless I pull rank on them, and I am loath to do so, they may delay until it is too late. Besides that, I simply detest receiving special treatment merely because I am President of the United States. What does a 'Square Deal' mean if not that every man in this republic is treated equally, regardless of social status or corporate position? No sir, Rowelly. This is our mess, and it is ours to clean up. We are going to bring these bandits to justice. Besides," he said with a grin, "This is more fun than a buffalo hunt."

"Rowelly, Craig, you men rest while I take first watch. I'm too keen to sleep now anyway. I'll wake you, Rowelly, in four hours. Now do not object. I insist."

He waved aside their unspoken protests and continued, "What good is being president if I cannot give my own men orders? Think of me as Colonel Roosevelt if it helps any. You do understand the chain of command, I take it? Good. Then let us have no more foolishness."

"Mr. President…"

"And please refrain from calling me that out here. It's a title, not a name, and it reminds me too much of Washington City. Thinking aloud, he said, "People call me T.R. or Teddy – but never Theodore. I wonder why," he added wistfully. "My parents liked it well enough."

"Yes sir, T.R. sir," Conner responded, clearly uncomfortable. "Actually, I'm a bit more concerned with the tracks of that big cat we crossed before we settled down up here in the rocks. He's a big one, he is, and what with all the settlers moving in around here, predators like the big cougars are becoming scarce, and those as remains are more unpleasant than ever before. Or so I've been told." He glanced at Rowelly. "So I will watch for the eyes in the night. I do not expect we'll see a hair of those rustlers though."

Whereas some men might relish the chance to sleep beneath a blanket of stars, Craig Connor, lately of Boston, Massachusetts, felt exposed and vulnerable. A huge man, standing 6'4" tall and weighing in at 250 pounds, he remained an urban man to his core. He relished the bustle of crowds, the clang of trolley-cars, and the new towers going up around him nearly every day, constantly enlarging and rebuilding the city he called home. He even missed the smell of the streets. The badland's silence, broken only by the wind and the night calls of bird and beast, nearly unnerved him.

The third man listened as he laid out his gear and sat on a blanket to remove his boots. While being asked, as the manager of T.R.'s ranch, to accompany the president on his western tour had sounded like a fine idea at first, promising a break from the tedium of serving as caretaker of the nearly defunct ranch, chasing badmen was more than Rowelly Sinclair had counted on. Upon returning exhausted from Cheyenne to the Roosevelt ranch with the President, and following a long day catching up on neglected chores around the ranch, he had turned the horses loose, untended in the corral, while he opened up the big house and put on some coffee, beans, and steak for their simple supper. By the time he remembered them out behind the barn, it was well after dark. And when he found the gate had been opened and the steeds missing, he flung his hat to the ground and let loose with a series of epithets he would not have wanted to share with the owner of the ranch. He felt a heavy responsibility for having let the man down and desperately wanted to set things right. What made it worse was that, after hearing his story out, T.R. had sat silent for a moment and then slapped the palms of his hands on the table. Rising abruptly to his feet, he gripped his ranch manager by his shoulders and shouted, "Bully. This is just the adventure I had dreamed of." He laughed. "We'll be on their trail by daybreak. Finally, I can breathe again and get some action."

Finally, the ranch manager carefully brushed off his well-worn hat and placed it by his boots, stroked the tips of his handlebar mustache, and sat for a moment, letting the peace of the night calm his spirit. That he was charged with protecting the life of the President of the United States, who apparently was completely at ease here, gave his worry for the man's safety an ironic twist. With a wry smile he lay back. T.R. may move a little too quickly for a Western man's preference, but doggone it, a man couldn't help liking him.

See Bird was not, at first, at all sure what had awakened him. He knew simply that some sound had, and that now he was fully and completely alert. He turned his head slowly to the side. The remains of his fire had burned down to a dull, pulsing glow. Kiamichi stood silently, staring off into the darkness. See Bird looked in the same direction but saw nothing. He heard a 'pop,' then two more in quick succession. They came from the general area where he had seen the distant light earlier. Gunfire. Someone was in trouble.

Generally, in the West, a man stayed out of trouble by not going looking for it. But in a place where people were still scarce, helping out a neighbor in trouble was more than a platitude. It was a necessity. In the time it took him to consider his options, See Bird pulled his boots on, unhobbled and threw a saddle on Kiamichi, shoved the Winchester in its sheath, and headed at a gallop toward the nearby hills.

The three-quartered moon was up, giving form to the shadowed nighttime landscape. Kiamichi's rhythmic hoofbeats pounded the turf as man and horse glided across the valley. The Choctaw did not worry, as some did, about his horse stepping in a prairie dog hole or injuring itself on some unseen obstacle. A lifetime on horseback had taught him that the night vision of a horse was vastly superior to a man's, that in fact, it rivaled a cat's. That fact, combined with the horse's sleeping habits, or lack of them, had taught See Bird that the animal was a trustworthy guard, better than most men when it came to keeping watch at night.

Kiamichi seemed to know where his rider was guiding him and effortlessly climbed the gentle slope, slowing to a walk. Just beyond a cluster of brush, on the edge of a copse of cottonwood, See Bird smelled a fire and sensed motion. He reined up. "Hello, the camp," he called out.

"Hello, yourself," called out a wary voice. See Bird heard the unmistakable click of a pistol being cocked. "Get down and come on in slowly, mister." He dismounted and, careful to obey instructions, walked forward toward the voice.

"I heard some shooting and thought maybe somebody needed some help. So I came. You fellers okay?"

Seeing the stranger was alone, unarmed, and apparently trying to be helpful, Sinclair lowered the pistol's hammer and shoved the gun back in a cross-draw holster he wore on his left hip. See Bird dropped the reins and walked with the man toward the campfire, which had been rebuilt. It was there that a sight greeted him, which left him speechless. The man he had last seen at the Cheyenne rodeo receiving the plaudits of thousands, the President of the United States was on his knees, sucking blood from a wound on the leg of a moaning man and spitting in the dirt. The blasted remains of a rattlesnake, headless, lay nearby.

T.R. rose and wiped his hands on his trousers. Introductions were made all around. "And that man on the ground is Craig Connor," T.R. said, thrusting his jaw forward in what passed for a strained grin, "a secret service agent, bodyguard, and friend from South Boston. That rattler decided to crawl in with him for a little extra warmth, and well, you see what happened. I shot the devil out of it, then cut off its head when it would not relinquish its grip. I got right after it sucking out the poison, so I do not believe the bite will prove fatal. But the man needs medical attention, just as we are on the verge of apprehending the buzzards who dared steal some horses from my ranch, Elkhorn. He pounded a fist into his hand, frustrated, as a judge might pound a gavel.

"Sinclair here," nodding to the steel-eyed man who had intercepted See Bird, "is the manager of that ranch. I'm planning on selling the whole spread. Just been too busy to get to it. I bought it years ago, following the death of my wife and mother on the same day. I needed to get away for a while. But it has been more trouble than it's worth lately. And I would sell the thing to the first person who makes me a decent offer. But unfortunately, at present time the West is just digging itself out of a depression and has never really recovered from the terrible winters it has suffered recently. I myself lost some forty percent of my stock a few years back and count myself fortunate." Never slowing his narration, he doused a towel with cool water from his canteen and placed it on the injured man's forehead. "The cold and snow buried the poor creatures where they stood." He shook his head in remembrance. Then, standing, he turned the conversation. "And what brings you out here, Mr. See Bird Carpenter?" He looked hard at his visitor, his strong chin jutting forward. "If you do not mind me saying so, you look a tad familiar. I am very good with faces, so tell me where was it I saw you?"

"Mr. President," See Bird answered, "I saw you at the Cheyenne wingding. I was lucky on a bronc, and my horse won the calf roping event."

"Now I remember," T.R. thundered. "I, myself, am only a fair to middling rider, and even though I work hard at it, I remain a modest marksman due to my nearsightedness. But you rode under a different name if I am not mistaken. I've been trying to persuade the Sioux in these parts to take white names. I believe it would help them significantly in their land and legal woes. But, alas, I seem to have made little headway."

He pointed a finger, speaking between clenched teeth. "And mister, from where I stood, it looked as though you were glued into that saddle. I have seen many a bucking horse ridden, but I've never seen anything like your ride. I am indeed dee-lighted to meet you." He reached out and pumped See Bird's hand vigorously. The callouses on his hand and strength of T.R.'s grip surprised him. Clearly, the president was not above physical labor. "Sit down here with us, if you please. Mr. Sinclair, would you please put on some coffee. We're going to have a long night to work out our plan of attack."

See Bird sat cross-legged on the ground, away from the fire. T.R. sat across from him. He had picked up another stick and was poking relentlessly at the now crackling fire, muttering under his breath with each poke. "Get action. Do things. Don't fritter. Be somebody. Be sane." Then he repeated louder, "Get action." His gaze took in the other three men as if seeing them for the first time. They looked at him expectantly. "See Bird, are you, by chance, any more familiar with the area to our immediate south than are we? And do you think you can pick up the trail?"

"To answer your first question – nope. I've never been here before. As to your second question, I do think that since I've been tracking and trailing for most of my 38 years, I do not expect it would be all too hard to follow the trail of these hombres, what with them mounted and dragging a bunch of horses down the trail.

But, sir, I just want to ask one question myself. Are you sure this is what you want to do, what with your man snakebit and all?"

T.R. nodded his head. "I know what you are thinking, See Bird. I've been considering just that. I know I must not be drawn into any rash action that would bring reaction and disaster after. But there is a way to proceed. This is my plan." He leaned forward, dropping the stick, resting his forearms on his thighs. "Sinclair, you will take two of the horses. At first light, we'll construct a travois and you shall return to Medora with Conner in tow. I left Dr. Bruster with my other secret service agent and secretary back at Elkhorn. See that this man gets proper medical attention and have them notify Washington City that I have been sidetracked enjoying the scenery and will report in several days. Then you and Roger Owens, the other agent, saddle up two fresh horses and high-tail it back down the trail to join up with See Bird and me. The two of us will be making quick tracks after those rustlers. If you bring fresh horses and switch off every couple hours, and if you ride hard you should be able to link up with us within two days, three at the most. These men we pursue are cowards and thieves, probably not killers. I should think that a proper exercise of power used fearlessly will do the job."

Sinclair's and T.R.'s eyes met. The President's agent broke contact first. He splashed out the remains of his coffee. Working to control his emotions, he said, "Mr. President, when you hired me, I took an oath to protect you whether you like it or not. I know I also serve at your discretion. It seems to me that there are too many holes in your plan. First off, we don't even know this man, See Bird. No disrespect intended."

"None taken," See Bird responded.

"And we don't know if he can track at all. Secondly," he bravely held up a hand to stem T.R.'s imminent eruption, "too many things can go wrong. These fellows may be watching their back trail and may bush-whack you. It's well and good to be the president and all. But these men may not find that out 'til after they plug you. Now, before you go getting all hot and bothered, I'm telling you I'll do what you order me to do because you're my boss. But that does not mean I have to like it."

The air around the campfire fairly crackled with energy. When Roosevelt spoke, his words were soft, his voice intense. "Rowelly, you've been with me for a long while now, and I respect your fears and concerns. They are rational, perhaps reasonable. But I have not gotten to this high office by equivocating or backing down when confronting an evil. And that's what this is. Back east men who would make these pathetic creatures we trail look like worms, daily squeeze honest men to work for a pittance and force miners to eat weeds while they hob-nob in their palaces, dining on shrimp and lobsters. When I get back to the White House, I mean to take on those malefactors of great wealth, to squeeze them until they cry 'Uncle.'

"I will not act expediently here and courageously there. Because they are here as well. The same types of men have overgrazed the land, destroyed the forests and wildlife, depleted the valuable minerals, and starved a brave people into a pathetic submission. If I am to take them on back east, then I may as well gird my loins now. Truthfully, I tell you, it all frightens me too sometimes. But I have learned that if you practice fearlessness, courage will come. Now, gentlemen," he rested his hands on his hips, "it's almost dawn. Let's construct that travois and get you on the road. See Bird, let's pack up and break camp. Then we have to go down there and clean up your old camp. I want to be on the trail of these miscreants before dawn." See Bird smiled to himself. This was a man, he thought, to ride the river with. He may have a funny way of speaking, but he would not be a man to wrong. And so it was that the President of the United States, having left behind his two secret service agents, his ranch manager, his personal physician, and private secretary, set off in pursuit of an unknown band of horse thieves, accompanied only by an American Indian cowboy.

If Bill Shorter, Web Cahill, and Dorsey "Bones" Blunt, would have had any inkling of the force of nature relentlessly bearing down on them in the person of Teddy Roosevelt, they would not have been sprawled around the morning campfire polishing off a second pot of coffee. Bill was the only one even to bother casting a glance down their back trail, but detecting not even a trace of dust in the still morning air that would warn him of approaching riders, he soon turned back to the fire and squatted down on a log.

"I tell you, Bones, that was pretty slick," Web said with a wag of his head, "the way you peeled off these cayuse from right behind that barn. I bet that four-eyed tinhorn is too dumb to notice they're gone, even now."

Bones appreciated the flattery, but thought that showing too much pleasure in the praise of the other horse thief would be inappropriate. "Yeah, he's a fool and a politician to boot. And you know that politicians is all a bunch of the worst kind of folks. He most likely stole that whole ranch off'n some poor sodder. So us boys taking back a few of his horses is just evening the score a bit, I'm a-thinking." They both chuckled at his display of wit and logic.

Bill Shorter scratched at the sweat-stained armpit of his discolored vest. He knew Web was just playing up to Bones and that Bones was wallowing in it like a pig in slops. Bones liked to think that he was the brains of the outfit. But the truth of it was that he couldn't think his way out of a barn with one door. Rustling that dude ranchers horses was just a spur-of-the-moment thing. The three men were out of work, out of money, and out of luck when the opportunity presented itself. Bill was the one who noticed the empty bunkhouse, the unlocked gate, and the handy to-be-taken riding stock, and brought it to Bones' attention. From that point on, everything just sort of happened. For Web to go all gooey over Bones' part in the action riled him to no end.

He tossed the dregs of his coffee into the dying flames, creating a hiss and puff of smoke. "Yeah, well, I'm a-thinking we should hit the trail. Dumb and blind or not, he most likely knows how to pick up a telephone and call to the towns hereabouts and have the John-Law on the lookout for them missing horses. He don't even have to come after us hisself. Why would he bother?"

The idea that even now, word about their raid could be reaching lawmen all around the area seemed to catch the other two off guard. Web grunted. Bones stood and tossed the remains of his cup into the dying embers as well. "You got a point there, Bill. And that's exactly why we're going to sell this lot as soon as we get the chance. Take what we can for them, and make tracks for anywhere else. The morning's near half gone. It's past time we cleared out of these parts. 'Sides that, I got me that itchy feeling on the back of my neck like I do if things ain't right."

Bill climbed into his saddle, leading the string of horses. "You got an itchy feeling, all right, Bones. We all do. But them's just fleas." He laughed and kicked his mount forward.

As Bones' gang was just hitting the trail, See Bird and T.R. had already been traveling at a mile-eating fast walking pace for several hours. The gap between the two groups was slowly but inexorably closing. Though the president was notoriously nearsighted and had one eye damaged in a boxing match, even he could have followed the thieves' trail, as clear as it was. And that was just what worried See Bird. Perhaps the horse thieves wanted to make it easy to follow, to lull whatever posse that might be trailing them into complacency. They may be cowards, but cowards were precisely the type of men who would not shy away from bushwhacking the unwary.

See Bird had cut his teeth on violent men who, in the name of a family feud, would lie in wait in the deep woods and hills of West Virginia or along lonely trails, to ambush and even scalp Hatfields and their allies so as to claim the reward for their pelts on the Kentucky side of the Tug Fork. The wide-open terrain in the Dakotas contrasted vividly with the forested and narrow hollers back east. But men with rifles could still find plenty of good spots from which to take their best shots. Consequently, his gaze was forever sweeping the horizons, searching for anything out of place, anything that would give away a man lying in wait.

T.R., on the other hand, focused his will and attention on the trail ahead. He was determined, no matter what was to come his way, he would surmount it completely. Once he set his sights on a goal, he would direct his iron will toward it unflinchingly. He may have ridden like a greenhorn, stiff in the saddle, but he sure enough could take punishment as well as dish it out. He was a tireless rider and if the pace bothered him, he never complained.

He was not a man to chatter aimlessly, but once in a while he would speak, almost as if compelled to express his thoughts out loud. See Bird seldom started a conversation, but at a mid-morning break to give the horses a breather as they crossed a small stream, he asked, "Mr. Roosevelt, I notice you're wearing a side-arm. I'm curious. Seeing as how these bad hombres are undoubtedly packing, and we might have to use force on them, well…"

T.R. chomped down on a strip of jerky. "You're wondering if I can properly use this piece of equipment, I believe." He smiled. At least See Bird interpreted T.R.'s toothy grimace as one. Teddy turned in his saddle and spoke directly. "I willingly admit Annie Oakley need not worry that my reputation will surpass her own. But I have led men in combat, and have fired in my enemy's direction on more than one occasion, likewise receiving their fire back. I suppose you could say I am an adequate marksman. A man in my position would be foolish to rely solely on others for his protection, especially given this country's recent history of presidential assassinations. The US Treasury Department, given the blessing by Congress, has assigned agents to protect my person. But a determined man can penetrate even a solid wall. So the sad fact of the matter is this: I wear a pistol almost always when I am in public, even to church. Thus far, I've had no reason to draw it. I would prefer to keep it that way. And what about you, Mr. Carpenter? I could not help but notice that you carry no side-arms."

See Bird chuckled. "No sir. And it's probably safer for all concerned that I do not. 'Adequate marksman,' you called yourself. Well, I guess that just about describes me as well. I do carry a pistol in my wargrip, but when I need firepower, I rely on this Winchester 85." He patted the stock of the weapon tucked in its saddle-sheath beside his knee.

"You say you carry the pistol in your 'grip.' But won't that rather defeat its purpose should you need it?"

See Bird thought a moment, listening to Kiamichi slurp up a final drink. "A man once told me that a lot of fools work hard at fast-draw but couldn't hit a wall. He said when it comes to .45s, 'Slow is smooth, and smooth is fast.' I reckon that's the truth. Fact is, I may not bring the barrel up first, but if a fellow's shooting at me, I will do my best so he won't have a chance to get off a second shot."

T.R. nodded, appearing quite thoughtful. "You express my feelings exactly, just exactly."

See Bird, embarrassed at possibly sounding like a braggart, twisted in the saddle and then pointed at the tracks they had been following when they paused. "Now look there, Mr. President. Unless I miss my guess, that hoof print is still damp where their horses walked out. That means we may be closer than we thought. We're probably no more than a few hours behind those galoots. We should keep our voices down from now on. Sound can carry far in these coulees. I do think that if we should run into them, it would be better for us if we drop back and tail along farther behind for a bit. Why don't we wait for them to set up camp, and then we make our move? Sound good to you?"

"Splendid, See Bird. That's just splendid." He laughed with pleasure as he reined his horse around and spurred it up the bank. "I haven't had so much fun in years. I feel like a boy again."

See Bird wagged his head and silently smiled at the back of his irrepressible traveling companion. T.R. seemed completely unaware of personal danger. Then he thought again. That's not quite right. The President was perfectly aware of all the potential dangers. But he looked at them as challenges to be faced and conquered, not threats that could destroy him.

# 15

The hot afternoon dragged on. See Bird slowed their pursuit to not press their quarry too closely. Veterans of the trail could sometimes sense the pressure of being hunted and become more cautious. See Bird's every sense was now on high alert. His deep black eyes, squinted against the sun and dust, constantly scanned in every direction. Occasionally, he would even turn and take a moment to study their back trail, searching for any sign that the men he hunted were now hunting him. Also, he searched for a brown haze that might signal Rowelly's return with reinforcements. But the horizon remained clear. Though relieved that they had found the thieves, See Bird now felt the pressure of figuring out how to reel them in. The feeling was similar to calf roping when he would race down a lasso with the piggin' string in his teeth just before coming to grips with the animal. Tension mounted. So many small things could go wrong at the last moment. And that must be avoided. The stakes were too high.

Looking at the sun starting its inevitable descent toward the rainbow streaked ridges, he spoke quietly. "Why don't we take a longer break? We're near abouts riding these fellers' hindquarters. It could be a bad mistake to come upon them too soon. Let's climb this slope a bit, stay below the ridgeline, and see if we can make anything out. They're going to have to pull up short in a bit anyhow. We'll have a cold camp, and then when it gets dark, we'll move in on them." T.R. nodded and the two men dismounted.

After hobbling the horses, they carefully made their way up the rocky slope. See Bird's moccasins made for silent walking. With T.R. in his high cowboy boots, such was not the case despite his best efforts. The scraping and crunching of leather soles on gravel guaranteed that if anyone were on the other side of this hill, the only surprise coming would be the one sprung on See Bird and T.R. Approaching the crest, See Bird lowered himself to his belly. T.R. followed suit. Together, they scanned the territory falling away gently before them. See Bird wondered what the man beside him could see without his glasses. But he was happy the President did not put them on. Sunlight reflecting off lenses was as good as telegraphing their exact location to anyone studying their back trail. Nevertheless, it was he who spoke first.

"See Bird," he whispered, "it is well that we have intercepted these men so quickly. Only about a day's ride farther on is a town called Hawkins. It doesn't have much to offer, not even a sheriff. But it does have a railroad siding. I would lay even money on the proposition that those banditos will seek to unload my horses there. That is why I am so determined to chase them down. By the time any authorities could have intervened, it would have been too late. By jingo, we've got them cornered now. Do you see anything?"

See Bird stared as if the very act could penetrate the unknown. The longer rays of the near setting sun provided even better reflectors than its rays did at noonday.

"Nothing," he was about to say. Perhaps he and T.R. had fallen farther behind than he had thought. Perhaps, after all this, they would lose them at Hawkins. He was just turning his face to T.R. when he caught something out of the corner of his eye. Was it a flash, a reflection? He looked back. Or was it his overworked imagination? For a long second there was nothing. Then, there it was again. It was caused, he was certain, by something shiny, a piece of glass, or metal. One thing for certain, though, it was man-made, and it was moving down a coulee soon to be wrapped in shadows. There, he thought, it flashed one more time before it winked out. T.R. caught his glance and stared into the soft shadows, seeing nothing.

"What did you just see?"

The Indian relaxed and exhaled. "We are right on their tails. See that low grey-green area between those little hills, about three-quarters of a mile off at about one o'clock?"

Roosevelt squinted. "Are you serious? About three-quarters of a mile away in that direction, you say, down in that shadowy vale. That's where you say they are. If you truly saw something, my good man, that is utterly remarkable. I must say I am duly impressed. Indeed I am."

See Bird leaned to the side, eyeballing his partner. He picked his words carefully. "What I saw was a reflection of something shiny. And as it passed into the shadows, it quit. It can't be natural. So it must be man-made. And since the only men we know of in these parts are your horse thieves, it only stands to reason, Mr. President, that the sparkle was made by the men who stole your horses. So, yes, I am serious."

T.R., realizing how his outburst might have seemed either patronizing or insulting, responded. "Mr.

Carpenter, what I mean to say is that your powers of observation are unusually sharp. I do not doubt for a moment that down there is our quarry, now properly identified. I dare say, men with your vision should be sought out and placed aboard every ship in the fleet. They would quickly become invaluable spotters and lookouts."

Mollified by the unusual apology, See Bird smiled and settled his back against a rock. "T.R., I think we've got those old boys cornered, sure as shootin'. That crew travels real lazy-like, so I don't figure they'll go much farther tonight. That means we can plan our next steps to end this game. We can make our play tonight when they're tired, or wait 'til daybreak when they're still sleepy. By then, Rowelly just might have caught up, and we'd have us a few more hands to work with. You've lived out here and know the land. What do you think?"

Roosevelt used to men whose job it was to worry themselves sick trying to protect him from any and all dangers, appreciated the fact that See Bird respected his opinion and treated him as an equal with valuable knowledge, given the situation. He hesitated not a moment. "The way I see it is this," he started. "As you say, they could dispose of those horses and get clean away before we close the noose tomorrow. We have no way of knowing if help will arrive in time to make a difference. I say we nail them tonight. Hawkins, from what I know of it second-hand, has not even a post office, much less a sheriff. It is probably just a cluster of settlers around a whistle-stop railroad siding. There are few streams around here, so it is most likely that the settlers gathered here because of the proximity of some small rivulet. If that is so, then the valley before us, down which those brigands passed, may provide them water along some feeder stream." He removed his glasses and wiped their sweat-stained lenses with his bandana and then replaced them.

"Drifters like them regularly stopped by Elkhorn, looking for a few day's work, often earning just enough to carry them on down the line a ways. They are not necessarily dangerous. But if they are following some rogue leader, they could be. Given their nature, I would not expect them to travel far in the dark, especially since the moon will not rise before midnight. By their accounts, they have traveled long and hard over the last few days. They will probably feel safe, being so close to their destination." He pounded a fist in the palm of his hand. "See Bird, everything I know and feel tells me that this is the place and tonight is the time to put a stop to their nefarious activities. I say, let's nail them."

See Bird watched the late evening sunset as the president spoke. The golden sky was turning a deep orange blending to crimson as it met the horizon. The valley below them was now completely lost in shadows. He looked at the man seated beside him as the last rays highlighted the lines of his face. Roosevelt was not a big man, certainly not when compared to the man's bodyguards. But he was burly. And beyond his physical strength lay, See Bird felt a strength of intellect and will that the Indian had never come into contact with before, and he sensed, he may never meet again. Should anything be allowed to happen to T.R. tonight on See Bird's watch, he knew he would never forgive himself. Nor would the nation. Yet the man T.R. was elemental and unstoppable. He could even be dangerous. See Bird almost pitied any of the men and outfits back east that might have the misfortune to fall into the cross-hairs of the president's political gunsights.

Soberly, he addressed the young president. "Well, sir, given your information, I agree with your conclusion. Now we have to plan for its success. I agree and think we should move on those hombres tonight. And here's how I see it. First, we wait for dark. We will walk our horses down toward that gap those fellers rode through. My guess is they'll be not far on the other side. With luck, they'll camp in a low spot, hiding, thinking that if they ain't seen, they won't be found. That's where we ground-hobble the horses. Then I'll cut around them on the east and come up from the south, while you climb up the ridge to their north. To the west is a ridge that looks too steep for them to get over fast, especially pulling a string of horses, and you'll be in position on high ground to brace them if they think to try their luck back in this direction."

"Do you really think that will work?" T.R. interjected. "Such a plan would put you in grave danger, my friend. Perhaps we should stick together and ride directly in a frontal attack, so to speak."

Such a course of action, See Bird feared, could lead to the worst possible outcome. "No sir, T.R. If you don't mind my saying so, this ain't Cuba, and that ain't San Juan Hill, and you ain't got a regiment to back you up – only me. And Mr. Roosevelt, this time the nation cannot afford to lose you. Whereas, I am expendable. Teddy looked as if he would erupt, but before he could say a word, See Bird resumed. "And besides, T.R., I really believe this is our best chance for success. They will not be expecting anyone to come at them from the south. And if we go riding down that little valley into their camp, shooting, and hollering, somebody may one day write a poem about us, but we'll still be dead. Think about it."

T.R. breathed deeply but listened. "And another thing to consider, I am not exactly overgrown. People have been misreading me for all my life. They probably won't expect much from the likes of me, even if they capture me, which I don't intend to let happen. So you climb to that ridge, but stay below the crest. When you come around the top, you must remain silent, or you will put us in grave danger. Try to identify and move down close to their camp. But stay away from their horses. They'll give you away for sure.

"That's where I come in. I plan to cut the horses loose and drive them right through that gap, back past you. We recover them and those poor boys can be corralled when we feel like it. With a bit of luck, nobody gets hurt. If they come after us, you sir, will have to stop them."

"Horatio at the bridge. The Spartan 300 at Thermopylae. Yes, your plan has some historical merit. And besides, I can think of nothing better involving action on our part. Let's move, See Bird."

Nothing betrays stealth more rapidly than the sound of iron on stone. So the first thing See Bird did was to take some extra leather he brought along for moccasin construction and cut it into squares. These were then used to muffle the horseshoes. It would have been quicker to proceed forward down the slope, but riskier. So the two men carefully led their mounts back down the hill they had climbed and wound around its western end. Here, after See Bird looped the string of his hat over the saddle horn, leaving it behind, he and T.R. parted company. Roosevelt, leading the leather-clod horses, would continue his slow, quiet approach to the next ridge, the one both men presumed the rustlers had set up camp behind. Then he would cautiously climb the hill and, spotting their campfire if they made one, edge his way into a shooting position.

See Bird worked his way around to the east, then south, in order to approach the camp from the direction of Hawkins. The moon had not yet risen, so the going was slow. The terrain was unfamiliar. But the sounds of the night, the chirruping of crickets, a distant screech of a night hawk, the scuttling noise of some small rodent nearby, surprised by the proximity of this silent man, all reassured See Bird that things were going as they should, that he shared the night with no others of his kind. Far from feeling threatened by the darkness of the night broken only by distant stars, he had to catch himself several times from falling into a complacency that might lead him to make a fatal mistake.

Judging that he had covered plenty of distance, enough to place him well south of where he expected to find the rustlers' camp, and using the stars as his guide, he swung to the west and then back to the north. The fact that the night remained peaceful enough and without the sound of gunfire both reassured and troubled him. Would T.R. be able to move successfully into position, at least enough to be able to help with supporting fire, should it come to that? Stumbling around in the dark could be treacherous. Perhaps, even now, the president was lying on some hillside grimacing, nursing a badly sprained ankle or even a broken leg. In which case, all that Roosevelt could do would be to lie there and wait to be found, hopefully by friends.

Realizing his anxiety was distracting him from his purpose, the Indian focused on the task at hand. He had to assume that T.R. would hold up his end of the deal and that he was okay. As he drew nearer to where he expected to find the rustlers, he could feel the adrenaline begin to flow. His senses became sharper. He paused to evaluate every noise. And then the moon rose, washing out the starlight along the eastern horizon. See Bird was startled by how open the country now appeared. No forests here, just sagebrush, gravelly hills and down to the left, a sparse stand of brittle cottonwoods.

He felt a momentary alarm, seeing nothing to his fore but a desolate landscape lit by the half-moon. Ahead of him rose a ridge that he presumed was the one separating him and Roosevelt from their quarry. Anyone moving on that hillside would be terribly exposed and vulnerable. He hoped the president was securely tucked in behind one of the large and plentiful boulders that littered the slope.

But maybe, he thought, the rustlers were not where he assumed they would be. The land on this side of the ridge varied somewhat from the other side. For one thing, there was that small stand of cottonwoods about a quarter-mile away to the west. He couldn't see it, but he figured there must be a water source nearby. Their leafless tops protruded from a low area. He studied the layout more carefully. Was that some movement he detected in those trees? Could that be where they kept the horses? If so, then perhaps their camp would be just on the other side. But if that were the case, what had happened to T.R.? He would have crossed the ridge directly facing See Bird only to find – nothing. No horses, no bad men, nothing. What would he do then? Would he even be able to provide support, so far out of position?

See Bird had to decide his next steps and they had to be right. He could backtrack, find T.R. and make a new plan for tomorrow. That was fraught with danger. This was dangerous, as well, but it was also an opportunity.

If T.R. was out of position, that could mean he was also out of harm's way. If the bad men's camp was over there by the cottonwoods, See Bird still might be able to sneak up and grab the horses, getting away before they could react. He thought long and hard about it – for about thirty seconds. Then, in a low crouch, he commenced his stalk.

When Teddy surmounted the ridge and the moon rose, he was crestfallen by the desolate picture before and below him. He saw nothing but a brush and boulder-strewn landscape devoid of any sign of life. For a heart-stopping moment he considered that perhaps the rustlers had pressed on, maybe all the way to Hawkins and that he and See Bird were too late. No one would blame them for coming up short. See Bird did not know the countryside, and Teddy hailed from the East, the land of big cities and civilization. But, he smiled grimly to himself; life was more complicated than that. See Bird was almost preternaturally comfortable with the land. He knew it and was at home with it. T.R. himself had come west at the age of 26, at a time when in his own words, 'the light had gone out of' his life. Following the sudden, catastrophic deaths of his wife and mother on the same day, he had thrown himself into ranching, learning about the land and the men who inhabited it. He became a good horseman and an 'adequate' marksman. Above all, he put himself through a crash course of learning about himself, his limits and ambitions, his loves, and hates. When he felt satisfied he had learned enough, then and only then, did he return to the East. But he never forgot the lessons learned in the West.

So now taking stock of his situation, he figured that his companion would behave similarly, and began to study the night-time landscape, knowing that See

Bird would be evaluating the same from a different perspective. The only thing that might be used to provide cover for anyone with horses would be perfectly aligned large rocks or trees conveniently placed, or cut banks along the dry washes. Unfortunately, although there were plenty of them, the rocks before and around him may be large enough to hide a man or two, but could in no way conceal a string of horses.

Trees were fairly rare, and a cut bank at night might be invisible until one stumbled over it. But there was a small stand of desiccated cottonwoods to his right front, about 500 meters off. It wasn't much, but unless those men had made a late push on into Hawkins, that spot appeared to be the likeliest place for them to make camp. Slowly and carefully, the President of the United States retraced his steps to the other side of the hill and began the long-angled descent to the bottom.

# 16

Bill Shorter leaned against a cottonwood and rolled a smoke. He was coming near the end of the first watch tonight, but following several untroubled nights, he did not expect there would be any problem here. He might even find a time to take a short nap before he had to roust up Web. He actually preferred the watches divvied up this way because Web snored so danged loud it was nigh impossible for a man to sleep through all the racket. It reminded him of thunder rumbling away in some storm, only to cease suddenly and completely. Then, just when he relaxed enough to start drifting off again, Web would explode with a snore that seemed to suck his body inside out. Then the rumbling would begin again, and the process would repeat itself over and over, all night long. It was enough to drive a sane man crazy. He scratched at his itchy crotch and daydreamed about what it would be like to have enough money to hire a real hotel room, with clean sheets and a hot bath, and to eat a real sit-down meal which consisted of more than beans and burnt beef. And best of all, then, just maybe he would be able to afford a soiled dove for the night, or at least part of the night. What more could a man hope for in this life?

But first, they had to push on into Hawkins and

get rid of these horses. It had been his idea to rustle them in the first place, though Bones liked to claim the credit. And it was also his idea to sell them in Hawkins. Even though he argued with Bones that their relaxed pace put them in danger and that they should push the trail harder, he had to confess that Bones had been right. Nobody seemed to notice the missing stock, at least not yet. And they would ride into town tomorrow afternoon, the horses in good shape, and should realize a decent profit from their efforts. The moon was up, the horses quiet, and the land, at least as far as he could tell, was empty. He took a long drag off his cigarette and exhaled. Only a bit longer and then he could catch some shut-eye. He could hardly wait.

See Bird noticed the dim red glow of the cigarette a few moments before he smelled it. So he was right. The rustlers had taken their rest almost within shouting distance of their goal. Now they would pay for their mistake. All he had to do was get close enough to grab the horses and make a dash for it. Lacking mounts, the rustlers would be as good as crippled and could be rounded up at the law's leisure. He had no certain idea as to the location of the President, but he would not be surprised if he were to turn out to be close by. The man was nothing if not resourceful. Given T.R.'s less than acute eyesight, he did not want to be anywhere near him if shooting started.

See Bird, himself, carried no firearms. His pistol was concealed in his wargrip. And his Winchester rested in its saddle sheath. The rifle was the last thing he figured he wanted to lug about in the dark. It would have slowed him down for sure or could have scraped on a rock somewhere, giving him away. The late moonlight glinting off the metal could easily have made him the target of a sharp-eyed guard. No. This was the best way. His only weapon was his knife, carried beneath his shirt, behind his left hip. He hoped he wouldn't need it.

He traveled steadily forward, crouched so low his face occasionally brushed some vegetation. He did not bother zig-zagging, knowing that an object moving across the line of sight at night was more easily picked out than one coming straight on. Still, he made use of any natural object that would present itself to catch his breath. Once, when none were available and he was within fifty paces of the sleepy-eyed guard, the man might have heard something, perhaps the brush of leggings against some chaparral. In any case, See Bird observed him turning in his direction and so dropped even lower, tucking in his head and thus, remained motionless so that in the vague light he appeared to the watcher as nothing more than one of a thousand large stones strewn about in the stark nightscape. Moving slowly enough to fool the hands of a clock, See Bird slowly raised his eyes. As he did so, the bandit turned and stepped decisively in the opposite direction, taking only enough time to stub out the cigarette before disappearing in the shadows of the trees.

See Bird saw his opportunity and seized it. It looked like the watcher was headed toward someplace with a purpose, most likely to wake another man to take over the watch. The Indian hoped the shift change would give him enough time to get in and out with the horses without being caught. He closed the remaining gap, flowing like quicksilver into the trees. Sure enough, for the moment the horses were unattended. They saw, heard, and smelled this unfamiliar human, but his voice caressed them in soothing tones, and they stood still, taking him in with their large, alert eyes. See Bird counted seven of them, one more than T.R.'s ranch manager figured on. And all looked to be in fine shape. They would indeed have brought a pretty penny at auction. Even unloaded at Hawkins for a bargain-basement figure, they would be a sore loss for the ranch and a large profit for the rustlers.

But it was not just these horses that needed to be released. The rustlers' own horses could not remain with them. It took a few precious moments for him to spot them hobbled a short distance away, and silently he made his way to them. He was about to free the first one when a sound stopped him cold in his tracks, the unmistakable click of a hammer being drawn back on a .45.

"And what do I have here?" The voice was menacing in its venom. But See Bird detected, just perhaps, a note of curiosity, as well. He hoped that somehow he could make that work to his advantage. He held his hands in front of him, palms up, as if in supplication.

"Please, mister. I'm just a poor Indian on foot. I saw you had more horses than you need. I would have returned it to you for sure after I got home." See Bird hoped the man saw what he wanted him to see – a small, desperate, poverty-stricken Indian, unarmed, a man who could not possibly pose a threat to him.

"How did you get in here?"

"I just walked. Your other man, he fell asleep and didn't see me coming in. I woulda woke him, but then he woke up. I got scared and hid, 'til he left."

The other man eyed him like a cat might a mouse before it pounced. See Bird realized that his helpless appearance might be just the thing to goad the man to action. "I knew Bill was worse than useless. But

I thought he could at least keep his eyes open long enough to spot a dirty, stinking, heathen savage. I should just plug you right where you stand. But…" he lowered the hammer of the pistol and waved it in See Bird's face, "I think the boys would never forgive me if they missed out on the fun. So what say we all have us a little neck-tie party." He took a step toward the Indian, standing now with his hands on his hips, his face a mask of terror. "Let's go, Sitting Bull," he ordered and lowered his gun just as See Bird dove for the man's feet, both arms extended, holding something in a two-handed grip.

Pain as sharp and intense as a lightning bolt surged through the outlaw's foot, up his leg, and ran throughout his body as the razor-sharp tip of See Bird's big knife plunged through the scuffed leather boot and bit deeply into his foot. A moment's hesitation as it caught on some bone, then slid off and continued its swift path through the foot and then the sole of the boot itself, pinning the outlaw to the earth where he stood. He reacted the way his body told him to. He screamed as his body spasmed with muscle contractions. The pistol fired twice, directly into the ground before he could drop it to bend and grab at his foot. By then, See Bird rolled to his feet and heard other gunshots coming from the direction of what he presumed to be the outlaw's nearby camp. That could only mean Roosevelt was in the thick of it. He knew he had to end this particular fight quickly. He kicked the grounded pistol away from the outlaw's feet, grabbed the bent-over man by the hair and rocked him back with a knee to the face. The outlaw fell unconscious, blood welling from his boot.

Stooping to sweep up the discarded six-shooter, he raced through the trees toward where he had heard the gunfire. With relief, he recognized a now-familiar voice giving orders. "I said it once and I shall not repeat myself save this one time. You men lie face down and lock your hands behind your backs." His voice lowered slightly and, if anything, became even more threatening. "Now!"

See Bird emerged from the trees to see the President standing guard over the two prone outlaws. Roosevelt spoke without moving his eyes from his two captives. "When I heard the firing, I figured you had somehow found this lair. I moved in to immobilize these two."

"And I am certainly glad you did, Mr. President."

Both outlaws swiveled their heads to take in their captor. Bill spoke, "What the hell, Bones. You mean to tell me we rustled Teddy Roosevelt's horses? Lordy, we are surely up the creek now."

"Shut up. You should have shot him when you had the chance," the outlaw leader responded. "Now they'll hang us for sure."

Teddy grinned that fearsome grin of his. "I am not sure horse thieving is still a hanging offense in this state. But if it is, you boys certainly deserve it. That will be for the law to decide, not me."

See Bird lashed the two men's hands behind their backs, collected their guns and handed them to T.R. Then he rolled them over on their sides. "Keep your eyes on these two while I go and check on their pal." Web was just coming around and moaning in pain where he lay. With a jerk, See Bird retrieved his Arkansas toothpick from the man's boot, eliciting yet another shriek, followed by some slobbering sobs.

"Was I you, old son," the Indian whispered in his ear, "I'd find me another line of work, maybe one that wouldn't involve getting all cut up like that." Then he removed the damaged boot and cleaned and wrapped the bloody foot. He couldn't do much of anything else with it. The big knife had slashed through almost from ankle to toes. "Yup, you'll be needing a cane to walk into the courtroom with. That's for sure. Best you start practicing now." With that, See Bird found a stick adequate to serve as a temporary cane, helped the man to his feet, and then stepped away, holding the man's own pistol on him. "Now walk."

By the time See Bird and the wounded outlaw made it back to camp, Teddy had the other two lashed back to back, lying on the ground. "Those navy knots I learned on the way to Cuba certainly came in handy tonight." While T.R. covered them, See Bird led the third man over, propped the other two into a sitting position, and sat him down beside them. "Well, my friend, it looks like we bagged the lot of them. Did you find the horses?"

"All of them and then some, T.R. They ran off a ways, but I don't think they'll go very far. Nowhere really for them to go. I'll round them up and grab ours while you pack things up here. I think we should push on into Hawkins. If we do, we should get there this morning yet."

"I concur. Most likely we wouldn't get much rest having to keep watch over these miscreants the rest of the night, anyway."

And so, with President Teddy Roosevelt leading and See Bird bringing up the rear, towing the string of horses, and with the dejected outlaws sandwiched between, they made their way into Hawkins about midmorning, having not even stopped to break their fasts. As expected, the village was little more than a cluster of clapboard single-story buildings along one side of a street. A muddy creek the locals called The Grand River provided water for the R.R. tower. Before they had traveled a hundred feet, T.R. reined them to a halt, and in his most commanding voice called out to a curious onlooker, "You there, would you be so kind as to summon whatever authorities may exist here to meet me at the telegraph office. And where do you incarcerate your drunks and scofflaws? We seem to have collected a few in our travels."

The man stared for a moment and barely stopped his jaw from hitting the ground. "By golly, you wouldn't be… but you surely are…" He stared, disbelieving. "I seen your picture. You're President Teddy Roosevelt. And you're here." He then drew himself up to his full height. "I'm Jasper Harris, sir, and I own that dry goods store. I got a room in the back that I use for new shipped goods and bolts of cloth. I keep it locked up tight. Once in a while a fellow might need some cooling off, and we stick him in there overnight. It's got metal hooks in the walls that I secure shipments to. I suppose that'll hold these hombres alright." Seeing the one man's bloody foot wrapped in a makeshift bandage, he added, "We don't have us a regular doctor yet, but Sam Connery is our barber, and he's willing enough to patch whatever needs patching. I'll send him over too."

He looked around at the slowly gathering crowd. "Willis, Jimmy, and a couple of you other boys. Help get these men into my back room. And lock them up good and tight. Joe, go get Sam and tell him to bring along his sewing-up gear. It appears one of those men might need a stitch or two." He threw his shoulders back. "I'm escorting President Roosevelt over to send a telegraph."

A few strides farther on and the two riders dismounted. With the help of a few bystanders, See Bird ushered the captives to the building Harris had indicated, while Roosevelt, accompanied by a growing crowd, made his way slowly to the telegraph office and stepped up on the porch. The telegrapher, a wizened man with sweeping grey eyebrows, and wearing a green visor, had come to the front door to see what all the commotion was about. When he saw the crowd, and recognized the personage leading it, and figured out that it was all headed in his direction, he scurried to his position behind the customer window and waited, trying with all of his might to look as alert and official as possible.

Teddy stepped up to the window. "I want to send a telegraph message to the Medora authorities for dissemination to all relevant news outlets. The telegraph operator grabbed a pencil and wrote as Roosevelt dictated. 'From President Theodore Roosevelt. STOP. Have arrived Hawkins. STOP. All is well. STOP. Will return by next train to Belfield and then to points west. STOP. Bring up Isabella STOP. Such a magnificent country. STOP.' Thank you, my good man. And what is your name?" His calloused hand reached through the window to shake that of the telegraph operator, who clasped the extended hand with flustered dignity.

"Dobbins, Mr. President, but my friends around here just call me 'horse.' I want to tell you what an honor it is for me to send your message. I voted Republican last time, and you can count on my vote for you next year too."

That Teddy was a political animal was now put on full display. He looked Dobbins in the eye and said with all sincerity, "I know I can depend on you, Mister Dobbins." He then turned and strode through the door onto the porch, raised two steps above the dirt-packed street. The mood of the growing crowd was festive, and as he appeared a vigorous cheer went up. 'Hip-

hip-hooray' and then 'For he's a jolly good fellow,' and then another rousing cheer. Someone yelled, "Speech." Teddy smiled as only he could and took one step forward to stand on the edge of the porch, behind the hitching rail. He wiped his monocle, waiting for the crowd to quiet, replaced it, and then began. "First off, I want to tell you fine people how dee-lighted I am to stand before you today." Then he lowered his voice, speaking softly at first, paying homage to the hard-working men and women who had weathered the worst that nature and man could throw at them and who had not only survived but thrived. Their children, he assured them, would inherit a country better than the one their parents tamed.

Subtly but steadily, his voice strengthened and the power in it rose. It was not a beautifully crafted speech. But it was his creation, and he poured himself into it. He placed one foot ahead of the other in a boxer's stance and straightened himself even more, so that he seemed to grow before their eyes. The audience was held rapt. When he excoriated the "malefactors of great wealth," the Jay Goulds and J.P.Morgans of the world, and punctuated his speech with jabs to the air and leaned forward as if to dare those villains to take their best shots at his formidable chin, the crowd too rose in fury. Had those titans of industry the nerve to make an appearance, they would have undoubtedly been whipped and ridden out of town on a rail.

Having made sure of the outlaw's restraints, See Bird stepped out of the dry goods store and stood watching, over the heads of the crowd, held spellbound by the president's energy and conviction. He had never known anyone like him. Upon reflection, he doubted that there ever had been another man like him.

T.R. concluded his spontaneous stump speech with a heartfelt plea for their support. "Indeed, I can do little without your iron spines. We must and we will reclaim this splendid nation and preserve it for untold future generations. Thank you. Thank you, my friends." He vigorously nodded his head to their rousing cheers and applause.

The man must be exhausted, See Bird thought, after everything he has been through the last few days, but if anything his energy had penetrated and charged the crowd, and then their energy flowed back, replenishing his own. Roosevelt smiled and waved and shook hands as if he had waited the entire year just for this opportunity. The crowd was his. He did not once mention the word 'Democrats,' yet See Bird seriously doubted that there would be a single vote for that party from this district in the next election.

The telegrapher brought out two wooden chairs for See Bird and Teddy. The wife of the dry goods store owner, carrying a covered tray, forced her way through the gawkers and stepped up to the porch. "Here you are, gentlemen," she said, as she placed a pitcher of chilled tea with two glasses and a plateful of freshly baked buttered biscuits along with a small jar of home-made blackberry preserves down on a small table. "It would seem that these menfolk would have no thought but for themselves, if somebody wouldn't constantly remind them. I'm sure you must be thirsty and hungry after chasing bad men all over the countryside." She wiped her hands on her apron and poured two glasses full of iced peppermint tea.

"Dee-lighted," T.R. said, picking up one and lifting a buttered biscuit. He slathered a spoonful of preserves on the biscuit, to the woman's smiling approval. Then she, having completed what she came for, nodded and stepped down, disappearing back into the crowd.

"Thank you very much, ma'am," See Bird called and drank deeply.

T.R. picked up his glass and, with a wide grin, touched glasses with his companion. "Here's to a thoughtful lady," he said loud enough for all to hear. Then he leaned in a bit toward the Indian and lowered his voice. "But I can't say as how I wouldn't prefer a long draught of a home-made mint julep laced with San Juan Rum."

The crowd seemed uncertain how to behave now that the initial shock of the president's sudden appearance had worn off. A few began drifting off to their various daily chores or errands, but then someone found an accordion, another man brought out a tuba, and a spontaneous party began to break out. The owner of the general store dashed into his building and emerged with two barrels. He plopped them down in the street and a clerk spanned them with a couple boards of rough lumber. A helper brought out a barrel of undetermined liquor, and the party commenced to pick up steam.

About one hundred meters away, at the far end of town, sat four recently arrived men on tired mounts, taking in the scene. Two of the men were ill-dressed in three-piece suits topped with bowlers, while the other two men wore regular cowboy working clothes. As the accordion player muscled his way through 'Oh Susanna,' the tuba player 'oom-pahed' along as best he could. Rowelly sagged in his saddle, beat the trail dust off his shirt and trousers with his hat, and said to no one in particular, "Well, boys, it looks like T.R.'s got here ahead of us after all, safe and sound."

"He sure didn't waste any time, did he?" asked the

other grinning cowboy, wiping the sweat and dust off his face with his bandanna, "'Cause we rode hard." The two Secret Service agents just sat stiffly astride their mounts, nursing their saddle sores, their faces betraying no emotions.

"No. I guess he don't," Rowelly replied. "Let's go find Mr. Roosevelt and see how he done it. Then I'm fixing to have me something that'll wash all this trail dust outta my throat." He clicked his tongue and gently kneed his horse forward. See Bird and T.R. sipped from their glasses of chilled mint tea as they watched the weary riders approach.

# 17

T.R. stood on the rear platform of the coach car, leaning over the railing, waving vigorously to the villagers clustered nearby and shaking any proffered hand. The short Northern Pacific train was composed of just an engine and coal car, a baggage car, which also transported the horses, followed by a single coach. Finally, the steam whistle blew and the locomotive slowly pulled away from the station. It was behind schedule, but who could blame it? What was originally supposed to be merely a water-stop had stretched into an hour-long stopover due to its illustrious passenger and the group that accompanied him.

Once the train pulled out of the station, the men in the coach deployed to their positions. The two secret service agents settled in at each end of the car, while See Bird, T.R., his ranch manager and ranch hand settled toward the middle.

For a little while no one spoke much. Hard riding and short nights had worn everyone down. However, the fine ladies of Hawkins made sure that the president and his entourage would not travel on empty stomachs. Before the train pulled out from the station, a large basket had been passed up to the rear platform. Rowelly now carefully placed it on a seat, took a brief glance at the contents and declared it fit to eat. "Grab it and growl," was his mealtime benediction. T.R. was offered first choice, but really there were no differences in the selections. The basket proved to contain a veritable cornucopia of good foods. The cold steak sandwiches were devoured first. They were followed by fresh apples, peaches, and pears, and for dessert, several still-warm fruit pies. For all the men, this was the best they had eaten since leaving Medora.

Once the meal was consumed and the secret service men resumed their positions, See Bird could almost have sworn he heard some soft snoring from the protectors of the president rocking gently to the sway of the carriage. Rowelly and the other hand found benches to their liking and settled in for a long nap. He could not blame them. They had ridden all night, trying to catch up with T.R., after having gotten a late start from the ranch. At least, See Bird thought, he and Roosevelt had found time to rest some along the way. But the President was not quite ready to sleep yet.

"I hope you don't mind, See Bird, if we talk for a little while before settling down. I find it helps me put things in a right order in my mind."

See Bird knew that, whether he minded or not, T.R. would hold forth as long as he chose to do so. It was his very verbal way of processing events.

"This has been a real eye-opener for me," the president began. "Of course, I own a ranch out here, but I visit it only rarely. This is all part of a six-week program on my part to journey extensively across the country. Back in the East, everyone comes at me with all their satchels full of expert advice, but I often find myself wondering if any of them really know what in blazes they are talking about. So I made arrangements to spend time with those who live here, whose very lives depend on their knowledge of the area.

"This is a grand and glorious continent we have inherited and populated at your people's expense. There is so much promise for the future. But so much of what I have seen makes me heartsick. So much has changed since I first bought Elkhorn nearly twenty years ago. Any man with half-a-brain could see how the land was being over-grazed. I warned them, but then who was I? Just some tin-horn Easterner. And to be perfectly frank with you, I was quite distracted back then. Sure enough, several brutal winters in a row and the butcher's bill came due. Now I am afraid that before long this land may well be ruined forever by rapacious greed." He looked at See Bird but finding his face unreadable, continued.

"Do you mind if I share something personal? It's just that I feel the pieces coming together, as if all the experiences of my life have been leading me to some cathartic event, and this trip may just be it. But the pieces are all jumbled up and often make little sense. I believe my Maker desires that I apply myself to bring it into some semblance of order."

"Be my guest."

"Here are the facts. I was born with a 'silver spoon in my mouth.' My father was a lion of a man, and my mother was the dearest person I ever knew. I was sickly and plagued with asthma. My father died when I was young, and my mother tried her best to see I got the best education she could afford, private tutors, the whole works. At an early age, I became aware that I was weaker than most boys my age, so I asked her help.

"What did my mother do? What any mother would do." T.R. laughed heartily. "She constructed a gym for me and hired men to work me into shape. It paid off. Going into politics was an easy decision for me, though I could have built a career as an ornithologist or businessman just as well. We mingled with all the money, 'old' and 'new.' I chose politics and was on my way up. I fell passionately in love with Alice, and she with me. My life was a veritable bed of rose blossoms." T.R. carefully set his mint-julep and rum down and licked his lips before continuing. See Bird, accustomed by now to T.R.'s overpowering personality, was struck by his introspection. It was unexpected.

"Pardon me, T.R., but a minute ago, you said you were 'quite distracted' back then, and that made you ineffective. Do you mind telling me what caused that?"

Uncharacteristically, T.R. hesitated, then continued. "I was in Albany when I received the news to hurry home, that my mother was failing. Alice was also struggling with the difficult childbirth of our first born. I raced home, dashed upstairs and held the hand of my mother as she died, then flew downstairs only to watch my dear Alice die after giving birth. I was devastated. I could not even bear to hold my new daughter, could not even say her name - Alice.

"I remember writing in my diary that evening, 'The light has gone out of my life,' and marking it with a big black 'X.' See Bird, I did not mean that figuratively. I felt a huge black sheet descending over me and smothering out all life and joy from my existence, and it took every fiber of my strength just to resist. That was the reason I came to North Dakota. Why would my Creator allow such a thing to happen? What was His purpose? What did He want from me? He answered me with silence. I eventually went back home, and against all my expectations, found that the passage of time, coupled with action, began to dull the bone-crushing pain. One day I contacted an old girlfriend from my younger days and found that when I talked with her, she seemed truly responsive to my state. Edith became my anchor and then my wife. Together we have a beautiful daughter named Alice and five more as well.

"So you see, I may come across to some as the proverbial 'bull in a china shop,' driven to action, but I am not without a smidgen of self-knowledge. Action helps keep me sane. Does that make sense to you?"

See Bird opened his mouth as if to speak, but before he could utter a word, T.R. continued. "If my Creator made me for a reason and then took those I loved away so suddenly, He must have desired my attention greatly. And if my Savior rescued me and gave me another chance at life, then I believe it behooves me to do as He wills. And to do that, I have come to believe that my job is to treat all men and women fairly, people of any color, race, or social status, so that all our people can share in our democracy. This is not a political stance. It is my belief, rooted in my very soul. But what can I do to help usher them to the greatness that a just and merciful God has planned for them? I must go about it in an orderly and systematic fashion.

"First, I need to collect the facts. That is why I have come here. I shall continue west to California. There I am to meet with a man who comes highly recommended. I contacted him, and he since has penned several letters to me urging me to see the land for myself. This John Muir appears to be an individualist with a mind and conscience. I know what you are going to say, but I've checked him out and he appears to be legitimate. Therefore, I requested that we meet. He has invited me to this Yosemite country in California, begs me in fact. So that's where I'm heading.

"On close reading of his correspondence, he appears to be a man with a head full of minerals, mountains, and canyons, and with not a birdsong to be found in any of them. But then, perhaps he can't hear." The president chuckled, "What do you think?"

See Bird might as well have not been in the car. He looked at T.R. and shrugged. "Perhaps I am making too much of his apparent lack of love for living nature," T.R. rumbled. "You may be surprised to learn that, had I not gotten into the political line of work, I most likely would have ended up an ornithologist." This did get See Bird's attention. "I've written a number of books on the subject of the birds of North America. I started when I was but a lad, and so I continue to this day, even doing my own sketching. Perhaps I shall continue in that vein when I leave this office after my next term. Do you not agree that a man should live his life, always exploring, always increasing his knowledge of the things that stir his essence?"

By this time, See Bird was beginning to lose the thread of this one-sided conversation. His experience with the man taught him that T.R. could continue in this fashion for hours. And though the man and the subject were interesting, he could not help drifting off now and then between lectures on the decline of America's songbirds, the disappearance of the passenger pigeon, even the waning of the turkey, the eagle, and the various waterfowl.

The Indian did not even realize how far he had faded into grogginess until he was jolted alert by a loud noise. He sat erect to see T.R. pounding his fist down on the wooden hand rest. "By golly, that's what I'll do then. As soon as I get back to the White House, I'm going to call in the man I just named to head my new

U.S. Forestry Department, Pinchot, Gifford Pinchot. We'll see if I can't just bypass Congress and set aside some lands for all Americans, not just the privileged few – National Parks, I'll call them. Yes sir, we'll just see about that. One thing is for sure. Doing nothing is not an option." In the dimming evening light, his eyes met and locked onto See Bird's. "Thank you, Mister Carpenter. You cannot know how much I value our little conversation. It is so refreshing to speak with one who appreciates and shares my national concerns. But now, if you will excuse me, I think I need to stretch out a bit and catch up on some badly needed sleep." With that, the president rolled over contentedly, folded a blanket under his head, and in only a few minutes, his soft snoring joined that of the other men. See Bird too soon fell asleep. The last sound he heard was the lonely call of the train whistle. It reminded him of what he feared may one day be the final call of the last American bison.

It had taken several days and nights of hard riding to reach Hawkins. But as See Bird rose to rub the sleep from his eyes the following morning, he was surprised to feel the train slowing as it pulled into Belfield. Here it halted to allow its passengers to stretch their legs, eat some breakfast, and for T.R. to check for any important news he might have missed while on his posse ride. While See Bird tended to his and Kiamichi's needs, Roosevelt, flanked by his suited escort, found the telegraph office and collected his messages. They then assembled in the hotel dining room. See Bird arrived first, T.R. a few minutes later. T.R.'s two ranch hands were the only ones missing as they saw to the sale of the outlaw's horses and gear.

See Bird was hovering over his second cup of Arbuckle's, savoring the aroma, as T.R. bustled into the dining room, carrying a handful of papers. Spying the Indian, he broke into his famous, tooth grinding smile, strode briskly over to the table, and settled himself in with a contented sigh. "You know, See Bird, back home in the White House I am not at all ready to begin my day without at least two or maybe three breakfasts, my appetite being what it is. Out here, however, I seem satisfied to take whatever I can get, and I still somehow manage to get in a good day's work. I guess I'll never understand it." The waiter timidly approached. T.R. impatiently waved him forward. "Come here, young man. Don't be afraid. I won't bite you. Though I am about hungry enough to give it a try. Bring me one of everything your cook is preparing in that kitchen, and tell her to put a rush on it." The waiter, given his orders, pivoted and moved on to the secret service men. "I told you to put a rush on it. That means do it now. Then take other orders. Got that?"

"Yes sir, Mr. President." The harried waiter did everything but salute as he dashed off to the kitchen.

T.R. laughed and waved some papers at See Bird. "What a morning! I take a few days off and the world goes to pot. Japan and Russia at each other's throat. Germany and England trying to gang up on Venezuela. Where will it all end?" Although Roosevelt's words seemed desperate enough, See Bird got the distinct impression that the President was enjoying each second of every blooming crisis. They were things he could focus his mind on and exert his mammoth will against. "At least Isabella shall be here shortly. That is a very good thing indeed."

See Bird slid the coffee pot across the table to him. "I don't know this Isabella, but I find if I have me a cup, and then one more, each morning, problems just sort of naturally work themselves into possible solutions. Drink and think. That's what I say."

T.R. stretched for the coffee pot handle, gazing thoughtfully at his breakfast partner. The waiter, emerging from the kitchen, noticed his reach with alarm and hurried toward the table. "It's okay, son," T.R. said, "I am used to pouring my own. Go on over and see what those men would like to order, and make sure that the United States government gets billed for it all, including a fair tip for all your extra efforts. The good Lord knows you deserve it."

As the waiter, mollified by T.R.'s words, turned to his other customers, the president pushed a sheet of paper over to See Bird. "Look at this. It says that the fellow who called himself Bones Blunt had earned himself a price on his head of $50. I would not have calculated that he was worth even that much. Since it was your idea to bring him down the way we did, and you took the major risks, I insist you take the money." He removed a fat envelope from an inside pocket and slid it across the table. "I will not have it any other way. I do not deserve it, nor do I want it. However, you are a working man who earns every dollar. And since I shanghaied you for a while, preventing you from earning your living in the rodeo, at least temporarily, I insist you take this." He lowered his voice, speaking sincerely, "Please, it is the least I can do."

See Bird listened carefully and weighed every spoken word. He observed T.R.'s body language as well, looking for any sign of condescension or a patronizing attitude. What he saw reassured him. With good grace, he looked T.R. in the eye, nodded slightly, and took the envelope. "Thank you, sir," he said. "I'm sure Sally will find a good use for it."

Roosevelt sat back, vastly relieved. He had come to be quite aware of See Bird's prickly pride and did not want to offend him. Quickly, he moved on to other matters. "Good. That's settled. Now," he paused slightly, "I am afraid I have one more request of you. You recall that when we first met, my man spoke of a certain big cat that was prowling the area of the ranch."

"Yes. I seem to remember him mentioning something about it."

"Well, I have received word just this morning that it, or one like it, has recently been ravaging our young stock. It struck twice recently, killing calves, eating little, and then disappearing. Perhaps it is old and can no longer hunt game. But from the condition of the torn remains, it certainly would appear to enjoy the slaughter. And that is something I cannot tolerate."

He shifted uncomfortably in his chair. "I gave instructions to my agent to place the ranch on the market and to begin an immediate search for a buyer. I find that present obligations make it impossible for me to maintain the property as it deserves. In the meantime, I have only one more request of you. See Bird, I would like it very much if you would accompany me to the ranch and help me track and eliminate this menace. I can see how this would force you to backtrack in your journey both in direction and time. So to help speed you on your journey home, I have cleared it with the Union Pacific so that you have, if you accept my offer, a Pullman berth back to Denver and from there as far east as St. Louis, if that is your preference."

See Bird did not know how to respond to the president's generosity. While the prospect of a big cat hunt intrigued him, it bothered him at the same time. He would take no pleasure in the death of such a creature. Still, he believed that it was a deed that could and should be done. Who knew if this cougar, were it injured somehow, might not attack some human, perhaps a child? If he did nothing to prevent this, then would he not shoulder some responsibility? And as for the president's offer to pick up his train fare. That, he thought to himself, would be a godsend. Not having to dip into his summer earnings would be a great boon for his family. With the $600 sewed into the lining of his 'wargrip,' coupled with the bounty on Mr. Blunt and the cash he carried, it all totaled up to well over $700. That would surely see his family through until next summer.

"I'll do it, sir. I cannot guarantee I'll find that varmint for you, but I'll give it my best. If my Sally were here right now, I suppose she'd jump up and throw her arms around you and give you a great big kiss to boot. I'll skip that part." They both laughed. "So let's just shake hands on it. T.R., you just hired yourself a big cat tracker." They both stood, and stretching across the table, shook hands to seal the deal. An arriving train signaled its approach with a whistle.

"And now, See Bird, it would be my great pleasure to introduce you to the beautiful Isabella." From Belfield to Medora was only a short hop west, but one could scarcely blame See Bird for wishing it could have taken longer. The 'Isabella' was a railroad car built especially for Theodore Roosevelt. It was part of the presidential train, The Elysian, and was to a normal coach what a palace is to a shack. Seventy feet in length, the Isabella dominated the short presidential train. Following brief introductions to the presidential staff, T.R. excused himself to handle some transcontinental communications with his secretary. See Bird felt it would have taken a day just to explore the Isabella, so he reined in his curiosity and found a comfortable seat. He figured that if the president wanted him to explore the Isabella, he would see to it in his own good time.

The interior of the entire car was paneled in mahogany. There was a dining section, complete with white linen tablecloths and fresh flowers. See Bird could only imagine how they were kept so fresh. The area of the car in which he sat must be the 'club' section, he decided. Beautiful stained glass surrounded picture windows which provided a panoramic view of North Dakota.

He was sitting there enjoying the sensation of true luxury, hearing the quiet hum of busy men trying to keep their voices down, when a well-dressed black man leaned over and asked him if there was anything See Bird would like for a refreshment. Not used to being catered to, he was a bit embarrassed, but then he smiled and asked for two iced sassafras teas. The waiter disappeared only to reappear quickly with two tall glasses. He handed one to See Bird and then glanced around to see who should get the second glass.

"Will someone be joining you, sir?" he asked.

"Yes, indeed. It's pretty lonesome in here. Everybody seems busy off working on national business, I suppose. So I was hoping that as T.R.'s special guest, I could persuade you to have a seat and chat a bit. Let's start with introductions, nice and polite. I am See Bird, and you are…" He extended his right hand and gripped the waiter's free hand.

Indecision warred with the man's friendly nature, See Bird could tell. Then the waiter reached a decision. "My name is Clark, William Clark, but folks just mostly call me Willie."

"Well, William, why don't you just pull up a seat and make yourself comfy." He waved his hand.

"It would appear there's plenty of room. Except for two men huddled over a table, locked in an intense conversation, they were alone. That did not come as a surprise. He had been told that Isabella contained two sleeping chambers, two restrooms, a private kitchen, dining room, and stateroom. In all, it was so well insulated that only the rush of the landscape beyond the windows betrayed the apparatus as being part of a locomotive.

William carefully tugged up at the knees of his flawlessly pressed trousers as he sat. "I believe I can take a minute to sit with such a distinguished man as yourself." He sipped at his tea.

"Now don't you go getting all fluttery flattery on me, mister. We're both people who have had to make our own way in this world. I was just wondering how you read the president. You've been working for him for how long?"

William's response was aborted when a short, balding man in a rumpled suit, puffed up with self-importance, breezed over and stood there, glaring down, demanding attention. "Willie, what on earth do you think you're doing? Boy, you are far above your station. You should be at the bar, not bothering the president's distinguished guest, Mister Carpenter. When I tell the Pres…"

"Now hold on there, mister. I asked Mr. Clark to help me pass the time. There can't be no harm in that." See Bird rose. As William started to get to his feet, See Bird waved him down. "Excuse me, Mr. Clark, but how old did you say you were? Somewhere well past forty, I reckon."

William smiled. "Somewhere well past forty, I think."

"Well then, Mr. what-did-you-say-your-name was? I believe I understand your mistake. You must have mistook us for someone else. My name is See Bird. I'm Choctaw. This is Mister William Clark, and he certainly is not a boy. Now, why don't you just run along and do something important."

"Hoskins is my name, See Bird." He nearly spit out the name as if it were distasteful to him. "Emmanuel Hoskins. And, Willie, you'll see me again." Having run out of air, Hoskins deflated, turned, and strode with all the dignity he could marshal, through a door on the opposite end of the car.

"Well, I want to thank you, See Bird, for standing up for me, but I do believe you may have cost me my position. Hoskins is a nasty little man who has gotten where he is today by playing the system and picking winners to back. He came from nowheresville and is deathly afraid he will end up back there. Uh-oh. That didn't take long. It's been nice knowing you, See Bird."

Both men stood as Emmanuel Hoskins, his cheeks cherry red, resembling nothing less than a boiler about to explode, strode down the aisle. Behind him, sleeves rolled to the elbows, walked Teddy Roosevelt himself, looking grim. See Bird studied that face, hoping with every fiber of his being that he had judged the man correctly. William Clark's future and perhaps the future of race relations in this country depended on it.

Hoskins started in. "Mr. President, I need not remind you of the importance of following the proper chain of command. This Negro blatantly disregarded instructions and was insubordinate. I can scarcely blame your guest, since he is but an Indian, for not knowing how to behave in a civilized manner. But Willie should know better than to sit around drinking when he is supposed to be on duty. I demand you take action this minute."

Teddy's eyes squinted to mere slits as he listened to Hoskins' irate rant. Then he brushed past him and stood directly before See Bird. "Tell me what happened."

Hoskins erupted. "I've already told you, and…"

"I know what you said, Hoskins. Now I am asking him. See Bird?"

"There was no one in the area, and I asked Mister Clark to share a sassafras and keep me company a bit. He was gracious enough to do so."

His soft-spoken recital of the bare facts seemed to deflate Hoskins, who began to realize that perhaps he had overreacted. Still, he gave it one more try. "Mr. President, if this were war…"

"Hoskins, will you never shut your yap?" T.R. turned on the man, and for a moment, it seemed he was likely to take physical action. Then he turned and faced See Bird and Clark. "I take a few minutes to go shovel some coal and talk to the engineer, and what happens? "Stupidity and prejudice, that's what happens." He glared at his chagrined aide. "Hoskins, do not ever again attempt to lecture me on the military or war. In war so long as his comrades stand with him, you don't care where that man's birthplace has been, whether a slave cabin, a reservation, or on a velvet cushion in Manhattan. You don't care a snap of your fingers how he worshipped his Maker. You don't care whether he was a banker, a bricklayer, lawyer, mechanic, or farmer. It's the same thing now in civil life. And by God, if I want to invite Booker T. Washington to the White House for dinner, then I will. Now send out that invitation. And get out of my sight."

They all watched the disgraced man exit the car. T.R. turned and spoke to See Bird and William.

"William, I expect you will have no more trouble with that man. I'll hate to lose him. He's good at what he does, but the times are changing. This is, after all, the 20th century. I know your character and the character of Mr. Washington. I do not believe it will happen in my lifetime, but I have faith in the basic sense of fairness in most Americans. So I truly hope and believe that one day a descendant of mine will one day vote a Negro into the highest office in the land. I would express the same for you, See Bird, but first, we have to make you people citizens. That'll be a job worth undertaking. Gentleman, please excuse me, but I am about at my day's end. I bid you both a good night. I must take my leave. We shall meet again in the morning."

From Belfield, it was only a short hop over to Medora. They debarked from the train early in the morning. Since none of the locals knew of Roosevelt's impending arrival, they were mercifully able to soon be on their way to Elkhorn, the Roosevelt ranch. They made their way at a relaxed pace, stopping for a mid-day break and arriving shortly before sunset.

T.R. may have been an Easterner by birth, but he had a Westerner's eye for the land. In the wagon leading Kiamichi, See Bird appreciated the scene unfolding around him as they approached the ranch house down the trail from the west. They halted the team so T.R. could point out the various buildings and the lay of the land.

See Bird was surprised when T.R. drew his attention to the house. A low, log structure, running probably sixty feet long and thirty feet wide, it was quite unimposing with a low sloped roof. But when Roosevelt spotted it, he became animated. "Look, See Bird, do you see there?" he pointed. "My ranch house stands on the very river brink. You cannot see from here, but on the east end runs a low, long veranda, shaded by leafy cottonwoods. And there, if you look across those sand bars and shallows, you'll see a strip of meadowland. And behind it is a line of sheer cliffs and plateaus."

"I don't imagine you ever got much use out of the veranda."

"If you think that, then you are mistaken. The veranda is a pleasant place in the summer evenings when a cool breeze stirs along the river and blows in the faces of the tired men who loll back in their rocking chairs," Teddy began to wax eloquent, "maybe reading a book." Then catching the skeptical eye of his companion, he laughed. "Okay, maybe not reading a book. But we would rock gently to and fro, gazing sleepily out at those weird-looking buttes over there until their sharp outlines grow indistinct and purple in the afterglow of the sunset." Perhaps captivated by his own words, T.R. fell silent.

"Mr. President, them's beautiful words. I expect that if you could put them into one of your books, maybe one not about birds, people would want to read them on their own verandas."

For the first time since they had met, See Bird could see that the depth of his emotion had left Teddy Roosevelt speechless. Flicking the reins of the team, he started the team down the road toward the Little Missouri River and the front of the house shaded within a stand of muscular-looking cottonwoods.

# 18

As was usually the case, See Bird found himself wide awake at the crack of dawn. The musty cot with his blanket thrown across it reminded him of the many nights he'd spent in those early cowboy years down in Texas. For that brief moment between sleep and full awareness, he was transported back to 'Big Jim's' ranch and ranch-hand duties. Those were pleasant memories of the time he'd spent learning the cowboy trade.

The house was quiet as he tiptoed down the hallway toward the front room, carrying his boots. That room was still bathed in shadows, the curtains pulled. The racks of elk and longhorn sheep leaned out toward him from their wall-mounts, claiming and naming this space. Carefully, he opened the heavy wooden door to the veranda and stepped out. "That you, See Bird?" a familiar voice asked.

"Yes sir, T.R. thought I'd check on Kiamichi. I just can't seem to lay there while the day gets away from me."

"Exactly my thoughts. The doves in the cottonwoods sang me awake. I do not think that in all the world there is a more heartbreaking song of unending grief then that sung by those birds. It is a song of loss, and I just cannot abide that for long, or it would consume my very spirit. Here, sit with me a moment before you get on with it." See Bird sat in a rocker next to T.R. and pulled on his boots as the President resumed. "I do not imagine, with the press of affairs of state, that I will have the time to come here ever again. Even so, it was here that the romance of my life began. Everything was so dark for a while I could not see my way forward. But now," he paused as the wind rustled through the leaves overhead, "I cannot imagine I would ever have become president without this place and that time." He turned his head to face his companion. "What do you think, how do you feel about this land, Mr. Carpenter?"

That was a question See Bird had never posed to himself, and if anyone else had tried to force an answer out of him, probably he would have shrugged it off. But T.R. wanted, and deserved, honesty. After collecting his thoughts for a minute while T.R. gently rocked, he responded. "I honestly think that the good Lord made us out of this land and set us in it as the thinking, feeling part of it tend it for Him. I know that we are never really very far away from rejoining it. Sometimes we ignore it or misuse it. Then we make both ourselves and the land sick. But sometimes we sense God working through it into us. I believe then we've still got a chance to set things right. And even if we can't, we're obliged to try because He told us to, and it nurtures us. And it's not just about us, but about our kids too." He shrugged. "But then I could be wrong."

T.R. stopped rocking and squinted at See Bird, seeing him as if for the first time. "I think, See Bird, you would do very well, indeed, among the philosophers and thinkers of the eastern cities. Your sentiments were more clearly and succinctly stated than many a volume filled with multi-syllabic vocabulary. I have felt bad enough for this land for quite a while now. I intend, when I return to the White House, to begin the fight to set things right, to restore some balance. Thank you for your thoughts. Yes indeed. Thank you." He took a deep breath. "Over breakfast, we will lay out the plans for our hunting trip." He smiled a predator's smile. "One rogue cat needs to be removed from His garden. And I do my best planning over a full plate."

President Roosevelt was not fooling about a 'full plate.' See Bird was amazed at the man's appetite. While they were on the trail of the horse thieves, they both ate what they carried, which was adequate, but hardly lavish. On this morning, T.R. laid into his food as though he hadn't eaten for a week. The prospect of a big game hunt with even a hint of danger seemed to deepen his hunger. While he had proposed a 'discussion' over breakfast, it was clear to See Bird that what it really amounted to was a listening session. Everyone listened while the president 'discussed.' There were, of course, interjections and objections, as when agent Roger Owens declared that his very career was at stake and that the agents were forced by oath and law to accompany T.R. as he tracked down the killer cougar. For his part, T.R. insisted he be accompanied only by See Bird, and that hunting a big cat as part of some traveling caravan would doom the entire enterprise. T.R. set his jaw as he summed it up. "I'm sorry, gentlemen, but that is the way things have got to be. Nothing else will do."

Seeing the misery and desperation on the red-faced agents' faces on one side of the table and the unflinching set of Roosevelt's jaw on the other, See Bird spoke up for the first time, surprising everyone else in the room. "Excuse me, but maybe I can help. It appears to me that you boys over here got a good point." He nodded in their direction. "And Mr. Roosevelt over here's also got at least one good leg to stand on." At this, T.R. pointed his fork in See Bird's direction as if he were about to speak. The Indian beat him to it. Looking directly at the man, he said, "Sometimes we get so tangled up in what we're against that we forget we're all on the same side." Instead of speaking, T.R. speared another chunk of steak and bit down hard on it. The faces of the agents slowly resumed a more natural color.

"What it boils down to is you fellers have to come along, but the question is, how close do you have to be? Tracking down a wild animal like this is delicate work. A mob barging around's liable to spook it up into the hills so's we lose it. Then it just waits 'til we're gone, and in a bit, it comes back, or it moves on and wreaks havoc for some neighbor. And we surely do not want to be the cause of other people's trouble." He paused, his eyes meeting Roosevelt's. "That could cost you votes, sir." T.R. vigorously nodded his agreement while chewing harder.

See Bird turned to the Secret Service men. "So how close do you men have to be to do your duty, a hundred yards, within eyesight, within yelling distance? I think if you boys were to stay within the sound of gunshot, say a mile or so, you could hold up your end of the deal without getting in trouble. And we would then have a better chance of running this beast to the ground. Most likely, it's not too far away, even yet. Its kills were recent and it may be feeling pretty safe. Looked to me like it headed off toward those buttes south-east of here. The weather is clear, so before we set up night camp, we could signal you fellows using mirrors. We could even leave messages along the way so's you'd know what we're doing. I don't imagine we'll be in much danger, for sure not as much as when we chased down those horse thieves. What do you say?"

The two agents considered See Bird's proposition. While still reluctant, in the end they realized that it was likely to be the best deal they were going to be offered. Owens chewed on the end of his walrus mustache nervously while the other agent, George Prescott fiddled with the brim of his bowler, then replied, "We don't like it and here's why. It could get cloudy and rain, so mirrors could become useless. Other things could still go wrong, even with us in the neighborhood." A hint of a smile teased his lips. "Another snake decides to climb into Roger's bag this time, and we could be late catching up to you. Still, our options, other than this, are limited or none. So we accept. But if we can't catch your signal or find your notes, you can set two more plates for dinner."

See Bird looked at T.R., who said, with just a hint of a smile, "See Bird, if you ever get it in your head that you would like to move to the nation's capital, I would have a job for you on the spot as my special advisor. I outgrew my need for nannies when I started my education, and while I abhor the idea of these two bears tagging along, I suppose I must accede to the necessity of their company. So I agree to your compromise, as well."

See Bird rose. "Well, gentlemen, that's settled then. It'll take me a few minutes to pack my 'grip and saddle my horse. I'll be in the stable when you're ready to head out. We should pack fixins' for three days. If we can't handle this business by then, Mr. President, I'm afraid you'll have to find a better tracker."

Later, in the stable, collecting his gear and saddling up Kiamichi, See Bird worried that the odds of them catching the killer cat within three days were not especially good. He knew from experience that the best way to track a cat was with dogs. But there was not a single one on T.R.'s seldom-used ranch. Also, cougars prowled a huge range. And the good Lord knew that there was a lot of that around the ranch. Added to the list was the fact that he was sorely lacking any contact with men who had experience tracking one. And with the big cat's excellent hearing and vision, any noisy, smelly camp would almost guarantee that their efforts would all be wasted.

But he was not the sort of man who dwelled unnecessarily on what might be lacking. As he cinched Kiamichi's saddle, he took stock of what they had going for them. Although they covered a lot of ground, cougars tend to stay near their kills or where they have a ready food supply. This dogless 'ranch' provided the perfect chow line. There would be little point in hunting the surrounding lowlands and valleys because he knew they would never catch a cougar on the run. The cats liked the highlands so they could keep a watch on things that might be a threat. And with all these hills and buttes in the neighborhood, there was a mighty good chance it was still around, maybe nearer than one might expect. As he walked Kiamichi out of his stall, he peered at the eroded landscape beyond the open door. 'Yes sir,' he thought. 'That old panther might just be closer than they think.'

He could hear the muffled conversation between the ranch manager and T.R.'s bodyguards as they hitched and loaded up their supply wagon. That was another point in the hunt's favor. The well-intentioned but unskilled bodyguards would be trailing T.R. and himself by a good distance. It would make for a smaller, quieter, and cleaner camp. It would improve their chance of success.

Though cougars can be proficient at swimming, unless forced to, they will normally avoid it. Given that the ranch buildings were situated near the banks of the Little Missouri, with no nearby bridge, and lacking a convenient shallow ford, See Bird believed it was most likely that the mountain lion's lair would be on this side of it. Also, given the fact that this was a lonely area with few neighbors, and the proximity of a number of rocky hills, some nearly barren, other sprinkled with pinon pines and junipers, See Bird decided to set off east by southeast, hoping to find some trace of their quarry there.

As See Bird walked Kiamichi toward the ranch house, Roger Owens fell into stride alongside leading T.R.'s packhorse. "A word, Mr. Carpenter, if you've a minute." See Bird slowed and glanced at the suited bodyguard. "I don't mean to take issue with you, but I am concerned about our president's safety. You've seen him in action. He has absolutely no fear for his personal safety. While he is admired, he is not universally loved. There are many who would pay top dollar to see him removed from the scene, violently if necessary, and he seems oblivious. What I am saying is if, for example, at one of his whistlestops, someone with an ax to grind were to shoot him down, the man would probably stuff a handkerchief in his chest and finish his speech before he went to the hospital." Both men smiled at such a thought. "He seems incapable of grasping the idea of what his life means to this country." Behind them, they could hear T.R. lecturing his ranch manager as they drove the bodyguards' wagon up to the veranda.

"Roger," See Bird said, "hunting those horse thieves down let me see the man in action. I know where you are coming from, and I promise to do my level best to keep the president safe. He has a tendency to rashness, but generally he keeps it well in check. He knows himself as well as anyone I've ever worked with. This man, if you pen him in too tightly, will react in one of two ways. Either he'll accept it, and shrivel up inside. Or he will bust out completely. Yes, he'd try to draw an inside straight, and expect to get it. But, doggone it, I trust his judgment, and if he wants to go for it, I suspect he has a fair chance of pulling it off. I never seen anyone like him. And here he comes now."

"Yee haw. See Bird, isn't this day spectacular!" T.R. was resplendent in what he certainly considered proper hunting attire. Despite the expected warmth of the day, he had donned a black Russian Cossack style fur hat. His shirt was tasseled buckskin that laced up the front. And his grey corduroy trousers were neatly tucked into his high and ornate cowboy boots. For armament, he wore a huge Bowie knife in its tasseled sheath, belted around his waist to the left and a shiny Colt .45 holstered and tied down on his right. He was a breathtaking sight, and the excitement on his face could not help but bring wide smiles to the two men. "I may never return to Washington D.C., that den of infernal political machinations," he beamed as he shoved his pince-nez back up on the bridge of his nose. "Well, what are we waiting for, men? The day's a-wasting. Let's ride." He spun his alarmed horse around in a circle and leaned forward on the saddle horn. "See Bird, what do you say we go and lower the boom on one nasty old cougar?"

See Bird grinned and shrugged, "You're the president. I'm ready." He slid into the saddle, and looking over his shoulder at the two Treasury men settling onto the wagon seat behind him, he reminded them, "You boys, give us plenty of room to pull ahead. I intend to make our camp on that second butte, the taller one, tonight." He pointed with his hat. "That should give you fellers a clear line of sight if you camp on the near one. And keep the noise down." He looked thoughtful for a moment, then added, "And remember, a cold camp tonight. We've got plenty of sandwiches and jerky. That's about it. I guess we're as ready as we'll ever get." He eyeballed the impatient president. "I'll lead," if you don't mind, sir." With that, the four men drew away from Elkhorn, T.R. and See Bird gradually putting distance between themselves and the trailing wagon.

# 19

See Bird knew that looks could be deceiving, especially when it came to gauging distances in the vast open but broken landscape of the Dakotas. The two hills See Bird pointed out to the men from the ranch seemed to remain frustratingly distant as they rode in their direction. See Bird studied the ground and the brush, looking for any sign that a large cat had passed this way, but found nothing. Once, he dismounted to examine some sagebrush, thinking he might have seen some hair on it blowing in the breeze. But, though it was some hair, it was clearly too coarse and short for a mountain lion. He decided it more than likely came from a smaller animal, probably a coyote. He showed it to T.R. They pressed on.

Finally, they approached the nearer and smaller of the two hills visible from the ranch. The two trailing secret service agents had disappeared far behind them. Perhaps four hundred feet high and covered with gravelly soil, the hill was eroded by water that over time had gullied out several shallow washes on the near side. No self-respecting big cat would call this place home, See Bird thought. It provided very little useful ground cover, and the gullies would provide any predator easy and protected access to the top.

He pulled a pencil stub from his shirt pocket and scribbled a note. Then he collected some large stones. "I told our nannies I would leave them a message." He tied it with a string to a stick, which he wedged into the pile of stones. Just for good measure, he attached a red bandana to the stick.

"They would have to be blind not to find that," T.R. commented. See Bird nodded, remounted, and together, he and T.R. quietly picked their way around the base of the hill and continued on in the direction of the larger and farther of the two hills visible from Elkhorn. It became clear, as they started across the intervening gap, that the hill was both farther away and higher than they had originally thought.

Partway across See Bird spoke lowly as he raised his hand in the universal signal to stop, "I've suddenly got an itchy feeling on the back of my neck. Do you feel anything?"

Roosevelt gazed warily about. "Nothing beyond a sense of total exposure." Not even a shriveled cottonwood graced the broken landscape before them. "Kettle Hill was a jungle by comparison. Any enemy up there would have us dead in his sights by now."

"Exactly." The unnamed hill they were planning to climb loomed before them, stark and boulder-strewn. Shadows filled the dry wash in which they stood, some six to seven hundred feet below the peak. They were just about to start slowly scaling its slope when Kiamichi whickered softly and edged to his right. See Bird looked toward where his horse directed his muzzle and ears and noticed a patch of low, dark green vegetation amid some boulders. In this country, pooling surface water was rare. But that, See Bird was almost certain, was just what his thirsty steed had smelled. "Hold on there a minute, T.R. Let's check that out." The two men dismounted and walked toward the vegetation, leading their steeds.

"Whoa there, fella." He stroked Kiamichi's muzzle and handed the reins to Roosevelt. "If you don't mind, sir, I want to check this out before we lead the horses in. There's lots of boulders strewn around a wild cat could hide behind."

"Yes, of course. I've got them," T.R. muttered, and took the offered reins.

The Indian silently stalked forward in a hunter's crouch. His soft leather moccasins enabled him to feel and grip the rocks beneath his feet. He became little more than a shadow flitting from boulder to boulder, blending into his surroundings. Having completed a circuit of the water hole, and being convinced that there were no other visitors in the immediate vicinity, he stood by its edge and softly called for T.R. to come on in. As the President led the horses, See Bird squatted to examine the area more closely.

"We're not alone here. This puddle isn't much more than six feet across, but with water scarce, a little oasis like this is a major draw for all the critters hereabouts. Do you see how these blades of grass are flattened? Something stood here recently. And over here," he gently swiped the ground with his fingertips, "it is still damp. Something probably heard us and ran off." He rose and scanned the rocky slope above. "If I was a big, ornery old cat who maybe was having a little hunting trouble, maybe I'm old or my teeth hurt, or I'm lame, I'd stake me out a place like this and wait for food to come to me. Bring the horses down and let them have their fill. They…" he stopped talking, his eyes fixed. "What have we here? Look at this." He stooped to pluck something off a prickly sagebrush. He handed it to T.R. "That's cat hair what got snagged. Our boy made off in a mighty big hurry right through there. He even left us a scuff mark where he kicked those stones over. And look at this pad print, an 'M' sure enough. Mr. President," he spoke formally as he stood, "I do believe our 'malefactor,' as you called those bad men back there, was drinking here just before we arrived."

T.R. smiled grimly, scanning the area. "But he's not here now, is he?"

"That, he ain't. But he's not far. We were downwind of him, so more'n likely he heard us rather than smelled us. Could be that he's got us eyeballed right now. I'm a bit surprised Kiamichi didn't clue me in, but that can happen. The old boy panicked, but cats are curious creatures, and I wouldn't be surprised if he paid us a little visit tonight – just to check us out. Let's camp upslope a bit away from here. There's no telling who else might mosey by during the night. No sense in asking for trouble."

"I agree. And since he knows we're here, do you think it would be safe for us to make a small fire for some coffee?"

See Bird nodded. "I don't see what that'd hurt. We'll keep watch two hours on and two off. I'll take first watch." T.R. nodded his assent. With that, the hunters moved upslope, away from the water hole and pitched camp. The sandwiches packed from the ranch had kept well. When the coffee was done, they let the small fire expire and doused the feeble embers with the remains of the coffee pot. See Bird, settled down beneath the North Dakota sky, watched and listened as night fell.

High above the camp, atop a rocky outcropping jutting from the brow of the hill, sprawled the big cat.

Though not technically classed among the 'big cats,' this puma was certainly a big one, tipping the scales easily at 150 lbs., and that was some forty pounds down from previously. At present, he was trying to rest his bulk to minimize the pain in his left hind leg. About a full moon ago, he had the misfortune to be spotted by a couple of cowboys riding their range twenty or thirty miles away. One had gotten off a lucky shot, catching the large male in his rear quarters. He dragged himself this far and was extremely lucky to have found the waterhole at the base of this hill.

The wound had healed ever so slowly, but the pain never left. When hunger drove him to hunt, he found he was less successful than before, more often than not. He surprised an occasional small animal at the water hole but for a while, steadily lost weight and strength. Now slowly recovering, his coat hung on him like a baggy suit of old clothes, and his previous lustrous, tawny coat, had lost all its sheen. Had he not heard the distant bawl of a calf for its mother that night and stalked it down, he might now be just buzzard pickings on the rocky hilltop.

His rage at the unrelieved pain and the creatures who had inflicted it on him was only slightly assuaged by the delicious feast he had enjoyed. It was not a neat kill. He had learned in maturity that his most successful hunting came from the silent stalk and the sudden leap from behind. A death-dealing bite to the back of the neck always finished the hunt quickly. But when he approached the calf and leaped at it, the pain from his wound threw off his balance, and he had landed on the side of the bawling, staggering creature. He had certainly killed it, eventually. That was foreordained. But it had all been very messy and far too noisy. At least the creatures who rode the large prey animals had not heard and intervened. That could have been catastrophic. As it was, he had eaten his fill, dragged off a haunch of it to stash for later, and limped his way back up to his lair. And now those same helpless-looking creatures who had so badly injured him had stumbled upon him here.

It was all he could do to control his rage and fury. The images that flashed through his fevered brain danced in blood red. He smothered a scream that struggled to erupt from within him. Instead, he lay there growling continually, the rumbling interspersed with an occasional hiss. This would be a night, he realized, that he would find no rest. But perhaps tomorrow he could punish the prey who sought to harm him.

Several hundred feet below the restless puma, See Bird and T.R. had made camp under a slight rock overhang on a fairly level spot. The horses had been cared for and ground-hobbled. See Bird did not expect a visit during the night, at least not from this cat. A hunter like this one needed a big kill only about once a week, and the calf kill occurred only a couple days ago. The sated and tired cat was probably resting and storing strength. And besides, the two horses would provide the best alarm one could hope for. They slept but little, had excellent night vision, almost as good as the animal they hunted, and furthermore, they feared the animal so strongly that even so much as a whiff of puma could send them screeching off into the darkness. Still, it never hurt to remain alert. It was See Bird's experience that just when a person lets down his guard, that's when trouble will surely strike. So he sat and listened to the song of the night and stared into the darkness until it was time for T.R. to sit the final night watch.

See Bird waked at the soft sounds of T.R. building a small fire to perk some coffee. Dawn had broken, but the valley they overlooked had yet to greet the first sun rays. He was a bit surprised when he realized his camp was higher upslope than he had thought the night before. Darkness, he thought, can make it hard for one to keep perspective. In such country, it was always good to camp upslope a bit. The valley may be no more than a quiet dry wash now, but should a late summer storm blow in, the rock-strewn valley and the nearby arroyos could become raging torrents of clashing boulders and swirling debris, impossible to escape.

When he returned from answering nature's call and seeing to the horses, the coffee was ready, along with some left-over biscuits from the previous day that T.R. had heated in a pan. He squatted down beside the president. As usual, T.R. spoke first. "I actually prefer the final night watch," he said as he handed a steaming mug to See Bird, who said nothing. "When I first came out west, I was young and crushed by disaster. As I told you, the light had gone out of my life. How the men who worked for me must have laughed at my feeble attempts to become like one of them. But I learned through sheer willpower, to ride, shoot, and work like them. And it was on a morning like this, quiet and clear, I watched the sky lighten from grey to soft pink to white. It was on that morning I felt the first ray of light return to me. And since then, my friend, it has never left me. That is why I love the West so much.

See Bird felt his own emotions swirl. For how many generations had his people sat and watched silent dawns such as these, believing that they would follow one another in unending succession. Now, it appeared there were only three options for them to consider. Option one was to resist and die. No. On second thought, he realized that option was gone. It had been tried and failed. Those who had resisted were all dead or fled to Canada. The second option seemed nearly as distasteful, to succumb and fall into a sullen hopelessness. He had seen this numerous times and in many places, the staggering drunken beggars living on the white man's largesse, hating themselves and resenting every moment of it. The third option, the one he had chosen, was to cast his lot with the victorious European-Americans, who even now were settling and changing this continent at breakneck speed.

These white people, he thought, were like brilliant children who could build incredible cities and invent marvelous toys, and yet, like children, give no inkling of a thought to the consequences of their actions on the world around them. But he did not believe and refused to accept the notion that they were hopeless and would never learn. The man squatting next to him, though childish in some of his ways, exhibited wisdom that, See Bird believed, proved his point. And that man was in a position of power and influence, able and eager to exert his will in order to accomplish his objectives. See Bird glanced sideways at this myopic Easterner staring into the distance. What was he seeing? And how far would he be willing to push to accomplish his ends? In a hundred years, would it even matter?

The president sighed and stood, shaking himself as if awakening from some dream. "See Bird, I feel almost sorry for that animal we must hunt to its death." He spoke, lacking any of the bluster he normally exhibited. "We have wiped out the buffalo and replaced it with cattle for beef. Grizzlies, elk, beaver, the list goes on. But we will make the desert bloom and feed millions.

Our greatest challenge will be to balance what is destined to be lost against the prospective gain. There must be a benefit to mankind, or all the effort is wasted. Perhaps someday the only place to find a cougar will be in the Bronx zoo. But today we must find and kill this one. I hope it will be worth the loss." He spilled the remains of the coffee on the embers and ground the ashes beneath his boot. "Let's go."

The two riders, See Bird walking in front, leading Kiamichi, T.R. astride a gelding, and trailing, circled the hill, slowly spiraling upward, hoping to cut the cat's trail. Periodically See Bird would stoop to squint over a small item or stone, seeking some clue as to the cougar's location. His intense expression never changed, yet Roosevelt noticed that See Bird's tension mounted as they rode higher.

The sun climbed to mid-morning and they were completing their second loop around the hill when See Bird hand-signaled T.R. to dismount. Roosevelt did so, and as quietly as he could, walked over to his companion, eagerly examining his face. See Bird handed him a small flat-sided rock and whispered, "He's up here, alright. Or he was recently. See that spot on the rock that looks like brown paint?" T.R. turned it around, found the spot and nodded. "That's blood. We cut across more down below along with a few cow hairs scraped off. Like most big cats, this one's carried some of his kill back to stash for later. If I was to follow the drip's line of climb, I bet we'd stumble on to his cache somewhere nearby. That means he is close by as well, and most likely has been watching us for a while, maybe since we started."

Both men paused to scan the higher elevations and the many rocky promontories. See Bird studied Roosevelt's face. His eyes were clear, face set in a determined look. His hands and body were steady. There was no nervous fidgeting. The man was preparing himself for whatever the future would bring. Some men, even men who thought themselves tough and hardened, would, when they realized they were considered prey by a wild animal, become jittery. That was one reason See Bird usually hunted alone, not because he was braver than other men, but because it was usually safer. Fearful men make rash decisions. Their minds become cloudy with worry and 'what-ifs.' A good hunting partner, like Sally's uncle Devil Anse Hatfield, or come to think of it now, Teddy Roosevelt, was a rare commodity. See Bird relaxed a bit. His concern over the reactions of his partner to the realization they too, may be being hunted, eased, and disappeared. Once again, he felt free to concentrate on the hunt.

"Let's keep on circling around. Two more loops should bring us to where we'll either spook him out or find out I was mistaken, after all, and misreading the signs. If that happens, we just start all over somewhere else. But I think I'm right. So ride cautious. Don't stare. Use the sides of your eyes to watch for motion. And trust them. You'll see more than you think possible." He took a breath and finished as T.R. remounted, "and make sure there's a round in the chamber."

Roosevelt drew up to See Bird, looked down at him, and smiled confidently, "I'm ahead of you on that one." He withdrew the big Colt from his holster, released the safety, and eased the gun back into the holster. "I'm ready." See Bird believed him.

As they rose above the surrounding countryside, See Bird could not help but notice the increasingly rocky nature of the landscape. Thousands of years of erosion had broken down much of the rock and washed it downslope, leaving the bones of the earth behind, protruding at increasingly steep angles. He carefully led the sure-footed Kiamichi around one huge boulder nearly blocking their way and looked back to see T.R. gently directing his horse to follow, loose reins in hand. A silver sliver ribboned across the land over his shoulder to the north-west, near the horizon. That would be the Little Missouri, he figured. His guess was confirmed a moment later when he detected a slender dark smudge against the sky in the same direction. That could only be from a chimney on T.R.'s ranch. A light breeze toyed with the brim of his black slouch hat. He reset it and considered the president's situation.

Something drove that man relentlessly. Perhaps it was ambition and the lust for fame. Perhaps it was the desire to do good deeds. Perhaps he was driven by the necessity to forget, to avoid going inside, to where the pain may very well be unbearable. Most likely, it was all these things and more. Whatever it was, See Bird doubted that the man would ever be able to stifle that drive and find rest for his soul. Despite his wealth, power, fame, or past accomplishment, Roosevelt seemed incapable of moving at less than full steam ahead. It made See Bird sad for a moment, but then he thought, as he rounded the corner and T.R. fell out of sight behind him, the man certainly lived an exciting life. It would not be the one for me, he thought, but it most likely was the only one for Roosevelt.

They were less than fifty feet from the crest of the hill, and See Bird was starting to worry. By now, he expected, they should have caused the puma, if it were still here, so much anxiety that it would have given itself away. But they had neither seen the cat nor had

See Bird detected any trace of it trying to sneak by them. Perhaps, it was not here after all. On such broken terrain as this, one could never be sure. The traces he had found were so faint and ephemeral. Perhaps he had willed more meaning into them than they deserved.

The warmth of the morning sun had stirred the big cougar from its restless lethargy. Its ears flattened against his skull, his fawn-colored hide blending perfectly with the sun-scoured outcropping, he shifted from position to position, slinking along the ridge top, following with his eyes the two-legged prey atop the four-legged prey as they made their clumsy way about the foot of his fortress. One of the two-legged ones walked ahead of his four-legged and looked about as if he could see anything with his little eyes. The swirling breeze blew their smell like smoke through his distended nostrils.

He did not understand why, but he was aware that he must be very cautious around these creatures. Although they had no claws or sharp teeth, weak eyes, and no sense of smell worth worrying about, every encounter he had with them in the eight years of his life had caused disappointment or pain or both. Prowling around their camps at night, he had found them to be noisy and stinky, but always alert. If he became overconfident and they spotted him, they would chatter loudly, like annoying magpies. Their noise and smell was nothing, however, compared to the noise and stench of the firesticks they always seemed to carry or have nearby. One night, as he stalked a camp, the explosion of fire from the end of the pointed tube nearly blinded him and singed his whiskers. He had fled in panic.

So the big cat had learned to give them a wide berth when hunting his territory. Sometimes it even worked to his advantage. Occasionally, when they had killed some animal, they would take or eat only the worst parts of it, leaving the juiciest, most tasty morsels behind as they would move on. He was a fine hunter, but he was not one to look a gift-horse in the mouth, so to speak.

Then came the time in the not too distant past when he had let himself get too close. They saw him, chattered loudly, their sticks bloomed fire and his hind flank seemed to explode in pain. For a long time, he had scarcely been able to move. He had lost nearly a quarter of his weight, and it was the specter of starvation that drove him down to the two-legged prey's den where he had killed that delicious calf. His flank was starting to heal. He could feel it mending today, but he was still nowhere near fully recovered. He could walk short distances without dragging himself about, but he hated these two-legged prey who could hurt him so badly. He would enjoy killing them both.

Attacking from ambush was his second-nature. Before long, their route would lead them directly below his rocky perch. He would wait for the walking prey to go around the corner so that by the time he could find a firestick, it would be too late. He would launch himself from his perch, so near the second prey, he could almost reach out and swat it as it went by. It would be fun to play with it for just a bit, but no, these creatures were not to be played with, at least not while they were still alive. He would use the method that worked the best for him, waiting for it to pass beneath, then leaping from behind onto its back and locking his vise-like jaws around the skinny little neck. He crept to the edge of his ledge tail twitching with nervous anticipation.

Kiamichi sensed something amiss before anyone else. The swirling air carried on it the smell of sudden death. He whinnied, snorted, then reared, screaming his fear. See Bird understood and instantly dropped the reins, circled to the side and smacked the horse on his flank, encouraging him to save himself. Kiamichi would not go far, he knew, just enough to guarantee his safety. Then See Bird spun to the rear and dashed back down the trail, around the corner he had just turned.

T.R. had heard Kiamichi's cries of distress and stopped in mid-trail. The Indian was about to yell when he saw the rock above Roosevelt's head rise up. The rock became the cougar they were hunting. It coiled to leap. See Bird pointed to it and yelled. Teddy Roosevelt may have been forty-four years old, but he was smart and nimble. He reacted instantly. The reins in one hand, he bent over and swiftly drew the Bowie knife from its sheath.

Death was in the air as the puma launched itself with a scream. So intent was he on killing his prey that momentarily he neglected to take into account his damaged flank. When he pushed off from his ambush site, the left hind leg gave way. This threw off his plunge onto T.R.'s back, bringing him up just a few inches short and to one side. At the same instant he leaped, Roosevelt had twisted to grab his knife. That combination of events saved his life. He felt the weight of the cougar on his back only as a heavy glancing blow, and then it hit the ground, rolling over, screaming in pain and frustration. T.R.'s horse bucked and spun away back down the trail in the direction it had come, but Roosevelt was not on it.

See Bird stood transfixed at the incredible scene. As the killer cat's claw scraped down his back, T.R. hunched and pulled his knife. Either he leaped or was thrown from the saddle, See Bird could not be sure. Perhaps it was a combination of the two. Roosevelt dove with knife flashing in the noon-day sun and his teeth set in what See Bird had learned to interpret as either a fearsome smile, or a smiling grimace. The arc of descent carried him directly onto the back of the cat, squirming and struggling to its feet. With no hesitation, T.R. straddled the animal and with a cry, plunged the knife down between its shoulder blades, once twice, three times. The cat screamed, managed one step forward, and collapsed. Roosevelt looked like nobody's vision of what the President of the United States should look like. Hatless and breathless, his fine shirt in tatters, he bestrode the puma nearly as large as himself, his big knife dripping crimson, wearing that now-familiar triumphant grimace. He looked feral and deadly. Then he spoke. "That was a close thing. You saved my life, See Bird."

"No sir," he said as he hurried up to T.R., "You saved your own life, Mr. Roosevelt." They eyed the body of the beast on the trail. "I guess those 'malefactors' back east you talk about better not get you too riled. It appears you can get plumb dangerous. Next time, though, you may be better off to use a gun."

T.R. guffawed and slapped See Bird on his back. "No time to aim and shoot. Good Lord!" he exclaimed. "That really got my juices going. And I believe I do feel a bit of a breeze on my back." He grabbed a strip of his fancy shirt and tore it off. "It looks like I'll be needing to refresh my wardrobe as well. Signal our nannies and let's collect our horses." He turned away in the direction his horse had taken, then turned back for one remark. "And won't this make a fine pelt!" He punched the air with a triumphant fist.

See Bird watched him walk away until T.R. turned a corner and disappeared. "Amazing," was all he said before turning to collect Kiamichi.

# 20

The following day Roosevelt was a veritable whirlwind of energy and activity. He wrote and had an aide fire off a handful of wires in all directions, saw to the packing up of the household items, disposition of the ranch sale, and following a mammoth four-course supper eaten out on the veranda, settled down in his favorite rocking chair in the cool of the evening. See Bird leaned against a post supporting the roof and watched the river, as if it were talking to him.

"It's too bad you have to sell the ranch, T.R. I see why you built it here. This place sort of grows on a man, don't it?"

"You feel it too, don't you? Yes, it does, and when I rode up the lane to it this last visit, I was undecided and unsure I was doing the right thing. But for some reason, I now believe that selling it is the correct thing to do. I do not see myself ever staying here again. It has provided me with everything I could have hoped for and more. Now it is time to move on, not just to California and then back to Washington City. It is time for me to move on with my life. I purchased Elkhorn at a time in my life when I needed it. Tonight, I believe I will never need it again." He glanced at See Bird, slouching against the post. "That may sound rather sad.

I hope not. I actually feel rather good about the whole thing. This has been an extraordinary excursion. And now it is time for me to plunge into the arena and make my political fight. I may get knocked around some. They may bloody my nose, but I am going to fight until I cannot lift my fists." He chuckled. "And then I'll kick. What about you, my friend?"

See Bird shuffled his feet, collecting his thoughts. He had seldom expressed his beliefs and dreams out loud and then mainly just to Sally. Speaking about them to anyone else embarrassed him. "I suppose I've earned about enough to head on home to West Virginia and maybe buy that twenty acres of wood Sally and my girl love so much. I'm not looking for a fight. I see myself as a peaceable man and a Christian. Jesus, as I learned about him, came from a small but smart tribe that was beaten down by a powerful empire." He glanced at T.R. and smiled, "Sound familiar?"

T.R. kept rocking. "He understood that his little tribe would never outmuscle that empire. He believed and taught that the way to beat them was by turning the cheek to them, staying honest, staying yourself, and taking the beatings until the empire can't stand doing it anymore and has a change of heart. After all, The Father made them too. Just stay true to yourself and let Him go to work. Sounds easy, I guess. Or maybe it sounds impossible. I don't know." He sighed. "I been trying, since it hit me all at once in fifth grade, that this was the best chance I had at getting along without getting bitter in this country." He looked at T.R., who stopped rocking. "Problem is I'm not very good at it. Seems like when I get in a tight squeeze my temper boils up. Then I do something I know I'll regret later, and I have to go to The Father again and tell him I'm sorry. That'll probably be the way it goes with me until the day I die."

"See Bird, my friend, I hope that won't happen for a long, long time. And I too pray for a forgiving Father. He certainly can be difficult to understand. I, for one, cannot understand how a God who created the dancing firefly that graces the purple dusk could be the same God who sends these swarms of pesky mosquitos to drive us crazy on what would otherwise be a beautiful summer evening. I do believe it is time to go inside. I've lost enough blood to satisfy them for at least one term in office."

The deep plush red velvet upholstered coach in which the president's party traveled back toward Cheyenne was a far cry from the rickety boxcar in which See Bird had begun his journey what seemed like so very long ago. Much of the time he spent gazing out through the stained-glass windows at the countryside flowing by. Occasionally William would come by to see if he needed anything and to share a laugh or two. Once, about midmorning, T.R. breezed in and slammed down beside See Bird for a friendly chat.

It seemed that 'chatting,' Roosevelt style, usually amounted to See Bird nodding and listening while the president went on at length about some issue he was currently wrestling with. Providing such a 'sounding board' for T.R.'s ruminations was something See Bird was glad to do. It required little from him, but patience and tact, traits that See Bird was certainly endowed with. Because of his natural taciturnity, when he would interject a comment, T.R. listened.

"William, I'll have a mint julep, if you please, and" glancing See Bird's way, "some fresh coffee for See Bird."

"Yes sir, Mr. Roosevelt, I'll put on a fresh pot right away. I'll bring it soon's it's done." He winked at See Bird and disappeared into the kitchen, glad to have made his escape.

T.R. sat and muttered under his breath for a few moments before erupting, waving a handful of papers before him. "It's those blasted Limeys and Krauts again." Seeing the puzzlement on his companion's face, he explained. The British and the Germans are ganging up on Venezuela. They are actually sending a combined fleet down there to 'collect debts.' Granted, their beefs are valid. The debts are real. But it's no secret what they are really after – the Isthmus of Panama. They know I'm going to build a canal there, and once they've wedged themselves in there, they may never be dislodged.

"Our navy has more ships available than either one of the two of them, but not as many as the both of them combined." He paused to catch his breath. "Oh, why won't that worthless Congress of ours give me the ships I need to build a modern navy? Do they think it is some kind of game we are playing? Men's lives and our nation's future is at stake. What are your thoughts on the subject?" He paused again for just a breath and then continued, thankfully for See Bird, because the truth was, he had not been giving the Venezuelan problem much attention lately. "Wasn't that a country somewhere south of Mexico?"

"I have half a mind to send what ships we can muster down there and call their bluff publicly. Those tired old European nations have no right to bully the nations of this hemisphere. They know about the Monroe Doctrine. Do they doubt I will enforce it?" See Bird shrugged helplessly. "Yes, they might. Then we will surely have to tally the butcher's bill. Can you provide any insight into how I can solve this dilemma without going to war?" T.R. paused to listen and take another breath.

See Bird spoke. "I do not know about such goings-on among the high and mighty. But I do remember growing up down on the Kiamichi River and how my father taught my twin brother and me a lesson I'll never forget. It was our job to make sure that every evening the horses were tended properly. So we took turns. One night in late fall, my brother forgot, or got lazy, or something. That night it stormed blue blazes and turned to driving snow. Next morning as we went out to walk to school, there the horses were, huddled against the barn, shivering and as bedraggled a lot as I've ever seen, miserable in the snow. And there, also stood our father.

"There was nothing we could say, so we walked over to the horses, put them in the barn, and tended their needs. Father never said a word, just watched us. They all survived, but I'll never forget the look in my father's eyes, hurt, disappointment, and anger. But the thing that really stuck with me was what he did next. He took both of us over to a calf pen where he had draped a wide, smooth, brown leather strap over the gate. We knew what was to come next and knew we deserved it. But against everything we knew we deserved and expected, he put his hand on the strap and stroked it like you might a puppy. Then, in a voice so quiet I had to strain to hear, he said two words, "Never Again." His hard face, quiet voice, and the sight of that big strap never disappeared from my memory to this very day. And after that our horses were always well cared for, I promise you that. My point is, Mr. President, there seems to be a lot of noise in all this politics stuff."

See Bird fell silent while T.R. thought. William used this moment to bring See Bird a cup of fresh coffee. That scent of fresh-perked coffee seemed to awaken something in Roosevelt. He stirred. "As I said before, my father was a lion of a man. Of course, I do not remember as much of him as I would like, but I do remember several items. Because I was such a sickly lad, I never went to school with the other lads, but was tutored at home. He made sure our home was filled to the brim with books, all sorts of books, anything that struck his or my fancy-- books on animals and Africa, of knights and fair ladies. One of those books was filled with African tribal sayings and proverbs. It seems I remember one of them most clearly. And though I did not understand it fully at the time, it has recurred to me now and again." T.R. stared at the ceiling as if it were inscribed there. "Speak softly and carry a big stick, and you will go far." And you, my good friend, with your father's example for guidance, have presented me with a perfect illustration.

"I think I can perhaps see the direction I shall take. What if we eliminate all the bluster of press releases and public statements, all the threats and counter-threats that could box all the participants into irrevocable and doomed positions? I know the Kaiser Bill and King of England. They are jealous cousins to each other and may not be the sharpest tools in the shed, but I cannot believe they would commit their countries to war over Venezuela. If I were to make no public announcements of naval or troop maneuvers, to carry on as usual, but see that they receive private notes stating clearly our nation's position vis a vis Venezuela and that I was sending our warships down there to protect those interests, they should see it is not a bluff, conducted for parochial political gain, but as a private statement of intentions and commitment. Thank you once again. See Bird for the wisdom of your counsel. I shall miss our little chats when we get to Denver."

The president rose and strode down the length of the car until he came to his stateroom, where he paused for a moment before pulling open the doors. See Bird heard his first words before they closed behind him. "Gentlemen, I have an idea…" and smiled.

At Cheyenne, there was scheduled a one-day layover, so the train could be restocked and some urgent official business could be taken care of. From here, the Presidential train would proceed to Denver, Santa Fe, Los Angeles, and Yosemite before it would begin its long journey back, ending in Washington D.C. It would have been quite a journey for any middle-aged man, let alone one under such constant stress. And the stress could only be heightened by the president's unflagging enthusiasm for speaking to crowds in every hamlet and crossroads from the rear platform of the Isabella. His secret service agents could only cringe and wince as, after every impromptu speech, the crowds would surge to shake his hand. Somehow, this funny speaking Eastern rich man was increasingly identifying himself as one of them.

Nevertheless, no man of power could wield it as did he without antagonizing other men of wealth and power. The story was told of how J.P. Morgan, the wealthy New York financier, phoned the White House in order to persuade T.R. to back off from his attempts to break up Morgan's Northern Securities Corporation, a holding company for a huge trust. He suggested to the president that he send his man, "and I'll send mine, and we'll fix things up."

"I don't want to fix things up." The president responded. "I intend to break them up." And removing such a public man would pose no great problem. Should even one of those hands reaching out to touch Teddy hold a pistol, another sad chapter in American presidential assassinations would be written. And, short of tying the President of the United States to a chair, there was absolutely nothing his protectors could do about it except to sigh with relief when the whistle blew and the Elysian chugged on down the tracks to the next hamlet where the entire event would be re-enacted yet again.

# 21

"In a few days it'll be September, and here I sit high and dry. And I still would like to know where in hell's bells is Maybell." There being no one else around other than the horse and his rider, the horse judged it was his call to answer. So perhaps reading the rider's frustrated tone of voice, or perhaps through sheer luck, he blew hard and vigorously shook his mane as if to say, "I'm tired of talking about it. I don't know either. Would you please change the subject?" See Bird laughed out loud.

Having said goodbye to Teddy Roosevelt and his beloved Isabella in Denver, See Bird was impatient to get back in the saddle. He was afraid too much train riding would make him soft. Besides, he had caught rumors of a few rodeos in the area still to be held. He had won a small purse in a local rodeo doing rope tricks and bull riding, an event he swore he'd never do again, and then set off for Maybell. A local rider had given him the tip that Maybell had one of the best late-season rodeos in eastern Colorado, sending him off with the mere nod of his head.

Unfortunately, it was looking more and more as though 'Maybell' had been only a ploy the cowboy thought up to remove some tough competition from the rodeo in which he wanted to compete. So here See Bird sat, looking at a treeless vista falling away as far as the eye could see. He had asked repeatedly about the elusive rodeo while working his way to the southeast of Denver. Mostly, the responses he received could be described as non-committal head-scratchers. A couple cowboys he crossed volunteered they thought it was still farther off to the east, towards the Kansas border.

So here he sat in the saddle, feeling more and more that he was on a fool's errand of a wild goose chase. "Well, boy, I'm not too keen on playing the fool, but I do it so well that I can safely say that this most likely will not be the last time. Down there is Kansas. Beyond that is Missouri. Past that is home. You got friends who've probably forgot all about you and are sleeping in your stall and gobbling down all your oats. I've got me a pretty gal and a girl child getting ready for school to start. Between the two of us, we've earned enough money to get us through some cold West Virginia nights. So we'd best be riding on." With that, he squeezed his knees just enough to convey his earnestness to Kiamichi, who felt the drive to start home too, and broke into a fast canter.

Some borders are determined by nature, land slashed by rivers, peoples divided by snow-covered spines of mountains, even oceans here and there. But most of the western American states' borders have little or nothing to do with nature. They were artificial constructs drawn on maps for the convenience of politicians. A map of Colorado appears crowded with mountains and Kansas looks like a flat plain. One would think they should be easy to tell apart. But on the ground, it is not so simple. True, Denver, resting on the eastern slope of the Rockies, is called the 'mile-high-city' while Lawrence, far to the east, rests not a whole lot less than a mile closer to sea level, but the land between the two cities is scarcely level and could in no way be called flat. From the western end of Kansas to the east, the elevation drops from 4,000 feet to around 1,000. And while there are fewer rivers in the western part, most of the rivers in the state follow that declining land and pretty much run from west to east, cutting the land into coulees while spilling eventually into the Mississippi River.

The chalky Kansas soil is some of the richest in the world so the eager farmers, often recent immigrants from Eastern European countries such as Poland, Bohemia, and Russia, pouring in to fill the void left by the defeat and expulsion of the Indians, along with the destruction of the vast herds of buffalo that until recently, migrated relentlessly from Texas to Canada, could scarcely be blamed for believing they could turn this prairie into a veritable garden of Eden. And for a number of years they prospered, drawing ever more settlers to the area. In 1863 there were 100,000 people in Kansas. Only forty years later, by the time See Bird and Kiamichi began their trek down from Denver in 1903, the population had mushroomed to nearly a million and a half.

If any of the settlers had taken the time to talk to the 'old-timers' or displaced natives, they might have heard a cautionary tale. Yes, there had been good rains for a number of years, but there was a good reason why in the western part of the state amidst the millions of wildflowers, the deep-rooted buffalo-grass was prevalent. And as one traversed the state eastward, the buffalo-grass gave way to blue stem, which in turn was replaced by bluegrass in the east. The trees went from non-existent in the west, to cottonwoods, to oak, maple, elm, and walnut in the east. Why such a huge divergence in flora from east to west? The answer, of course, is water. While the eastern part of the state may, on average, receive some forty inches per year of rain and snow, the west must make-do with half of that.

In wet years farmers could earn a good living by plowing up and turning over the prairie to raise their thirsty crops. But as more and more acreage of drought-resistant plants was replaced with wheat and corn, as more and more surface was stripped of its natural protection, when the dry seasons came one following another, when that relentless western wind blew, the very land itself began to disappear. When that happened in the not too distant future, the grown children of these very farmers and ranchers See Bird would wave to or chat with when he stopped to pass the time along the road, would pack what little they could and flee to anywhere else. The population in many counties in western Kansas, to this day, have not recovered from the drought that was to strike the region just two short decades after See Bird passed this way.

Of course, as See Bird plodded slowly through the countryside, neither he nor any of the people he met could see this impending disaster. Indeed, that summer the area had only recently recovered from some monumental floods, floods that had killed dozens of people, and which were already being referred to as the floods of '03. And no city in Kansas had suffered more than did Manhattan, a small city of some 3,500 people at the junction of the Big Blue and the Kansas River in northeastern Kansas, where See Bird had stopped to clean up and spend the night. A place where 57 people had perished just last May.

The oppressive summer heat had lingered into late August promising temperatures in the upper nineties, but cooler and certainly even wetter times were just ahead. One had to remain optimistic.

The first rays of the Sunday sun were already dissipating what little coolness the night had provided. The day promised to be another hot one. He had originally thought to spend more time in the area but found he had missed the local rodeo by nearly three weeks. At this time of year people's attentions were turning more toward the upcoming harvest, and the season for cowboy cavalcades and such shindigs was passing. It truly was the time to be heading home to West Virginia. His thoughts were increasingly turning to the woman he loved, and the small six-acre plot of tobacco he had planted would need harvesting too. This summer had provided enough excitement and adventure to last a lifetime. It was time to once again settle into life's calmer routines.

See Bird reflected on these things as Kiamichi carefully stepped onto the bridge spanning the Big Blue at Manhattan, heading east. Below and off to the sides were stacked tools and parked equipment workers were using to build and reinforce levees in the effort to restrain the floods. But the river of forces that shape and test men's lives were not yet finished with See Bird.

The early afternoon found him sitting off on the roadside beneath a huge cottonwood, listening to the west wind rattle through its drying leaves and eating a pan of oats he fried up for himself. Kiamichi shared his rider's taste for oats enthusiastically, but he preferred his oats raw and with plenty of water. Occasionally, See Bird would fry up just such a pan full in the morning, eat what he wanted, and pack up the substantial leftovers for later. Today though, he had broken his fast at a small roadside diner on the edge of Manhattan. He was surprised to find one open so early, and on a Sunday, as well. So as to be on the road more quickly, taking advantage of any coolness the morning had to offer, he had eaten his fill and left quickly.

With his horse ground tethered nearby, See Bird had just leaned back with his head resting on his 'warbag,' his black slouch hat tipped over his eyes. Even the turkey feather he wore on its brim seemed to wilt in the midday heat. Cicadas, however, were making their presence known. The buzzing of the insects singing their once-every-seven-year love song seemed to be growing louder by the second. Annoyed, he sat up and looked around. The buzzing noise increased in volume and then altered its texture, sounding more mechanical. He looked to the west and saw speeding towards him in a cloud of dust down the dirt and gravel road, one of those new mechanical marvels, an automobile. He had seen a number of them in the cities he traveled through, but in those cities the roads were paved, at least with stones or bricks. For one of them to be traveling down this road at such a breakneck speed seemed poor judgment bordering on insanity.

This apple-red flash barreled along until it struck a rut too deep to avoid. Then it slowed to a crawl, traversed the rut with a wiggle, straightened out, and then came on as rapidly as before. Kiamichi paused on a mouthful of oats, judged the noisy apparatus to be no threat, and contentedly resumed his munching. A smile played on See Bird's lips as he raised a hand to wave at the vehicle's two occupants. A young woman in a balloon-sleeved blue dress and topped by an outrageously wide-brimmed straw hat acknowledged his wave with a salute of her own while never releasing her grip on the automobile. Little other detail of her appearance was apparent. Her hat was secured snugly beneath her chin with a light blue ribbon, and the entire upper part of her face was concealed behind large goggles. Her male companion, wearing similar goggles, and topped by what looked to be a flier's leather cap with earflaps, seemed not even to notice his audience, so intent was his focus on the road before him. The small horseless carriage corkscrewed slightly as it navigated a particularly deep rut, straightened itself out, and with a bang and a puff of exhaust smoke, accelerated and soon disappeared from sight around the next bend.

"Looked like those folks were in a mighty big hurry to get someplace. I don't expect we'll be seeing them anytime again soon. And we ought to move along too, boy. Might be we'll get to Topeka tomorrow night. What do you think about hitching a ride on the eastbound from there? We can afford it, what with the railroad ticket to anywhere east that our friend the President gave us. Does that sound good to you?" Kiamichi seemed either uninterested or unpersuaded and continued his munching, swishing his tail just a little bit harder than usual to swat at a particularly pesky fly. See Bird had trouble translating his response. "Well, fella, let's just see how it goes then. Maybe yes. Maybe no." He saddled up, and soon the pair turned back onto the road, following the trail taken by the recently departed automobile, along the north bank of the Kansas.

See Bird's expectation that he would not soon see that particular vehicle again was proven to be mistaken. He was admiring a field of ripening corn, so tall that though he was mounted, his head barely cleared their tasseled tops when he detected a flash of red just up ahead. He thought he recognized it, but why would that vehicle stop way out here in the middle of nowhere? He picked up his pace and in a few minutes, without having to ask a single question, the answer became obvious. The contraption was stuck where a small stream drained a cornfield on the north side of the road across that road on its way to the Kansas River nearby. Left to itself, the stream was harmless. But the daily traffic of horses, wagons, carts, and the occasional automobile, had churned the area into a mud hole ten yards wide by a couple feet deep. And every time the woman in the big hat accelerated, it seemed to bury the wheels a few inches deeper.

Against the rear of the steaming auto, the goggled man who had been driving braced himself. At least See Bird presumed it to be the same man, now so covered in brown mud he was unrecognizable. He was applying all of his strength in a futile attempt to free the machine that seemed intent on burying itself. Occasionally, just as it seemed the floundering auto might actually be gaining some traction, inching forward, the driver would try to encourage it by giving it more gas. Inevitably, it would then lose what little forward momentum had been gained and slip backward, sending the mud-covered man in the rear, slipping to his knees amid an explosion of profanities. So intent was he on the task at hand, or perhaps his goggles were also too mudded up, that he failed to see the approaching rider or the amused smile on his face. The lady behind the wheel, looking over her shoulder spied him first, turned back toward the front and shut off the engine. Leaping over the door of the roofless horseless carriage, she managed to land on nearly dry ground. From there she turned, waved, and yelled for help. It was only then that her mud-soaked companion noticed See Bird astride Kiamichi scarcely ten feet behind him.

See Bird did not hesitate a moment. As he kneed his horse forward through the wallow, he slowly uncoiled his lariat and played out a loop. As he came abreast the woman, he handed her the loop and told her what to do with it. "Drape it around that entire front end, then you get back inside and do not start that thing up. I do not intend to have my horse become the first victim of that infernal machine. Make sure it is out of gear and steer it straight down the road behind me. Do not let it turn itself off to the side. When you're clear of the wallow and apply the brakes so it don't roll back. You got all that?"

"Yes, I do. And thank you, mister. This mud hole nearly swallowed our car."

"Thank me after we get you two out of this muck. You to the rear," he called, "when I start pulling, you can lean into it some. But if we lose it, get out of the way. You got that?"

"You bet. Let me brace myself. Okay, I'm ready when you are."

By this time, the young woman had climbed back behind the steering wheel and looked expectantly at See Bird. He walked Kiamichi forward, taking the slack out of the rope which was tied to the pommel. "I'm going to rock it once," he called to the man. "When she rocks forward, give it all you got."

The powerful quarter-horse haunches leaned into the pull, and with muttered encouragement from his rider, Kiamichi freed the auto's wheels just a bit. Then See Bird urged him back as if he were in the rodeo arena maintaining tension on a calf throw. "Now," See Bird sang out. Kiamichi knew just what was wanted. He had pulled cattle out of wallows using just the same technique, years before. But his memory was good, and he had learned his lessons well. With a powerful forward lunge, he ripped the wheels of the car free of the muck and it slowly edged forward out of the slime, coming to rest on dry roadway. It coasted a few feet before it stopped and the rope went slack. The woman behind the wheel applied the brake, while the man at the rear dashed around the side to dry land and, raising his arms to the sky, shouted, "Hallelujah! You did it."

See Bird dismounted and retrieved his rope, eyeing the still steaming auto suspiciously. "I guess we all did it." He looked up and down the road and then at the hissing machine. "It don't appear that there is likely to be any harm in leaving this thing here for a few minutes to cool off. You are some sight, Mister…"

"Benton. Oliver Benton. But my friends call me Ollie. This mad young woman traveling with me is Miss Julie LaLaine. And you are?" As he spoke, he lifted his goggles off, exposing the only clean area of his body, a circle of skin immediately surrounding his eyes, those icy blue eyes.

"Carpenter. Red Carpenter." See Bird could not have said why, at that moment, he used his white name to introduce himself. He reached out to shake hands, but Ollie laughed and declined.

"I'm sorry, but I am such a mess. If I touch anything I shall most likely contaminate it. I need to clean up somewhere."

See Bird caught himself staring at the mud-man standing before him and said, pointing off to the left, "There's a river over there, the one this trickles into, right behind those trees. You could take a clean change of clothes and rinse out those things you're wearing while Miss Julie and I wait over here."

"Yes, that would be the proper thing to do. Unfortunately, there is no clean change of clothes. That valise contains Julie's overnight things. We planned to be in Topeka this evening, where my parents live. I intended to introduce her to the family. I truly do not know what I am to do now. I am a total mess."

"That's okay, Ollie dear. I'm sure I can tolerate you in your present condition for a few more hours. But we really must be going if we are to make it to your parents," Julie insisted.

See Bird thought for a moment as he reattached his rope to the saddle. "I might have an idea. I've been riding rodeos all summer and have some pretty worn out duds that'll need replacing soon. But at least they're clean." He detached his warbag. You got a couple inches on me, but if you roll up the sleeves on the old red shirt, it should fit you okay. And then there's a pair of denims I never liked too much because they were an inch or two long. But they're clean and should get you to Topeka. When you get home, just throw them away. It'll be more'n likely two more nights on the road for me before I get there anyway. You've had enough trouble for one trip. Take them, and you folks can be on your way." He shoved the bag into the young man's hands and pointed him toward the thick maples and elms growing near the shore. "Now, git to it."

"Red, you cannot realize how much your kindness means to me. I promise that one day I shall repay you. Thank you." With that and See Bird's warbag in hand, he disappeared in the trees.

"Red, that really was kind of you. You could have just ridden by without saying a word."

"Julie, I read once in the Good Book about a good Samaritan. I reckon that story was included for a reason."

"Yes, certainly, but Red, you must realize that not everyone you meet is either kind or honest." She leaned his way, lowering her voice. “There are those who can hide their bad intentions behind nice words and smiles.” See Bird was standing with one foot resting on the front of the car. Julie had climbed into the passenger seat.

See Bird found himself becoming uncomfortable with the direction of the conversation, so he switched subjects. “Say, what kind of vehicle is this anyhow? Know anything about it?”

Julie seemed relieved to talk about something less personal, as well. She laughed, revealing a slight but attractive gap between her front teeth. “I should say I do. My father figures these are the wave of the future. He ordered one of them from Mister Egburt. He has the only license to sell them in all of Manhattan and Topeka. I helped Daddy decide on this brand. It is a Ford Model ‘a,’ with a ‘flat-2.’ That’s a two-cylinder engine. On the open road this buggy can produce 28 miles per hour, and if you want it in black or any other color, well, that’s just too bad. It only comes in red.” She giggled girlishly. “If you need any more information, you’ll have to ask Mister Egburt. Everything I know about this car, I learned from him.”

“No, no thanks. That’s enough to chew on. You clearly know your stuff. The wave of the future, you say. I’ve never ridden in one, but I have to admit, I would like very much to take one apart to see what makes it tick.” He caught some movement from the corner of his eye. “Well, look over yonder. It didn’t take Ollie long to do his switcheroo.” He waved, and Ollie returned it as he walked toward the Ford.

Julie looked at See Bird and speaking quietly but earnestly said. “Yes, we seem ready to go. Thank you again, Red. You have a safe trip home to your family. And if I could say just one more thing,” she hurried as

Ollie approached the car, "Oh, never mind. Just you please be careful." She turned her head and smiled, "Hi, Ollie, you handsome devil you."

"Hello, sweetheart." He handed See Bird his warbag and tossed his wadded up wet but wrung out clothes behind the seat. "Red," he said, "I would really like to stop and visit with you, but my parents will be worried if we are too late. Your help was a real godsend. If you give me your address, I will be sure to wire you something to pay for all you've done."

See Bird waved it off. "Think nothing of it. You needed a hand today. I'll most likely need one tomorrow. Besides, I was glad to help out. You might want to slow down a bit, so's you get where you're going in one piece."

Ollie shrugged as if to say, 'Don't worry about it.' Then he jumped up behind the wheel, turned the ignition, and, remarkably, to See Bird at least, the little Ford turned over and started immediately. Then, putting the car in gear, he started it down the road, with nary a backward glance.

See Bird walked over to Kiamichi and tied down his warbag again, then mounted and slowly they walked on down the road. "Now that was an odd young couple," he said to no one in particular. "He's a cold fish, and she's definitely worried about something."

It may have been her quiet admonitions to him that drew his thoughts back to her. She seemed almost secretive, as though she had something to tell him, but did not want Ollie to overhear. Perhaps it was their different attitudes or Oliver's cold blue eyes. Eventually, he decided, it must have been all of those things and something he could not identify that roused his suspicions, until when once again, they paused give Kiamichi a breather, See Bird untied his warbag and lowered it to the ground. Upon opening it, the first thing he did was listen for the tell-tale crinkling sound of the big bills he had sewn into the lining and check on his stitching. It was untouched. His unique stitch knot insured that. Relief was his first feeling, followed quickly with shame for having suspected the young man of duplicity.

Certainly the bag seemed lighter. It was minus the denims and shirt he gave to Ollie to replace his ruined clothing. But by the time he had emptied the entire contents of the bag, he grimly faced the fact that he was also missing three more items, his sock with nearly two hundred dollars in it, his Colt .45, and a box of cartridges.

# 22

Sunday morning had begun at 4:30 AM for Manhattan, Kansas, resident Stella Granger, a.k.a. Julie La Laine with a soft but insistent tapping on her ground floor bedroom window. The groggy residue of a troubled sleep evaporated, leaving her vaguely disquieted. She sat up, tossed back the coverlet and stood fully clothed, prepared, she thought, for the adventure this day promised. She hurried to the window, and seeing the man she expected standing there in the predawn dimness, threw up the sash and wrapped her arms around his neck as he wrapped his about her slim waist and lifted her through to set her gently down again. "We must hurry," he whispered. "It'll be light soon. C'mon."

It was only then, with the reality of what she was about to do confronting her did she ask, "But what if we're caught?" This entire scheme that Stan Burke, the man See Bird knew as Ollie Benton dreamed up, had seemed, oh so much more attractive and exciting while they sat on a picnic blanket, day-dreaming over a bottle of inexpensive wine. She had listened to Stan as he described the exciting life lying just before them, there for the taking. She had even added a few touches of her own. But in truth, she had never really considered all the ramifications of stealing a car from a man she had known and liked as a family friend for practically her entire life, robbing the jewelry store, and fleeing her family and friends, most likely never to see them again.

It was sadly true that her father was an ogre. At least that's what she called him behind his back. He was a successful practicing attorney with eyes on a judgeship. Such being the case, he was terribly severe and would tolerate absolutely no behavior from her that would in any way impede his future rise in politics. The very idea of his only daughter having a drink of alcohol or smoking a cigarette or going dancing unchaperoned was intolerable to him, no matter how much she would plead. He even refused to sit down for dinner without first donning the appropriate jacket.

And her mother was just as bad. Sometimes Stella wondered if perhaps she wasn't even worse, pushing and egging her father on the way she did. Often her mother acted as if she wanted to be the lawyer in the family. She would talk to Stella's father nearly every evening about what cases and such he was working on, and act as though she found it interesting. Ugh!

Worst of all, recently she had heard them talking about sending her off to some 'finishing school for young ladies,' from where she was certain her parents dreamed of her eventual return, tamed and docile, trained on a classical piano and ready to wed some simpering, totally proper and boring young man, and then be forced to produce a pack of squalling babies, spending the rest of her life cleaning dirty baby bottoms and listening to the ticking of the grandfather clock in the foyer.

Well, she would have none of it. In her heart of hearts, she knew she was born to be an actress in a moving picture, like the one she had seen when her family visited her Aunt Lucy in Topeka. The Nickelodeon experience was a revelation to her, and she dreamed of someday 'trodding the boards,' as she thought it was called. Her parents' plans for her were total 'yuck.' "Oh, why couldn't they see she was destined for greater things?"

Everyone knew the Stan Burke was a bit of a rake. Her father warned her that he was bad company and to be avoided. He said it seemed impossible for the young man to keep steady employment. And Stella had heard the lurid rumors concerning him, of the girls he had lured 'beyond the tracks.' She knew he was 'experienced.' When he walked by, girls would turn and stare. Some said he really wasn't that much to look at, medium height and weight, thick brown hair combed straight back that he had to grease to keep flattened, and always wearing what seemed to be a permanent pout on his thin lips resting beneath those piercing blue eyes. They were easily his most striking feature. His eyes were the bait, but it was his lips that were the hook that really convinced her that he was the one for her.

Stella remembered the first time she had 'walked out with him.' She had seen and smiled at him a number of times with absolutely zero to show for her flirtatious efforts. He did not even seem to know she was alive. Then one afternoon as he strolled by the park where she stood chatting with her friend Doris, he stopped a moment and slipped a note in her hand, then continued walking. She read it to Doris. The note said she was to meet him that evening inside the entrance to the fairgrounds. Both girls looked at each other with open mouths.

A doubt assailed her. "What do you think, Dorie?"

"Stella, you're going for sure, right? Oh, I wish he'd asked me."

That settled it. It was easy to lie to her parents. She knew Dorie would cover for her. That very evening she met him as planned. Those lips. The memory of them all over her face and neck still made her shiver with delight. She had never felt that way before. And when she kissed him in return, pressing herself against his body, she could tell he loved her too. Their trysts became more frequent. He taught her so much. Soon she was as bold an experimenter in lovemaking as was he, until she was convinced he was as enamored with her as she was with him. Soon it was common knowledge to everyone in the city of Manhattan, with the possible exception of her parents, that Stan and Stella were an 'item.'

At first, their trysts were filled with small-talk, but it was not long before their personality differences became apparent. Stella was a fantastical dreamer, but Stan was always the practical one, always searching for ways to implement their dreams. She would laugh and call him, "Stan, Stan, the man with a plan." Their conversations went from "Wouldn't it be nice if…" on her part to "What if we were to…" on his. Then one recent evening he presented his 'escape from Manhattan' plan to her. She listened politely over a second or third glass of red, could not think of a single reason for them not to do as he desired, and in the end even suggested a few ways to improve his scheme.

But now, as she stood in the cool of the pre-dawn on the dirt outside her bedroom window and realized that all of their pie-in-the-sky dreams were moving toward reality, she had second thoughts. She suddenly felt so unsure of this enterprise. It wasn't fair to Stan, she knew. He had worked so hard on it, and with her complete approval. If she got cold feet and backed out now, would he think her a coward and hate her forever? Tears welled up in her eyes. And then he kissed her, a hard, passionate kiss that promised her heaven, and she forgot her reservations.

She banished her hesitations. "Let's go, Stan. You're right. Just a second." She reached back through the open window to grab her favorite "traveling' hat from the lampstand, the hat her mother said went so well with her blue dress, plopped it on her head and tied it down. "We had better hurry." She took his hand as the two dashed off in the early morning gloom.

Gerald Egburt was one of Manhattan's most successful entrepreneurial stories. A German immigrant handyman and tinker, he had become one of the area's most respected mechanics and salesman of rebuilt buggies and wagons. When he read about what the Fords were doing in Detroit and other rapid advancements in transportation, he heard his future calling. He answered by withdrawing most of his savings and obtaining a loan from the local bank. Then he sent a money order wire to the Ford Motor Company requesting delivery of three of their new Model 'a' Fords. Lloyd Granger, Stella's father, had been his first customer. But he was sure he would have little trouble selling the other two.

He had hired Stan Burke to prepare the autos for sale and delivery. At present, all three were stored in a large barn just across the river, scarcely a mile from Stan's house. Since he had complete access to the cars, obtaining ignition keys for them was no trouble. So when he and Stella concocted their robbery plan and they realized they would need to get away from town fast, what could be more natural than to steal one of Mr.

Egburt's cars? As Stanley so cogently put it, "If the old man didn't want them stolen, he should have locked them up. It's his own fault if your father's new Ford gets stolen."

"Yes," Stella added. "And it's not like we're really stealing his stupid car. We're just borrowing it until we get to the Topeka train station. We could even leave a note telling who to return the auto to." Stan grunted what she took to be his assent, and phase one began.

Stan entered the storage barn through an unlocked side-door while Stella waited outside. He moved swiftly but carefully in the dim light to the vehicle he had prepared for the occasion. It had a full tank of gasoline and an extra can in the back – just in case, right next to the empty valise. The new Ford started right up. Leaving it on 'idle,' he smoothly rolled the barn door open and drove it out. Stella slid the door closed and jumped in beside Stan. They looked at each other with forced but excited grins. Stella thought she detected a hint of fear in his eyes, which frightened her. To bolster his courage, she placed a hand on his leg and squeezed. "Let's do it, Stan," and, thus, phase two was begun.

Leo Edelstein was a Russian Jew who fled a pogrom with his wife Ruth to family contacts in the Netherlands and eventually found himself, along with others like him, on a liner on his way to America. Enchanted by tales of fortunes being made in the American West, the erstwhile gold miner made it all the way to Manhattan, Kansas, before becoming aware that there was a better way to mine for gold in America than digging in the mountains out west. Tapping those same contacts in Rotterdam, he was able to open up a jewelry store he promoted as 'The Best and Only' store in the whole city that sold diamond jewelry. What kept him in business, though, was his scrupulous honesty. His reputation for putting a fair price on his merchandise was what brought customers back, and that, he swore, was the real key to any business success.

But this was Sunday morning. The Diamond Emporium would not be opened again until Monday. Stan, in his studied walks around town, had kept track of the local police on the beat. If last week's patrols could be counted on as a predictor, he figured the final security check on the store would be prior to 5 AM. Stan stashed Lloyd Granger's car behind a wooden fence by an empty lot just a half-block away from the store at 4:50, according to his pocket watch. With the empty valise in hand and Stella standing behind him, he peered through a crack between boards and, sure enough, in the slowly brightening light, could see the patrolman slowly walking his beat down the street, occasionally checking a store door or cupping his hands to look in a window. But he did not linger and after another minute, he turned a corner and was gone.

"All clear," Stan whispered. The two stepped through a spot where two missing boards opened a gap, and strolled across the street, hand in hand, just in case anyone was watching at this early hour, and together walked directly past the Diamond Emporium to the corner, which they turned. A narrow dirt alleyway ran the length of the block behind the stores, and it was into this they turned. They paused behind the store and checked in both directions before turning to the door. It was, as expected, locked, as was the neighboring window as well. They heard a sudden rustling noise inside and for a panicky moment plastered their backs against the wall. A cat, disturbed by their approach, dashed from under the building and scurried between their legs, exiting down the alleyway. They both released their breaths at the same time.

Stan reached into the valise and withdrew a glass cutter. Within seconds he had cut out a small rectangle of glass and gently tapped it inward. It fell, tinkling softly as it hit the floor. Swiftly he reached up inside, turned the lock mechanism, and raised the window. Before Stella could even catch her breath, he slipped inside, closed the window and opened the back door. "Enter my lady. The place is ours." Carefully he closed and latched the door behind them. "You stay here and keep an eye out for anything."

Donning a pair of white 'kid gloves' and avoiding the front windows of the narrow store as much as possible, Stan walked down the row of glass-faced counters, sliding each one open and carefully sweeping the contents into his valise. Stella kept watch at the back window, nervously starting at every sound. Then Stan was beside her again. He must have read some misgivings on her face for he said, "I avoided all the stuff upfront and his big garish pieces as well." He tapped his now much more heavily laden bag. "But believe me, darling, we'll be set for a long time to come. Out we go." And so was completed phase two.

'The getaway' was the most problematic of their considerations. Too many things beyond their control could go wrong. Nevertheless, it started off without a hitch. The couple strolled back to their hidden car, determined not to appear rushed. The vehicle started up directly, and they were soon on their way. Back across the bridge, they turned east as the sun rose. Their future looked bright, indeed. Now they only had to get to the big Union Pacific train station in Topeka, ditch the car, and hop on the 3:15 to St. Louis, where they could begin living the good life.

Becoming stuck in the mud-hole and having to be rescued by See Bird, was definitely not part of their plan. Nonetheless, Stan was proud of himself for turning even that to his profit. That hick of a cowboy had stashed some two hundred dollars in a sock in the bottom of his bag. Stealing their rescuer's money also solved a problem he had been worrying about, a gap in his plan. Certainly, the diamonds were worth a lot of money, but he hadn't considered how he was to support the two of them on the little money he started with. One could scarcely buy a train ticket or pay for a meal in a restaurant with a diamond. A couple hundred dollars in cash would see them nicely on their way.

And for him to have left that pistol behind would have been only asking for trouble. An angry cowboy with a gun, hot on his trail, was not something he wanted to encounter. So he took that too. Now, even though the get-away was behind schedule slightly, he was armed and better off financially, as well. All in all, he figured, considering the little time it had cost him, things had turned out not so badly at all. Stella seemed a little off her mark this morning, but then, he thought, that's just the way it is with women sometimes. He was confident she would perk up when they were on the train to St. Louis.

# 23

After spending all of maybe thirty seconds kicking himself for being, once again, such a gullible fool, See Bird decided what he was going to do, or at least what he would try to do. His situation was not hopeless, but it did look to be poor bordering on bleak.

If he were to just shrug off the theft and continue on his way home with the funds that remained to him, he and Sally could probably make it through the winter – no guarantees, but probably. Maybe the small tobacco crop he planted would be more profitable than he expected. He certainly would not be able to purchase that piece of woods that Sally loved so dearly. And there would be no frills for his daughter Gertrude either. He would report the two thieves when he got to Topeka, but he figured they would be long gone by them. Thinking about all this frustrated and saddened him.

And then there were the two thieves themselves. He had been taken in by their lies completely, for that is what he was sure their story was. It was his own willingness to take people at their word that had cost him his hard-earned wages and Sally's dream. There was little doubt in his mind that having been successful robbing him of his money, gun, and by golly, even his fancy red rodeo shirt, the two would continue their banditry until they were stopped. As he stepped back into the stirrup, another thought occurred to him. Why were the two of them traveling so fast and so light if not to get away from something or someone? Probably, he decided, they had left behind other victims like him. It was all too bad, and the more he dwelt on the situation, the madder it made him. Slowly a plan began to shape itself in his mind.

"Well, big boy, it looks like we got our work cut out for us today. Those two played me for a sucker, and it's up to me to set things right. It ain't likely that we'll catch them, but if there's any chance at all, I gotta take it. Looks like that means a 'long run' for the two of us, so we might as well get on with it." With that, he kneed Kiamichi into a mile-eating gallop, riding as easy as he could, letting the horse have his head. About fifteen minutes later, without completely stopping, See Bird slid out of the saddle to run alongside Kiamichi. He dropped the reins, certain that his companion would keep pace. His running pace was slow enough so that Kiamichi could slow to a canter. Without having to carry a rider, it was almost a resting pace for him. About fifteen minutes later, See Bird remounted, and Kiamichi picked up the pace again while his rider gained his breath. Then the sequence was started over again.

Having repeated the process a number of times, See Bird noticed that instead of growing tired, he was actually catching his 'second wind.' Given the way he felt, he believed he could continue such a run nearly indefinitely. He watched Kiamichi for any sign of exhaustion. Many a rider ruined a good horse by running it until it was blown. After that, the beast really wasn't good for much at all. That scenario had to be avoided at all costs.

Kiamichi's main need would be for water, and so periodically they would stop where it could be found. Running, as they were, pretty much along the river, there was little lack of it. They would stop, Kiamichi would guzzle while See Bird drank his fill from his canteen. Experience taught him that skipping water breaks could spell disaster for a long-distance run. Then, after checking his horse's hooves and sides, they would resume their chase. Miles disappeared along with the hours.

What traffic they encountered was all local and sparse. See Bird did not bother to ask passers-by if they had seen an apple-red Ford driving hell-bent for leather. He knew it would be a waste of time and just an excuse for him to stop running, allowing his quarry to pull ever farther ahead.

His biggest obstacle while he ran was the heat. He tied his hat to the pommel and wrapped his bandanna around his forehead to stop the sweat from clouding his eyes. The triple-layered, laced moccasins he had sewn together were perfect for a run such as this, supple enough for comfort, and dense enough to shield his feet from small rocks he inevitably stepped on.

At one point along the road, he met a young man in bibbed overalls driving a mule-led wagon on some farm errand. The boy smiled and raised a hand in greeting and then let his hand fall with his smile. What was he to make of this Indian man, moccasin-clad, a yellow bandanna around his head, running silently down the road with his black hair gleaming with sweat, as his horse jogged along behind? He had never seen anything like it. To make sure it was not an apparition, he halted his mule and sat watching until the Indian running ahead of his horse disappeared around a bend.

See Bird saw the young man but had nothing to say. He was on a mission not only to retrieve his lost goods, but to retrieve his and his wife's dream. It was his mistake that had set this disaster in motion. It was up to him to devote all his energies to set things right.

The hours stretched on, and when See Bird realized he could no longer run beyond a slow jog, he stopped trying and walked at a furious pace. Kiamichi walked behind. When he mounted and kneed the horse into a trot, he monitored every stride of the horse as he monitored the rhythm of his own heart. Steady and as fast as he could safely travel, as Kiamichi could safely travel.

In spite of everything he knew and used to maintain his pace, as the afternoon wore on, he found himself beginning to flag. He did not know where he was, only that he was headed in the correct direction. He knew Kiamichi also could not keep this pace up indefinitely and would soon need a real rest. He was a large animal who burned a lot of energy and needed to replenish not only water but food as well.

At this point, See Bird ran into a bit of good luck, almost literally. The traffic on the road was increasing, leading him to believe he was approaching another town when he found himself gaining on another of those horseless carriages. At first he had vague and tired hopes that this would be the one he was chasing, but even in the dusty, hazy light, he could see it was not the one. The rear end of it was too tall and besides, it was black, not red.

He considered for a moment grabbing hold of some rear appurtenance and letting it tow him forward, but then discarded the thought as unworthy. He pulled alongside and then ran even with the driver, who glanced his way, startled. Looking rearward, the driver saw Kiamichi doggedly keeping pace with the runner. And so the odd trio continued for a short while, the Indian running alongside the vehicle, with the horse trailing both.

Curious, the driver, a prosperous-looking middle-aged fellow with a considerably protruding paunch, waved his free hand to gain See Bird's attention, then patted the seat beside him, indicating that he should jump in and ride along. See Bird considered a moment, evaluated his situation, including the fact that there was more traffic ahead, maybe gave the smallest of nods, and then leaped inside, plopping down on the seat. The first thing he said was, "Have you seen a red Ford motor car recently, headed in this direction, carrying two people, a young man and a woman?"

He scarcely credited his ears with what he heard in reply, "Why, yes, I have, now that you ask, probably not more than a half-hour ago, as a matter of fact, passed me going like sixty."

See Bird felt a wave of elation replace his exhaustion. "Thank you, mister. That sure is good to know. I am in a race with that pair of thieves, and I have to catch them. What town is this coming up?"

"Rossville. We're just a small burg, only about ten miles from Topeka. You're not kidding about those being thieves, are you now?" The look on See Bird's face told him all he needed to know. "The town constable's office is dead ahead on the right, and one of those new-fangled telephones was installed on the wall just last month. They can speak right to the police office in Topeka, assuming that's where your thieves are headed. Maybe they can nail them."

The driver pulled up before the Rossville Police Department, which was really nothing more than a small brick building with a hitching rail in front. See Bird hopped out, thanking him for the lift while he grabbed Kiamichi's reins and swung them over the rail. Stepping quickly through the door into the bitter smell of old coffee and stale tobacco, he saw a man, or at least the shiny bald head of a man, poking up from behind a newspaper. He would be the officer in charge, See Bird supposed. The police officer hurriedly slid his feet off the desk, and with a combination of irritation and embarrassment etched into what looked like a permanent scowl, balefully directed his attention to See Bird. The telephone that the driver had spoken of hung next to an open door, exposing a short hallway between two empty cells.

"And what can I do for you, Chief?"

See Bird was flummoxed for a moment before he realized the scene he must be presenting, from his moccasin-clad feet and dirty clothes, all the way to his sweat-stained headband. To the surprised officer, he must have appeared the stereotypical Indian from the 'old days,' and one who was most likely drunk and didn't speak English well either. He smiled at the thought.

He took a calming breath and slowed down, keenly aware that success in his nabbing the thieves rested on his ability to convince this man in a faded blue, too tight tunic to believe and help him.

He began with a simple plea, flatly stated. "Officer, I need your help. Early this afternoon, traveling from Manhattan, I was set upon by two thieves who stole nearly two hundred dollars from me, earnings I won in summer rodeo competitions. They were driving a new red Ford motorcar and headed in this direction. If what I suspect is true, they may be running from the law in Manhattan, which you can confirm in a minute's telephone call. But they're traveling fast." He nodded toward the phone, but the police officer made no move toward it.

"The man who gave me a ride here said he saw them little more than a half-hour ago, driving fast toward Topeka. They should be getting there about now, is my guess. If they are guilty of some crime in Manhattan, I would not think they would be going to Topeka as a destination, but rather as a place to jump off from. Lots of trains out of town, I suspect. So I suggest when you call Topeka, you ask them to keep an eye out for a young man and woman traveling very light, with only a hand valise, buying a one-way ticket to anywhere else."

"Mister…"

"Carpenter, Red Carpenter."

"Well, Mister Carpenter, that was quite a story you told. And at first, I was prone to just dismiss it as some drunken fairy-tale. But if so, you told it quite convincingly and sound quite sober. And like you said, it can be easily checked out. This here's the twentieth century, and wonders never cease." See Bird was unsure if the policeman was talking about the telephone or about a sober, well-spoken Indian. He let it ride.

"In any case, unless you have someplace you must be, I would appreciate it if you would just have a seat and make yourself comfortable while I make a few phone calls." The vaguest hint of a smile might have tugged at the corners of his mouth. "You can help yourself to a cup of coffee, though I wouldn't really recommend it, or read the paper if you like." He indicated a worn, wooden chair against the wall.

"I think I'll pass on the coffee, thanks, but I have been a mite out of touch, so if you don't mind, I'll catch up on the news." See Bird sat and picked the newspaper off the desk. Turning to the front page, he grunted in surprise at an article about Teddy Roosevelt's recent appearance at the Cheyenne Frontier Days celebration and the President's ongoing tour of the West. The policeman stared at this unlikely scene for a moment, rubbed his shiny head, and walked to the phone, muttering to himself.

He first called the Manhattan police department to follow-up on See Bird's suspicions. What, to See Bird's ears, started off as a semi-serious, skeptical inquiry on the local constable's part quickly turned quite serious, and before long the bald policeman in the too-small tunic was doing more listening than talking. When he hung up, he glanced See Bird's way as though he was thinking of saying something, then thought better of it. He then picked up the telephone again and rang up the Topeka Police Department, telling them what he had discovered from Manhattan. Finally, he ended that conversation and carefully replaced the telephone on the hook. He tugged at his blue tunic to cover his protruding belly and slowly stepped back behind his desk, resuming his seat, leaning on his elbows, and eye-balling See Bird, who carefully returned the newspaper to the page the officer had seemingly been reading and laid it back down on the desk, only then meeting the officer's eyes.

"Mister Carpenter," he began. See Bird thought he detected a hint of apology in the tone of his voice. "You appear to have these two characters dead-to-rights. I no sooner got through to Manhattan and asked about the red Ford than they told me that the whole town is in an uproar. A storage garage was broken into and a brand-spanking-new red Ford, bought but undelivered, was just driven away, either last night or early this morning."

See Bird nodded. "That's about what I expected."

"But that's not the half of it. Next, the thieves broke a window of a jewelry store, and pert-near cleaned it out. It looks like the automobile was to be their get-away car. I imagine we'll find it stashed somewhere near the Topeka train station. And hold on 'cause there's more." He held up his hands as if to restrain See Bird from interrupting. "Later today, after church, a local citizen reported his seventeen-year-old daughter missing. His wife actually found her gone this morning when they called her for breakfast. They didn't report the girl gone through until this afternoon because I guess they were told she was staying with a friend. And the corker is that her daddy is the owner of the stolen vehicle. So it would appear that she and her partner stole her daddy's new car. Your description of the female thief matches her father's description exactly, right to the curly brown hair and the gapped-teeth. Now how's that for a rotten kid?"

"Any idea of who the male might be?"

He shook his head. "Nobody for certain. Manhattan police are checking around. But I'll bet my bottom dollar that if we find the girl, or the car, or the jewelry, we'll find that scamp, too. You said he looked to be about her age, maybe a few years older, with blue eyes. That's not a lot, but it's something anyhow."

See Bird shook his head sadly. "It's a bad business. But there's two things I forgot to mention. The first is that the man is armed. When he stole the money from my bag, he also stole a Colt .45 I've had for years and a couple dozen cartridges along with it.

"The other thing is, I'm not so certain about the girl's part in all this. She tried to warn me about something, but he came back from changing clothes too soon for her to finish what she was saying. So I'd go easy on her if you have the chance. She may be his captive or something."

"That's good to know. Anything else you remember that could be helpful?"

"Can't think of a thing. If I do, I'll let you know, Officer. I should be going now. They're probably in Topeka by now, but I think I'll just ride down the road a piece to check it out."

"That's a good idea. I'd go with you, but I'm the only one on duty and can't leave." See Bird started to rise to leave. "But, Red," he rubbed his head again and this time smiled for real, "Good luck, and be careful."

"I plan on it."

# 24

"Stanley Burke, I've about had it with you, with this worthless automobile, and with your whole crazy scheme. You don't even know anything about this machine. How did you ever expect us to get away in it?" Stella had rehearsed her words and even considered her pose, concluding she would strive to attain the perfect blend of righteous indignation and exhausted forbearance. She sat by the side of the road, fanning herself with her hat. Her hair hung in sweaty brown curls down the sides of her face. She felt absolutely nothing like the eager adventurer of earlier in the day.

What had seemed at the time a gallant rescue by a handsome knight, and a dashing flight to freedom had become a tiring flight into embarrassment and fear. Every muscle and bone in her body ached from the pounding of the road, from the hours of being slung first one way and then another. For this she was unprepared. And when she begged for rest, Stan would just look at her from behind those stupid goggles and smile, like he was enjoying this lark immensely. "Just a little while longer," was his constant rejoinder to her pleas.

She touched the place inside where her true emotions dwelt and surprisingly found she missed her home, her lovely bedroom with its flowered wallpaper and lace curtains. And then she realized she missed her parents as well.

She was also terribly unprepared for the small things they had forgotten. Neither of them had thought of bringing food. They had started early in the morning, and it was now mid-afternoon – without having had a single bite. "We'll be dining on shrimp and caviar soon, my dear. Just you be patient a little while longer," Stanley told her. Shrimp and caviar, indeed. Right now Stella would have been satisfied with a peanut butter and jelly sandwich and a cold glass of milk.

She understood now that Stan was only able to think of himself, that he never really loved her like she hoped he would. When she told him she had to relieve herself, another little thing she had failed to consider in her plans, he positively leered at her and then said, "Can't you hold it just a little while longer, dearie?" Those skinny lips of his and those frog-eyed goggles, coupled with his demanding, patronizing voice made her want to just scream and stomp off. But then, where could she go? And what if he didn't call her back? And, speaking of 'going,' she had to right now. But Stanley seemed oblivious to any of her concerns and merely amused by her dramatic efforts.

She was at first shocked when they had finally stopped and he stepped out of the auto. Right there, in front of God and whatever man might happen to pass by, he opened his fly and with an audible "Ahh," sent a stream of urine shooting into the ditch by the road. And then he topped it off by lewdly grinning at her as he tucked himself away. Never in her entire life had she been so embarrassed. But then he made something that could not be any worse, worse yet. He said, "I feel a whole lot better. Now it's your turn to go," like he expected her to bare her bottom there in the weeds beside that infernal machine. This man, she now realized, who stood before her in his blousy red shirt and too short denims, was a man she did not know and did not want to know.

While he stared after her, she strode off with all the dignity she could muster to find a bush behind which she could relieve her bodily needs. Her face burned with shame. Thank heavens he couldn't see it. She understood now that the man she thought she had fallen in love with, that handsome, gallant, loving man, was really a selfish, ugly, mean-spirited cad who saw her as merely a tool to be used and probably, when she had outlived her utility to him, discarded.

But what could she do to extricate herself from him and this whole mess? When the Ford overheated this final time and Stan had been forced to pull over, she had tried to reason with him. "This is getting dangerous," she complained. "I know we missed the 3:15 and I am afraid that soon the police will find and arrest us and send us off to prison. And that auto is so unreliable. If it keeps overheating soon it might break down completely. Please, Stanley dear," she pleaded, "I want to go home. I want to be honest, and I want you to be honest with me."

Stan listened to her, his expression slowly darkening. Then he reached over for the valise, and from it pulled out a big pistol and a box of shells. Without saying a word, he began loading the gun. Then he held it, pointed skyward. "They are not going to catch us if we just see this through. And if someone tries to stop me, they'll find I'm no pushover. You want me to be honest with you, well brace yourself.

"You've got to show some guts too, Stella, because I cannot afford to leave you behind. I thought you were made of tougher stuff, but now I'm beginning to worry that you're no different from all the other sluts in that stinking town." His ice-blue eyes fixed on her like the eyes of a predatory hawk might focus on a mouse. "I figured that with your dad being such a big-shot lawyer if things get bad, he'd work himself to death to save his precious baby girl and me along with her. If his little darling is not with me, then I lose my best bargaining chip. I'm sure you appreciate my being honest with you. Right?"

His threatening words sent a shiver of fear down her spine. What had happened to the Stanley who so gently lifted her through the window only this morning? It all now seemed like ages ago. Did a bag of stolen jewelry mean more to him than she did? Something in her spirit died at that moment. Perhaps it was her girlhood, as she came to grips with the knowledge that the Stanley she dreamed of never existed, except as a construct in her own childish imagination. And, yes, it was clear now that the bag of jewelry was more valuable to him than anything else in the world. The only question now for her to answer was, how was she to shake off this waking nightmare?

"You are right about one thing, though," he said as he placed the pistol back in the bag with a flash of his former bluster. "I also think this car has outlived its usefulness. Come here and help me push it off to the side of the road down into those weeds. If we're lucky, no one will see it until we're long gone. Besides, we're only a short hike into Topeka, maybe a mile or two. We have to expect that by now, the Manhattan police will have sent out word who they are looking for. Come on now, darling, and lend me a hand. We'll be out of this stinking state in a couple of hours. We just have to tough it out."

This was her father's prized possession, this filthy, faulty thing that she had hoped to park and leave as good as new in a train station with a note to her father that would make him weep and repent for his prior cruelty to her. Now it felt like, as she leaned against the rear of the vehicle to push, that along with it, she was also pushing her girlish fantasies into the ditch. Now everything was ruined, and she foresaw only a dismal future for herself. This was not at all what she had desired. It made her want to cry.

"Push!" he cried.

Silent tears trickled down her cheeks as the apple-red Model 'a' Ford disappeared, along with her dreams, into the muddy ditch.

# 25

See Bird's sense of optimism, fired briefly by his encounter with the driver who had picked him up and driven him to Rossville, and then by the unexpected helpfulness of the town constable, was waning with every minute that ticked by and every bend in the road that revealed only another empty stretch of highway. To the south on his right, as he rode, stood mainly cottonwoods and other varieties of deciduous trees covering low shrubbery that concealed the Kansas River. To his left were mainly farms and fields, interspersed with the occasional woodlot. But nowhere to be seen was any trace of the fugitives. He was increasingly convinced that by now that the pair had safely made their getaway and were probably, at this very moment, congratulating themselves on their audacity as they relaxed in the comfort of a coach car on a Union Pacific train speeding off to wherever they planned on going.

Within two miles of Topeka, he began to notice the change in scenery. Road traffic was increasing and so were the number of buildings and dwellings, no longer just widely interspersed farms, divided by township roads.

He had spent the better part of his life learning to track. He could recognize the footprint and habitat of most, if not all the native creatures he would encounter, from squirrel to buffalo. But this was something new. He had never lent himself to tracking an automobile before and found it intriguing. If he were to apply animal tracking techniques to vehicular traffic, at least as it occurred on such a rutted dirt and gravel track as this highway pretended to be, he discovered that his skills were useful indeed.

At first, he was baffled by the confusion of information the road provided. Slowly, though, he began to sort it out. The principles for tracking game could be applied to tracking vehicles. He could soon tell when a mule-led buggy, or an ox-drawn wagon had passed. Riders on horseback were the easiest. He had been reading their track for decades.

The width of the wheel rims, the depths of the ruts they cut, even the wobble of the tracks told him something of the nature of the cargo or the steadiness and skill of the driver. Then he began to notice another type of wheeled track, ones that left a fingerprint, so to speak. One was distinguished by a number of grooves all running parallel to each other. Another had no grooves at all, to speak of, and yet another could be discerned by the cross-cuts across the parallel lines. But all, when they traversed the occasional wet areas or puddled track, were soft-sided and rounded compared with steel rims of animal-led wagons or buggies.

He was leading Kiamichi by the reins when another thought occurred to him. The very depths of the grooves and tread in the mud told him of the history of the vehicles. The deeper and sharper the outlines of the tread, the less wear they had suffered. That meant that the newer vehicles should leave the sharpest tread marks. With that as his premise, he ceased worrying about all the traffic and focused on the deepest tread patterns, ones that might be left by a brand-new Ford. He identified the one most likely to be left by a new Ford and remounted Kiamichi, picking up the pace.

About 150 yards down the road, he noticed where the treads pulled over to the right side of the road. Anyone traveling to Topeka would probably be on that side, as well. A well-worn path, probably used by local fishermen, led toward the river. A damp stain, perhaps where a radiator had overheated or water carried from the river had spilled, darkened the ground between the wheels. See Bird could almost see what had happened here. He winced at the idea of pouring water scooped up from the dirty Kansas into the motor of a new car. He didn't know that much about the machines, but it could not be good for its internal workings. But then, if the driver did not intend to take it much farther, it really would not matter all that much.

A horse-led cargo van approached and See Bird flagged down the driver.

"Excuse me, mister, but I'm on the tail of a red motor car carrying a young man and woman. You wouldn't have passed anything like that would you have?"

The driver, a round-faced bull of a man with a walrus mustache and wearing a bowler, shook his head. "Can't say as I have, but then I just turned onto this highway about a quarter-mile on." Disappointed, See Bird thanked the fellow and started past. "But, mister," the driver added, "you'd best be careful where you take your horse. There's a causeway up ahead as the road cuts near the river. It looks like grass, but if you get down in it, you'll get stuck for sure. I know. Been there before. Good day to you now." And with a flick of his wrists and a whistle, his wagon rumbled past See Bird.

"I've got me a good hunch, big fella, that we're mighty close. That car of theirs has been acting up. It's been driven too hard for too long. I wonder if it can even make it into town. Let's go." With that, the steed stepped into a fast walk while See Bird studied the roadbed from the saddle, trailing what he hoped were the tracks of the fugitive Ford. If he found nothing within the next mile or so he figured it would be all over. Topeka was a large city of some 35,000 people. No doubt, the streets would be paved or bricked, making tracking the Ford impossible. So if he was to find it, it was now or never.

Had he not had his encounter with the cargo wagon driver, he most likely would have missed the Ford. The road here was high and dry, just as the man had said. That meant there were fewer tracks to be seen in the firmer pavement. But it also meant there was little to no shoulder to the highway. His eyes were skimming over what looked like a grassy field when he caught a flash of light on shiny metal. When he looked more closely, nearly at his side, there protruded a corner of the rear end of the red Ford from among the long reeds.

See Bird leaped from the saddle. There was no doubt that this was its final resting place, but had some terrible accident suddenly thrown the two passengers to their death? It was with considerable relief that he could clearly see and identify the tracks of two people walking away, one wearing narrow pointy shoes and the other, the male probably, wearing larger, more square-toed shoes. And they were headed on down the road across the causeway. He knew they were close now.

Carefully, he walked Kiamichi along, constantly scanning the shoulders of the road. If the two thieves spotted him, they would certainly take cover in the deep grasses bordering the road. And See Bird was keenly aware that even now, his own Colt .45 could be sighted directly on him. Without consciously thinking about it, his hand rested reassuringly on the stock of the Winchester in its sheath. Not desiring to make an even easier target of himself, he dismounted and led Kiamichi along the road, using his peripheral vision to scan for any movement to the sides. The end of the long causeway drew steadily nearer. Already, up ahead, he could see a cluster of low wooden buildings resting on the higher ground. That would be the start of the suburbs. He became aware of the almost painful sensation of time passing, of falling behind. It reminded him of the recurrent dream he had where he would run to exhaustion, but he could never seem to close some undefined gap or draw even a foot closer toward his goal. And then their tracks disappeared.

The female footprint, he realized, was in the lead, walking ahead and slightly to the left of the man. His shoeprint often obliterated, or stepped on her right imprint. But it was in her print that he found a piling of dirt to one side, as though she had here made a decision to run for it, to dash off to the side, down through the long reeds. The man had turned and followed. See Bird led Kiamichi down off the road and ground tethered him so he would graze without wandering off. He trusted the horse to remain, at least for a while. He considered taking the Winchester but decided it would be ineffective and cumbersome in the close quarters of the marsh. Taking a deep breath, he parted the long grasses and followed the trail as quickly and silently as possible.

The female accomplice must have acute vision to have spotted this path winding through the slough, angling toward dry land. Or maybe she had not seen it at all and in her mad break for freedom just lucked out. Whatever the case, See Bird realized he was extremely close now. The grass stems had not even had time to straighten up following the fugitives' passing.

He floated like a ghost, silent and invisible through the chirruping reeds. He sensed a desperation, not his own, in the wind and decided it must belong to the girl. He did not know how it was that he was certain of things like this, only that he was. At times like this he felt almost as if he were indeed floating or more accurately, being carried to where he needed to go to do whatever was demanded of him. He felt again, as he had a number of times before in his life, the sensation of being a tool, of being used. And he did not mind. In fact, he thrilled to it. In this state, he felt lifted up and certain, full of purpose. Doubt and fear dissolved and disappeared.

As expected, he heard them before he saw them. Two voices, a male, loud threatening and demanding, and a female, breathless, tired, yet with no trace of fear.

"That was the last straw, you stupid bitch. I'm through with babying you along. I've offered you the world and you just spit in my face. I don't need you anymore. You're just a millstone around my neck. Do you realize that you've now caused me to miss the next train for St. Louis? Do you?"

"Stan, poor Stan, I am so ashamed of myself for not recognizing you for what you are before this happened. You're a sour, shriveled soul, a conniving…"

"Shut up, I said. Shut your mouth, Stella, or I'll shut it for you."

See Bird read the menace in his voice and almost broke through into the small clearing, but paused as she responded. “Oh, yes,” Stella answered bitterly, “my sweet lover. You have the gun you stole from that decent cowboy. You can shut me up forever, I’ve no doubt. So go ahead. What’s stopping you? I can never face my family and those I’ve wronged so badly. I’m ruined.” To See Bird’s ear, her pleadings sounded a bit over the top, but then she choked down a sob and steadied herself. “But I do not have to swallow your schemes anymore. And I won’t. Please, Stan, stop.”

Perhaps responding to the change in her voice, Stan’s voice changed also, his tone almost pleading. “Why, Stella, why did you betray me? Can’t you see this is our one chance to make it big? My one chance to break out of that trap of a town? I still want you.”

She stared at the ground. “You want me? That’s a joke, Stan. And I have never betrayed you. I thought you were exactly what I needed. But I was so wrong. I’m only trying to stop you from making the hugest mistake of your life. Please put that gun down and think.”

The gun never lowered, but the man paused a moment before he spoke. “I have been thinking about it, and you. A lot.” his voice became cold and hard again. Their eyes met. Those pouty lips she used to find so sexy, now repelled her.

See Bird slowly parted the blades of grass to peer between. Stella, her curly brown hair totally disheveled, sat hatless on the ground. Her pretty blue dress now had a tattered sleeve, and the ragged fringe of a petticoat protruded from it covering scuffed shoes.

Stan Burke hovered over her, feet apart. His hair was no longer greased back, but now stood as if aimed in several directions at once. He had a ragged, raging aspect to him that was at odds with his attire. Wearing

See Bird's cheery red rodeo shirt and his denims that rose above Stan's ankles, the man looked more than incongruous. He looked laughable. All but for the shiny pistol he kept waving about.

"I've been thinking about you a lot, Stella," he repeated and took one step back. "And before we permanently part company, you need to be taught a lesson. And I intend to be your teacher. Stand up." She rose to her feet, fists clenched. See Bird could see the angry red welt rising on her cheek where Stan had knocked her to the ground. "Now let's see my little actress at work. Take your dress off." When she made no move to comply, he pointed the .45 directly at her. "Do it now before I rip it off."

To her credit, Stella stood her ground and faced Stan. See Bird realized that she was going to defy the man with the gun. A thrill of admiration for her new-found courage resonated in him. If she were acting, this would be her greatest scene.

"You'll do this thing to me at the point of a gun? Oh, Stanley. You could have taken me willingly many times, but not now, never like this. You'll have to kill me first."

See Bird knew exactly what she was about to do and was amazed that Stan seemed caught completely off guard. He also knew it probably meant the young woman's death and stepped out into the clearing. "Stanley Burke, drop that gun!" he shouted just as Stella launched herself screaming at the man, all claws and teeth, hurling two handfuls of dirt into his face.

Stunned by the sudden appearance of the cowboy he had left so many miles and hours ago, and totally confused by Stella's transformation from pouty princess to screaming banshee, Stan stumbled backward a few steps, granting just enough time for Stella to clutch his neck and clamp down with her teeth on his ear while he frantically rubbed at his eyes with the sleeve of his shirt.

With a scream of agony, he smashed the girl to the ground with the barrel of the gun as blood cascaded from the place where his earlobe used to be. Stella lay still where she fell, while Stan staggered over her and, with a maddened look on his face, pointed the gun directly at her head.

See Bird knew it was now or never. In a few moments, the young woman and perhaps he as well would be dead at the hands of this thief, would-be rapist and murderer. "Father guide my hand," he prayed as he seized the big knife he always wore and hurled it with all the force he could muster at Stan. It flew with lethal accuracy, meeting him squarely in the mouth.

# 26

See Bird's Arkansas toothpick smashed into Stan's mouth, hilt first. See Bird saw flecks of teeth fly and heard the jaw crack as the heavy handle did its damage. Stan's reaction was automatic and completely predictable. He gurgled a moan, dropped the gun as he grabbed for his damaged face, and then cried out again as his fingers caused him even more pain. Then he fell to his knees, cradling his injured jaw.

See Bird hesitated by him only to retrieve his knife and gun before stepping over to the unconscious Stella. Untying his bandana, he dipped it in the water to wipe and cool her face. The pistol had opened an ugly gash on the side of her head, matting her hair with blood. Clearly, she needed a doctor's attention. He spoke to her gently, applying a cool compress to her forehead. She moaned, her eyelids fluttered briefly. When she opened her lids, her eyes appeared out of focus. She moaned once more and passed out again.

See Bird wished he could do something to restrain Stan, now sobbing and moaning as he lay on his side, but he had to do something to get help and notify authorities. "Stop. Breathe. Think," he told himself. And the answer came to him. He stood and whistled twice sharply. He knew that if Kiamichi could hear him, he would come to his rider immediately. There was no immediate response. See Bird was about to whistle again when he saw the tall grasses along the trail rustling and knew that help was on the way.

In a moment, the sorrel pushed the reeds aside and appeared with a nicker, as if to say, "Hold on. I got here as soon as I could."

"I don't think I've ever been happier to see your long face before," he said, stroking the horse's muzzle. Then he took his lasso and lashed the broken Stanley to a nearby willow. "Don't worry none, mister. I'm just making sure you don't wander off the path into deep water while I take this girl to a doctor. I'll be sending folks to pick you up directly, don't you worry." He snugged the knots tight and stood.

Carefully, he scooped Stella up in his arms and carried her over to Kiamichi. "I better carry her. You follow behind." Then he started back up the trail to the road. Approaching the end of the trail, as he was about to step up to the roadbed, he recognized something lying in the weeds. It was the same carpetbag valise he had first seen fifty miles ago. Placing Stella down carefully, he reached over to the bag. It was open.

The first things he found were some wet and wadded up, not so muddy clothes that Stan was wearing when he first saw him trying to push the Ford out of the wallow. Along with it were shell cartridges. Moving them aside, he found his damp sock. From the feel of it, most of his cash was safe. Obviously, Stanley had little opportunity to spend any of it. Upon removal of his money sock, at the bottom of the bag lay a fortune in sparkling diamonds and gold and silver jewelry. He buckled the bag shut, carrying his money sock over to Kiamichi, and secured it in his wargrip. Then he walked out onto the road, in no mood for any further delay, his Winchester resting comfortably in his arms.

Within minutes a vehicle approached headed into Topeka. The grim-faced man cradling a rifle and standing in the highway beside the prone young woman could not be avoided. When he held up his hand to signal the driver of the mule-led buggy to stop, the driver did not argue.

When See Bird explained that the girl lying by the road needed a doctor, and a fellow tied up farther down the trail needed a doctor and the police, the driver visibly relaxed and became positively solicitous. He rearranged a couple of bags of grain he was hauling into town to sell, so that Stella could be made comfortable. She was beginning to come around slowly, but was clearly in distress and nauseous. See Bird tied Kiamichi to the rear of the wagon and took a seat beside the driver. "Gee, haw, Molly," the driver called, and thus they entered Topeka.

A couple hours later, having seen Stella to the care of a doctor, the West Virginian sat in the Topeka Police Department headquarters, answering questions and filling the police in on missing details. They, in turn, filled him in with what they knew, confirming most of his suspicions.

The police found Stanley Burke exactly where he had been left and transported him directly to the same local hospital as Stella. There he was treated and released back to the police custody. The butt-end of See Bird's big knife had done its damage, knocking out four teeth, damaging the gums, and causing Stan to nip off the tip of his tongue. But other than that, his mouth was functional. The jaw was not broken. His ear was a mess, though. Angry and desperate, Stella had nearly bitten the appendage off. The doctor had sewn it up the best he could, but it would never look the same. "Perhaps," the doctor suggested, if he let his hair grow long and cover it…" See Bird stopped listening. He really did not care much about the appearance of Stanley Burke's ear. At present, the man lay on a cot in a cell, not twenty feet from where See Bird was talking to the police chief.

The chief himself a tall, white-haired man, younger than the color his hair would indicate, seemed intrigued with the case and listened carefully to everything See Bird said, interrupting only to ask clarifying questions or add some detail See Bird did not know.

"The girl's father and mother will be on their way here tonight. The 11:20 should get them here tomorrow morning. The girl's mother sounded nearly beside herself."

"That's understandable."

"I talked to the Manhattan police chief. He told me an interesting thing. Egburt and Edelstein pooled their resources and put a $100 reward out for the thief. Looks like that'll pay for your clothes nicely indeed. And that Egburt fellow did a pretty smart thing. Seems when he bought those automobiles, he also bought some insurance for them. So he should be reimbursed for the wreck of his new car. So, all in all, Mr. Carpenter, it looks like things turned out okay, thanks to you."

"All except for Stella. What's going to happen to her?"

"Yes. It appears she got the worst of it all. That was a nasty cut on her head, and she'll have a knot there for quite a while."

"I was thinking of her legal situation."

"That might be a bit more dicey. Certainly she should have told somebody from the start about Burke's scheme. That's her problem. But that looks to be her only problem. She's a minor girl who fell for a man who toyed with her, using her to further his illegal plan. When she woke up to see what was really happening, she tried to set things right. And it very well could have cost her her life. She owes that to you, Mr. Carpenter. And I wanted to ask you just one personal question. How on earth did you do that knife trick, sending it tail-end into his mouth?"

"It wasn't a trick. I just threw the knife with a prayer. Someone upstairs took it from there. And as for Stella's part in this, from what I heard her say to that snake in the marsh, she has spunk, some brains, and tried her darnedest to do the right thing. I'll be glad if you use my written statement to that effect if it ever should come to a trial. And I should think her daddy would have something to say about it then too."

"You're probably right about that, Red. I would appreciate it if you would stay in town tonight. Her parents said they would very much like to meet you and thank you personally."

"It was my plan to get a good night's sleep. My horse is about worn out. I don't want him off his feed. Ain't neither of us had a good meal since so early this morning it might as well be yesterday. And her folks should hear it from me what a brave daughter they have. It might help some. Anything else?"

The police chief rose and shook See Bird's hand. "I think that about does it. The Harrington Hotel has an in-house restaurant that's open late and is as good as anything else in town. They also have their own livery out back." He reached out his hand. See Bird shook it. "And thank you again, Mr. Carpenter, for all you've done."

The bone-weary Choctaw stepped out of the police station and walked slowly down to Kiamichi, who was patiently waiting at the hitching rail. His legs felt rubbery for a moment and then reminded himself that, besides everything else that happened today, he had probably run thirty miles. Kiamichi looked at him as if to say, "You sure did, and I ran with you every step of the way. Let's call it a day."

See Bird rubbed the muzzle of his friend affectionately. "And then let's go home."

# 27

**Covington, Kentucky, January, 1925**

Charlie sat by the fire, slowly feeding small pieces of wood into it in order to keep the temperature inside the tent comfortable for his wife, Gertrude and his newborn son Stuart. Stuart Carter, she named him. He asked why and she just smiled and said she liked the sound, said it sounded smart. Left to his own devices, Charlie most probably would have chosen something else, but then he shrugged and sighed. That is what she chose, and so that would be his son's name for all of his life. As he sat there by the flames, he tried to imagine what kind of life that would be. He gave it up in a minute, grimly aware that no imagining could ever come close to foretelling what a person's life would become or produce. When he was a child playing in the woods and helping his pa, he could not have possibly imagined what the years would send his way, both horror and love, and both unbounded.

Horror. He still could not accept what he had seen in the Great War in Europe. He entered, a young pilot with dreams of glory. Flying a Sopwith Camel, he was shot down in a 'no-mans' land between opposing trenches, on a day splashed with rain. He had survived the crash when the plane flipped, but had been forced to endure three days and nights crawling and burying himself in the churned-up muck before he could reach an abandoned trench, and ten more days scavenging among the rats and decomposed bodies for scraps of food before he was found. But even now, sitting here listening to his son nurse at his mother's breast, the horror threatened to wash him away once more. He fiddled and worked another stick into the flames. Nervously, he rifled his belongings, digging out the bottle he stashed there. A couple stiff drinks would help him sleep better and hold the nightmares at bay. He uncorked it. "One thing for sure," he thought as he took a deep swallow, "I will protect my son so he will never have to experience a war like his father had."

See Bird snuggled closer to Sally, deep in quilts and concealed by shadows on the other side of the fire, far from the hot flames. He kissed the back of her neck tenderly and smoothed her hair back with gentle fingers. Nestled like spoons inside one another, he marveled at his constant desire for this woman. Now, as she slept, her spirit at rest, he considered and weighed his life as it had turned out.

Rodeoing had been good to them. With the money he earned, he had bought three farms, including that twenty-acre woodlot she loved so much. Even though it didn't look like they would ever move to Oklahoma, if it was not meant to be, that was alright with him too. Together, for most of the year, at least when he was not off riding the rodeo circuit, they raised a beautiful daughter, saw her become a fine woman and now, he was confident, a loving mother.

As he struggled to find a comfortable position, his aching and aging body whispered that his rodeo days were drawing to a close. What would he have to show for nearly a lifetime in the saddle? What would he do next? "Well," he thought, "there was that broken-down jalopy his neighbor Duncan Holmes back in Warm Holler had towed over to his place. Duncan left it there last summer, dropped it off in front of the house and told a befuddled Sally,' if cain't nobody won't fix the durned thing, it'd be See Bird.' And there it sat 'til this very day. Now wouldn't it be a terrific thing to unlock the mysteries of the gasoline-powered internal combustion engine?

Sally and he had never created a child together. That was the only cloud that drifted across an otherwise blessed marriage. But even that blow had been softened by the beautiful grandson his daughter presented him with. He was a slender infant with hair as black as his mother's. See Bird wondered absently as he drifted off to sleep, what traits of his father would the boy carry and where will the trail he would choose in life carry him. But most importantly, would he ride it well?

THE END

# Afterword

One of the most difficult aspects of writing historical fiction is knowing when to rely on the history and when to develop the fiction. It can also, when done to the author's satisfaction, be the most rewarding. "Kiamichi" opens and closes in the winter of 1924-25. Yet the story is set in 1903, not a year the gets much respect from the casual student of history.

Yet that year, 1903, truly could be called the real start of the twentieth century. That was the year Teddy Roosevelt finally shook himself free of McKinley Republicanism, taking on the big money trusts of the 'Robber Barons.' It was the year he decided what kind of president he would be. It was in 1903 that he faced down the combined fleet of England and Germany over the fate of Venezuela, and it was in 1903 that the United States formally recognized the new Republic of Panama and in the same year, began planning for work on the yet to be constructed Panama Canal.

In the summer of that same year, T.R. took an extended tour of the West on the presidential train, The Elysian, riding in the Presidential car he named Isabella. It was, by the way, while he was speaking from the rear platform of the car in Milwaukee WI that a gunman shot him in the chest. On his hands and knees, he stuffed a handkerchief into the wound, rose and finished his speech. It was following that incident he made the now-famous pronouncement, “It takes more than one bullet to kill a bull moose.” Currently, the Isabella is serving as a diner in northern Illinois. It is said that the food is good.

It was on that western tour that he served as an honorary judge at the Cheyenne Frontier Days, as described in the novel. He also put his ranch, Elkhorn, in North Dakota, up for sale. From there, he continued west to Yosemite, meeting up with John Muir. This was a seminal trip for the young President. It helped him come to grips with the great issues then facing the United States regarding private property and mineral rights vs. the rights of the American people at large to possess and control the natural resources.

His accomplishments regarding conservation are staggering. Here are a few:

- He set aside 150 million acres of National Forest.
- He helped create 23 sites that would become national parks.
- He created 18 National Monuments such as Devil’s Tower and The Petrified Forest.

Much of Roosevelt’s extended dialogue in the novel was modeled on, and in some cases, lifted almost verbatim from what he actually said or wrote. Such is the case towards the end of Chapter 15 and in Chapter 16, paragraph 4, as well as in other places. The author tried to stay as true to Roosevelt, the man, as possible. To capture the flavor of the man’s feelings, I include here a T.R. quote on the subject.

“It is vandalism wantonly to destroy…what is beautiful in nature, whether it be a cliff, a forest or a species of mammal or bird. Here in the United States, we turn our rivers and streams into sewers and dumping grounds, we pollute the air, we destroy the forests, and exterminate fishes, birds, and mammals, not to speak of vulgarizing charming landscapes with hideous advertisements. But at last, it looks as if our people (are) awakening." What would he think of us over one hundred years later?

Sometimes truth about Teddy Roosevelt is stranger than fiction. He did once chase down thieves and bring them to justice. Also, he did, indeed, leap onto the back of a mountain lion and stab it to death. It is also true that, while he worked tirelessly to set aside forests and land to preserve for posterity, he was proud of being a big-game hunter around the globe. Even in his post-presidency, he remained physically active, exploring Africa and unknown and unnamed Amazonian rivers. In short, he was brilliant yet naive, sensitive yet oblivious, principled yet willing to compromise, but he was always dynamic, seeking to move forward.

No 'Afterword' could even come close to describing so complex an individual. Should the reader wish to know him better, I would suggest several good books: David McCullough's *The Path Between The Seas* and Edmund Morris's tour de force *Theodore Rex* are two of my favorites on the man.

As for See Bird, he did try in 1924 to lead his family from West Virginia to Oklahoma. But a late start, Gertrude's pregnancy, and a vicious December snowstorm, caught them near the White River in Indiana, forcing them to retreat. They made it back to Covington, Kentucky, where in early January 1925, Karl Stewart, the author's father was born, as described, in a yurt-like tent constructed according to See Bird's design. His experiences in World War II are portrayed by the character of Stuart Carter in the subsequent novel *The Seventh Cruise.*

But See Bird was never one to lament the past. He built a good life for himself and his family on land near Glenwood, WV. He, Sally, and their daughter Gertrude are all buried in the same church cemetery there. When he could no longer 'go rodeoing' every summer, he built and repaired things to earn a little money and keep busy. That was his genius. My father always said that if See Bird could get into something, he could fix it and if he could walk around it once, he could build it. "He had magic in his hands." Told that as a child, I always wondered about it. That is the origin of the special powers he displays in the books I have written about him.

He bought a car, I do not remember the make or model, probably a Ford, and he kept it running for years. I vaguely remember riding in the thing. Dad called it his jalopy. It was open with a flat front windscreen, but the thing I found most wonderful about it was that it did not go up hills very well, so when Grandad would get to the bottom of the hill, he would turn the car around and back up the hill. Reverse was the only way to go forward then. It still seems funny.

He may have been soft-spoken, but he loved a good time, whether it was a rodeo, county fair, or even his birthday party, which was always a 'blow-out.' It was held at 'the farm,' and began early in the evening. Guests and friends would arrive, men like 'Cowboy Copas' and Hawkshaw Hawkins. They would play their guitars and sing while Sally would play the 'mouth organ.' Somewhere along the line, See Bird would begin to dance, 'clogging,' they called it. And the party was on.

There would be a countdown at midnight. At the stroke of which See Bird would take a shot of whiskey and slam down the shot glass. Everyone would cheer, he would clog, and that would be the last drink he had until next year's birthday party.

Charlie, my grandfather, lost his life to the bottle. Following the untimely death of Gertrude to cancer, probably ovarian, the disconsolate man drifted to California, where it was reported he was killed fighting with someone over a bottle of booze. He was buried there.

Sally outlived them all. It was from her I heard most of the tales of the 'Olden Days.' The little house she and See Bird retired to in Huntington still stands as of this writing, a small, single-story house with a white picket fence, on what's left of Monroe Avenue.

This concludes the Western trilogy begun with *The Legend of See Bird: The Last Long Drive*, *The Legend of See Bird: Devil's Backbone* and *The Legend of See Bird: Kiamichi*. All three books may be purchased on Amazon.com or through Headline Books, Inc. of Terra Alta WV. Inscribed or signed copies may be purchased directly through the author at kcstewart71@centurytel.net or the author's website at karlstewart.net or on the author's Facebook page.

Other books by the author:

*Good Night, Sweet Dreams*- an illustrated children's book on race

*The Seventh Cruise* - a novel of WWII

*Up Harvey's Creek* - a child's memoir of WV

*Fare Thee Well, Harvey's Creek* - sequel to *Up Harvey's Creek*

Synopses of the books can be found on the author's website – karlstewart.net

# Acknowledgment

To my publisher Cathy Teets of Headline Books, Inc., who never stopped encouraging me to come back to write this book, even as my intentions wandered.